Wilson's Island

Ralph has come home. The face of the town he once lived in is changing - roads have been built, houses demolished - but his family remains entrenched in old habits and rituals. His father, Cliff, draws him into the murky half-world of his 'business'; the sinister Charlie casts an intimidating shadow over both their lives, and Ralph's grandmother and her sidekick Eric bicker and observe from their rooms above the games arcade. Before the story is over, Ralph experiences evictions, darts matches, deals, violence, and, perhaps, love. And Wilson's Island, and what happened there, recurs like a watermark throughout the story - an event which has left a lasting trace on all their lives.

Subtly compelling, beautifully written, and shot through with a dark comic streak, *Wilson's Island* establishes Stephen Blanchard as a major British novelist.

STEPHEN BLANCHARD was born in Hull and now lives in South London, where he works as a postman. His first novel, *Gagarin and I,* won the Yorkshire Post Best First Work Award and was shortlisted for the Whitbread First Novel Award.

By the same author

Gagarin and I

WILSON'S ISLAND

Chatto 87

Stephen Blanchard

p.1 Eric & Marion
p3 Cliff & Ralph
p.16 Jean
Colin

38 Alison 39 Frank
46 Mrs Cromer
42 Alma

PP 7 & 8

Ralph is (Cliff's?) son &
Marion's grandson.
Eric, who lives with Marion,
is not his father.
Cliff's "Not quite family"

Ralph has a wife Jean &
son (John?)(little boy)

Chatto & Windus
LONDON

First published in 1997

1 3 5 7 9 10 8 6 4 2

Stephen Blanchard has asserted his right under the Copyright,
Designs and Patents Act, 1988 to be identified as the author
of this work

First published in Great Britain in 1997 by
Chatto & Windus Limited
Random House, 20 Vauxhall Bridge Road,
London SW1V 2SA

Random House Australia (Pty) Limited
20 Alfred Street, Milsons Point, Sydney
New South Wales 2061, Australia

Random House New Zealand Limited
18 Poland Road, Glenfield,
Auckland 10, New Zealand

Random House South Africa (Pty) Limited
PO Box 337, Bergvlei, South Africa

Random House UK Limited Reg. No. 954009

Papers used by Random House UK Limited are natural,
recyclable products made from wood grown in sustainable forests.
The manufacturing processes conform to the environmental
regulations of the country of origin.

A CIP catalogue record for this book
is available from the British Library

ISBN 0 7011 6615 0

Typeset in Sabon by
Palimpsest Book Production Limited,
Polmont, Stirlingshire
Printed and bound in Great Britain by
Mackays of Chatham PLC, Chatham, Kent

To my daughter Catherine

The author would like to thank the London Arts Board for their generous provision of a bursary.

One

Before Eric had finished at the sink, the cat came in through its flap and rubbed against his ankles. He pushed it away with his heel and set a pie dish to soak on the draining board. He glanced at the wall clock and then jammed the lead into the electric kettle. The creature returned to him, twining itself between his ankles with a wavering cry of hunger. He ignored it and reached up to open the door of a cupboard and take down the tin caddy. He spooned black tea into the pot and by that time the kettle had boiled and switched itself off. He unplugged it and poured boiling water into the pot.

While the tea was drawing he fed the cat, squatting to fork meat into its red plastic bowl. The handle of the fork he used was marked with a strip of black waterproof tape to distinguish it from the rest of the cutlery. The meat had a strong smell of offal. The cat made gagging noises as it ate. He rinsed the fork under boiling water from the tap, then flicked it dry and returned it to its place in a jar in the cupboard under the sink. He looked at the clock again. There was the noise of the TV from upstairs and then came the fainter stutter of a payout from one of the gaming machines at the front. When it had emptied itself and fallen silent he could hear the TV more clearly.

He climbed the stairs with the tea things on an enamel tray. The arcade was separated from the hall by a single metal-faced door. He shifted the tray to avoid the chair lift stalled at the bend of the stairs. The door of the office was open and he pulled it to, balancing the tray along his other forearm and listening for the click of the latch. The door of Marion's room was closed as he had left it and he shifted the tray again to free a hand to knock. He could still hear the racket from the TV.

'Yes?' she called.

Who else could it be but him? At this time of day, what else could his business be? He opened the door. The room was filled with the noise of clapping.

1

'Why are they standing and making that noise?' she asked. As if her attention had just been drawn to it.

Eric put the tray down on the bedside table. The china shivered. The glass sugar bowl caught the light of the lamp. 'That's the PM. She must have just given a speech.'

Marion peered at the screen. 'Does she have a goitre?'

He shook his head, arranging the cups and saucers. 'No, that's the proud way she holds her throat.'

She pulled a face, holding her reading glasses in her big hand. 'I could speak too and set them back on their arses.'

Eric reached to turn down the volume. He poured for her, lifting the pot to let the tea stream from a height. He took pride in the steadiness of his hands. She watched him as he added milk and sugar.

'My bones are aching,' she told him. 'Has there been a change in the weather?'

The blow heater was purring in a corner. The room was too hot for his taste but then he kept himself active. 'The weather is just the same.'

'Then it must be something else that's changing . . . You've fed the cat, I hope.'

He nodded, closing his eyes. He adjusted the little table on its casters so that it was nearer to the bed. 'No doubt it'll be up here in a minute, stinking of the stuff and snuggling in your lap.'

'As long as it isn't *your* lap,' she said.

'It had done its business again under that armchair. There were little pellets of it gone hard as iron.'

When she sipped her tea she could not resist a shiver of luxury. 'She wouldn't be attracted to that spot if there was no dust.'

'My fault then! If the thing shits, then it's my doing!' He laughed to himself, bitterly. The tea was piss-weak as she liked it. 'The tea's to your liking?' he asked.

She didn't answer but stared at him, her features gathered around her fleshy elderly nose. It made him feel uncomfortable. As if she read something there he did not know himself. He could hear the chirrups of the machines below his feet, coming faintly through the carpet with its rubber underlay.

'I gave the lad downstairs his lunch,' Eric told her. 'Meatballs and gravy, mashed spud with tender sprouts. He was pleased. He says he's sick of that café place. That's the kind of work that makes you hungry, you see. Standing around – a big feller like

2

that: you'd expect the opposite. There's been a fifty-quid jackpot, he said.'

She looked dismayed. 'Already?'

'Someone needs to win to keep the rest coming back. Everyone loves a winner.'

She stood her cup back on its saucer, missing slightly so that the china squeaked. 'My joints ache: you can see that my wrists are swollen.'

'You can only expect it, Marion. At our age, I'm meaning.'

'I don't expect it. I never do . . .' She lowered her eyelids. 'You can read to me now. My eyes are tired.'

Eric looked at the pile of books beside the bed. He'd brought them from the library in the box of his moped and didn't need to read the titles. He picked up the one that was lying on its face. It had a dampish smell and was printed minutely on yellowing paper. Handling it gave him a faint twinge, like a little flow of current.

'You may as well start at the top of the page,' she said.

'Which page?'

She laughed. 'Whichever takes your fancy.'

She lay back against the bolster, settling herself to listen. She massaged one hand gently with the other and Eric noticed that her fingertips were blue with cold. He felt pity for her and then not. He changed like that, couldn't predict it.

A station with no trains now, weeds and gravel on the empty bed of the rails. Foxes would cry in the night – like babies but with different intentions. When Cliff was working late or just sitting, he thought, Sign of life anyway, better than the bastard silence. A faulty strip light flaring but never getting there, the tube filling with spooked dishwater, the doors hooked back on aisles of suites and bedroom furniture, shopsoiled mattresses in plastic valises, linoleum and carpet oddments, very slight seconds, white goods – washer-dryers, cookers, fridges.

Our prices are suicidal.

In his swivel chair through midweek afternoons, pushing stockinged feet close to the blow heater. Racing on the Sony. He watched the delicate, jittery stepping of the horses at the tape. Starter's orders. The riders like crabbed foetuses recalling the state of his heart. Dr Chandraniaker with his hands clasped over his small potbelly prescribing another course of Warfarin.

You need look no further.

Pursing his lips, he unwrapped another Edward VII slimline, then lifted the heavy table lighter – Louis Quat with the chrome worn thin. He sprung the flame and leaned towards it, the cigar twitching between his lips. The phone went and he tried to hook it with two fingers and missed – off balance somehow, the chair rocking. He caught it at the second try and brought it backhanded to his face. He stabbed the gizmo to kill the sound of the TV. He checked the office clock out of habit and waited.

'. . .'

'Excuse me?' he asked. 'Anyone there?'

'. . .'

He watched the clock until the second hand swept out a full minute, then propped his cigar in the ashtray and put the phone to his other ear. He listened for the faintest sound of a breath.

'You are the lowest of the low,' he said into the receiver. 'You are lower than shite. To be as low as you I'd need to dig a pit.'

He put the instrument gently into its cradle. The crisp clack of the plastic cheered him. The warmed weight of the lighter was still in his mitt.

A woman and two men played darts against the roll of the ship. The young woman was the best, throwing snake-armed with a snap-wristed flick at the end to send the dart on its way. Her eyes when she turned were bright under the dowdy lights. She wore her dark hair in a roll at the back of her head, held by a jewelled clasp. Strands of it were escaping. The men were bulky and roll-shouldered, coloured holiday shirts open on their sweating chests. Father and son, maybe. They looked sloppy with fatigue or drink.

Ralph watched them from where he sat in the corner of the saloon. The woman took the last double and he clapped his hands for her. She smiled back at him after she'd retrieved her darts. Her teeth were tiny and gapped. The older man sent him a stare as he wiped the score from the board, hostile at first but then changing to interest or speculation.

Ralph waited until they had gone back to the bar and then finished his drink and crossed the floor to the steep stairs leading to the deck. The narrow double doors pushed open into coolness. The breeze carried a smell like oiled metal. Low tide, he thought, or approaching, the tops of the sandbanks uncovered. He took hold of a stanchion as the deck leaned another degree. At the side

4

there was nothing visible except a stretch of glass-brown water caught in the deck's weak lights. He could sense the drag of the one stationary paddle as the boat turned.

He leaned against the rail, thinking that they must be midstream by now, nosing back into the current and towards the port. There was not enough light to separate water from sky. He glanced down towards the afterdeck with its vehicles. A couple of lamps glowed and he could just see the top of his black five-ton van.

When he heard the swing of the saloon doors he kept facing into the other direction, looking into the moving darkness. They released a snatch of music from downstairs, the woman's high laughter.

'She's my wife, you know . . .'

He turned on his elbow. It was the older, fatherish man.

'Cig?'

Ralph shook his head. 'No thanks.'

The other man stayed with his arm extended, as if the refusal had left him off balance. Then he took one for himself and lit it. 'People take her for my daughter, you see. As it happens, my daughter is almost the same age.'

'A friend for her, then.'

'Oh yeah. They're too bloody close, actually. When they compare notes then I start to worry.' He grinned around the cigarette, then took it from his mouth, nodding over the lit end. 'Christ, that starts me thinking.'

'I can see it might make life difficult.'

'Oh yeah. *Bloody* difficult, I'd say. Impossible is more the word.' He laughed as if he were recalling something, then leaned down and laid his forehead against the iron rail. He murmured.

Ralph bent towards him. 'Sorry?'

The man was cooling his brow against the rail, rolling his head very slowly. He sighed and stood up, blinking. A narrow chain he wore caught a shine. 'I said, the Dormobile's mine. Parked down there.' He nodded in that direction.

'Been along the coast?' Ralph asked.

The fatherly man looked back blearily, drunker than he'd seemed downstairs, maybe because the fresh air had hit him. He stared at Ralph's face and then at his clothes and broken shoes. He blew out his cheeks. 'Oh, here and there. The feller we're with is her brother, you know. In a thing that size you could say three starts to be a crowd . . .' He stood back to take another pull on his cigarette.

At the faint signal of a bell, the other paddle came into play. The slack water at the side ran backwards for a second and then turned to foam.

'That your van?' the man asked.

'That's right.'

'Thought so. I try to match people with vehicles. A game I play. Been away long yourself?'

Ralph left a second to show that he might not care to answer. 'A while. A fair while.'

'Business, not pleasure. From the look of you.'

'This and that.'

'The this-and-that trade . . . And you're going back home?'

Ralph stayed silent even longer. 'Not really. Not really that.'

The older man looked towards the lit windows of the saloon with their little caught-back curtains. 'Oh, you're hard-pressed to tell where that lies after a while. When you're always on the bloody move. You only have to take your eye off it once and it's gone.'

Ralph said nothing. He could see the lights of the coast now, a luminous string. They both heard the woman's laughter, carried towards them on a breath of ventilation. The man moved closer, nudging with his elbow.

'Truth of the matter is, she's younger than my daughter . . .'

Two

Eric hoovered the rug and then went back through the room with the hose-fitting, cleaning along the skirtings and around the bases of the machines. The rug was worn in front of the door and before the most popular of the games. The old boards showed, scuffed to paleness and studded with the heads of nails. He bent to flick a switch, reaching for it, grunting. The screens of the machines lit and started their silent cycles. He could smell the circuitry starting to warm. He turned off the Hoover and the vacuum collapsed with a wheeze. He listened for a noise upstairs and felt pleased with himself when there was nothing. Why so pleased? he wondered. After a minute he turned the machine back on.

When it was nearly seven there was a single thump against the shutters with the meat of a fist. They shivered with the noise. Eric leaned the Hoover against the side of a machine and went through the connecting door into the hall. It was lit by a dim lamp with a parchment shade. The pictures of Egypt shone in their thin frames. The Giza group of pyramids. Temple of Luxor. Avenue of Sphinxes, Karnac. He put one hand flat against the front door and leaned forward to the fish-eye. He could see nothing at first, or only the grey field of the lens. Then Cliff stepped into sight, made tiny and distant. He was looking not towards the house but along the street at something. Maybe his son's garbage tip of a van. Humming to himself, happy for whatever reason, Eric felt for the fat brass key on his chain.

'Ralph's here,' Cliff said as soon as he opened the door.

Eric stepped back, grinning and chiming softly with the keys. His grey dust jacket hung pocket-heavy from his sloping shoulders. 'Then you're another one that's psychic.'

'He was seen. Someone saw fit to tell me.'

Eric dealt with the door, making a show of first things first. 'He came in the small hours: I thought there was no point in troubling you.'

'No point?'

7

Eric nodded and worked the bolt at the door's foot back into its staple. 'That's right – I thought it could wait until the morning.'

Cliff gave him a look of puzzlement and distaste. He had just shaved but had left a bristly patch along the jawline. He smelled of that stuff he smoked and sleeplessness.

'So when did you hear?' Eric asked.

'An hour ago.'

'Someone woke you with it?'

'I wasn't asleep.'

'He was dead beat,' Eric said. 'I'm not sure how we got up the stairs.'

'You mean he had trouble walking?'

Eric nodded. 'I tried to help but he shrugged me off. You know what he's like. I put up the army cot for him. He was out the second his head went down.'

Cliff looked through the doorway into the arcade. The machines were generating wheels of colour and flashes of silent light. 'That's his van outside? We'd better move it before it attracts the police.'

Eric slapped his pocket. 'I'll take care of that. He's given me the keys.'

'Does Ma know he's here?'

'Marion?' Eric asked. He did not like the shortened form, couldn't take to it. He shook his head. 'She'd taken a pill – for a touch of her migraine.' He sent a look towards Cliff, who was already climbing the first flight.

'Thank Christ for pills,' Cliff said.

He felt it or imagined it: something shoved between the shoulder blades at the point between one vertebra and the next. He shrugged it away and climbed past what had been his wife's room – the office now, a six-lever Banham on the reinforced door. He nodded towards the old girl's bedroom.

'You'll have to break it to her gently.'

'Her lost boy back,' Eric said. 'Her darling grandson. It'll take twenty years off her.'

'Will it? Maybe until he's away again.'

'Oh, she'll have her own ideas on that . . .'

The stairs to the attic rooms were uncarpeted. Their bare deal treads were specked with paint. The paper had been stripped from the walls and ceiling, leaving the plaster mouldings standing proud. A fine dust lay in the angles of the walls.

'Still hard at work?' Cliff asked.

8

Eric stopped and ran his finger along the banister rail he'd newly sanded. He was in love with the slow movement in the grain. 'Oh, you know it's a religion with me.'

They went into the front one of the two rooms. Ralph was lying under a plaid rug, one bare foot pushing from the fringed end and his shirt still on. The room's furniture had been pushed into the far corner and covered with a dustsheet. Eric's trestles and ladders occupied the rest of the space. One bar of the fire was glowing in front of the tiled hearth, the coal effect sending out little shivers of red light.

'I wanted him to feel cosy if he woke,' Eric said. 'There's nothing worse than a cold room.'

Ralph's breath stalled for a second but then recovered. There was something slow and thorough about it, as if he'd expel every atom before he took the new breath.

Eric smiled, tilting his head. 'Sleeps like the Rock of Gibraltar, always has done.'

'Good little sleeper,' Cliff said. 'No problems there.'

Feeling that he maybe shouldn't, he looked at the spiral of his son's hair, the untrustworthy way in which it sprang from his scalp, straight and doggish but thinning already at – what was it? Thirty-one? Two? Should know these things. His hand grasping under the cover, plucking at something in his sleep, and then the other tucked into the side of his face with the knuckle shiny with saliva. A black arc under the thumbnail, which meant he'd had trouble somewhere with that rustbucket of a van.

'What the tide's brought in,' Eric said, grinning.

'The cat, you mean.'

'Oh, I wouldn't say that. I suppose he'll be staying here now that he's arrived.'

'Not necessarily. And whatever brought him here might drag him back again.'

Cliff took off his raincoat and looked for somewhere to hang it. He was sweating from the climb and his heart was beating with a fast, lurching rhythm. A scavenging gull made a squeak of sound over the roof. He glanced at his watch. Just turned seven.

He looks done in, Eric thought. The hours he keeps. In the back bar of the Lamb or that other place he uses. The kind of shites he spends his time with. 'I'll make us some tea,' he said. 'I expect he'll sleep the clock round.'

Cliff shook his head, staring at his son's yellow heel. A black shoe lay on its side below the couch, spilling a waxy roll of sock. 'Don't bother for me. I only came here to see if it was true.'

'And now you know.'

'That's right.' He fidgeted through the pockets of his jacket and found one of his cards. 'Give him this, then.'

He held it out. Eric took it without comment and dropped it into the pocket of his shirt. 'The help doesn't arrive until nine,' he said.

'Help?'

'Man, if you like. To open the place downstairs.'

'Ah.'

Eric shrugged. 'Oh, I've plenty to do before that. Then she'll be waking up, I suppose.'

'You don't sleep much yourself, Eric?'

He looked cornered for a second but then laughed. 'Sleep? What's that?'

'Read to me,' Ma said. 'Read that to me, Cliff.'

'. . . the poor, if buried at all, were buried in the sand with a few pots of drink and food beside them. It is, however, not certain that the poor were always buried. It is very probable that the peasants were not supposed to have a future life, and their bodies would be cast out either on the desert or into the river. It is not for nothing that the scavenger creatures who live on carrion – the vulture, the crocodile, and the jackal – were all deified.'

Ralph woke with a memory of talking to Eric. Or Eric saying a few words – something about paint. He saw the tea left on the seat of a chair next to the cot and reached for it. The side of the mug was still warm but the tea was almost cold. He propped himself on his elbow and drank it.

Ah. Light fell in an oblong from the window which was filmed with pale dust. He knew the room but wasn't sure where he was in this space which seemed to have swivelled about on itself. Then it turned back again.

Years since, anyway.

He freed his legs from the rug. The heads of tacks studding the bare boards felt like points of ice against the soles of his feet and there was the mouse scratch of a radio. Talk. He thought it was elsewhere in the house but then realised that it was in the same room – behind him, on very low. For a second, he did not want

10

to turn. The walls had been stripped back to their plaster and tatters of paper were swept into a pile near the corner. Blockish shapes gathered under sheets. The light fittings had been removed and the ends of dark, braided cables pushed through a rough hole in the centre of the ceiling. The radio buzzed with talk. He stood, pushing at his bare knees, and turned.

'I am one of those who like to watch paint dry,' Eric said.

He sat on a folding chair behind the door, dressed in powdery overalls, with one leg resting on the other. His foot twitched in its worn plimsoll.

'I thought you'd sleep your life away,' he added.

'I still might.' Ralph looked for his trousers and saw them carefully folded on a sheet of clean newspaper.

'It's not my place to welcome you,' Eric said. 'But welcome anyway.'

Ralph looked about the room again, as if he hadn't heard. Eric followed his glance with a pained smile.

'Is Ma awake?' Ralph asked.

Eric laughed and laid a finger on the glass of his watch. 'You might say she is; it's nearly two o'clock. Your father's already been and gone.'

Ralph stared at the shrouded furniture. 'Cliff was here?'

Eric nodded. 'What you call him is your own affair.'

'Did you phone him?'

'No need: he has his own informants.' Eric worked his neck to take a crick from it. 'Marion will be waiting for you, I expect. She had me run out for a bottle of port wine.'

Ralph bent to lace his shoes. He could smell the staleness of his own clothes. 'Where did you take the van?'

'Around the corner. That exhaust is knocking itself to bits, y'know.'

'I know.' He stood and smoothed the creases in his trousers. 'Are you joining us, Eric?'

Eric looked sly and sorrowful at the same time, an expression like a child's. 'Oh, I'm busy up here. Besides, it's something for the family.'

'You're family, almost.'

'And almost means not quite. Tell her I'll be down if she needs me.'

'Right.' Ralph drew a hand across his face. 'I'll need to shave.'

'There's a razor of mine in the bathroom. Though you needn't

11

bother, you know – she'll take you as you are.' He stared from his chair, tipping his head back against the wall. 'So where've you been sleeping? In that vehicle of yours?'

'Last couple of nights, yeah.'

Longer than that, I think.

Ralph teased a scrap of paper with his toe. A part of the pattern caught his eye. 'What are you doing up here, Eric?'

'She wanted these attics more presentable.' He sighed, resting his knotted hands on his thighs. The fingernails were crusted with white paste. 'What better thing is there than to decorate a room?'

Ralph shaved and then washed himself over the handbasin. He found a stick of deodorant and rubbed some under his arms. A sun column stood like a sentry in the corner. The frosted pane of the window had a clear oval in its centre and he looked through it into the garden. He could see the whitewashed back wall and then the little square of lawn with its perimeter path of herringbone brickwork. The grass was trimmed and vivid. A hole had been punched in its centre the diameter of a four-inch flowerpot. Water shone at the bottom.

He looked at himself in the mirror again. There was a flaw in the glass that he remembered. He stepped out on the small landing. The door of the office was locked when he quietly tried the handle. New wood had been let into the frame and then planed clumsily flush, left unpainted. He looked down into the narrow hall. He could hear the chirrups and dull explosions of the machines downstairs. A lorry passed in the street and made the front door shudder. The pinpoint of the spyhole went dark for a second.

His grandmother was sitting among cushions in the high-backed chair, reading through the illuminated lens of her desk magnifier. White flex trailed from her lap towards the skirting. When she looked up, her eyes were clouded and sore-looking. Ralph wondered for a second if she could see well enough to recognise him. A two-tier trolley of polished mahogany stood near the foot of the bed and dark slices of cake were arranged on a plate alongside a bottle of wine and four dimpled glasses.

'Your father was reading to me,' she said.

She smiled. For a second her face looked as fresh as a young girl's. She marked her place with a slip of paper and closed the book, resting her hand on the blue cover. The shine of her rings was nearly lost in the flesh of her fingers.

'I heard he couldn't wait,' Ralph said.

She examined him for another second. 'That's right; he had to go.' Her smile turned painful, open-mouthed. 'Aren't I worth a kiss, then?'

He kissed her on the cheek, tasting the scented powder she wore. She put the tips of her fingers to his face. Their coldness disturbed him. He stepped back. She wore a thick cardigan of pale blue wool, open over a dark dress with a waxy shine to it. Little pearl buttons clustered below her throat.

'He left you his card,' she said.

He laughed. 'His card?'

'His business card. He lives on the premises nowadays. Just like me.' She took up the little oblong and held it out to him, turning her face as if it was no concern to her. 'Have you been talking to that fool upstairs?'

'Eric?'

'Who else is a fool on these premises? What's he been telling you?'

'Nothing much,' Ralph said.

'Then I'm thankful for small mercies.' She looked at him again, observant. 'Shall I ask him to cook you some dinner?'

'I'm fine for now. I'm still a bit—'

'You're still a bit delicate.' She nodded. 'You can wheel that trolley over if you like.'

He pushed it close to her. The cake had a rich, fermented smell.

'I knew you were on your way,' she said. 'I had a sense of it. It had to be someone arriving or myself going on a journey. And I don't stir much nowadays.'

He drew up a chair with a frayed embroidered seat. The frame shifted as he sat down. He glanced towards the bed and saw for the first time the cat curled asleep on the wrinkled cover.

'Still Mrs Foster?'

She followed his look fondly. 'Who else would it be? We're both of us too old to change now.' She frowned and looked lost for a second, as if she'd forgotten what she'd been about to say. Then the lines of her face eased. 'A glass of wine then. So that I can drink your health.'

'I don't drink, Ma. Not now.'

13

She sighed, leaning back. 'Not even a drop for the occasion? Wet your lips with it.'

He smiled. He still felt light-headed with sleep. He took a piece of the cake.

'The cake is Mrs Cromer's,' Ma said. 'She gave me it out of the blue last week. She must have been expecting something too.' She smiled across at him. 'You'll need to do the honours, Ralph – my hand isn't as steady.'

He picked up the bottle. The cork had already been drawn. The wine looked almost black in the daylight filtered through the nets. He poured two equal measures and then held the neck over a third glass.

'Let him come down if he wants to join us,' Ma said.

'I asked him, he said he wasn't family.'

'A silly game he's playing,' Ma said. 'That sort of cleverness will only take you so far.'

He put down the bottle. The cat on the bed raised its head to yawn. It saw him and froze, staring his way. Its eyes looked sightless. A wave of its fishy breath carried on the air.

'Well, cheers,' Ma said.

He chimed his glass with hers. He took a sip and then put it down. His mouth was still coated. 'So how are you keeping, Ma?'

'Oh, better for seeing you. There's not a lot that keeps me going. Force of habit, mostly. I'm like a machine somebody turned on and forgot about . . . Don't ask who.'

'I think you're looking well, Ma.'

She laughed almost silently, the folds of her throat shaking. 'That's the sort of remark Cliff makes. He thinks I'm soft enough to be pleased by it.' She took a tiny sip of wine, then a larger one. The cat stretched and jumped to the floor. It began to clean itself, cocking a leg. 'That animal has a better view when it licks its arse,' Ma said. She pointed to his glass. 'Finish that, won't you? It's bad luck not to.'

'Best if I don't, Ma.'

'How long since you had a drink?'

'More than a year now.'

'Finish it then. You can cork the bottle after that.'

He felt the heat of the wine in his throat. He was drunk in a second and then it passed as suddenly. She was still staring when he put down the glass.

14

'I'd say you'd lost a stone, Ralphie.'

'Been doing my own catering, you see.'

'You're one of these men who'll turn gaunt in their middle years. You'll take after our side of the family.'

'Thank God for that.'

'You mustn't mock your father: he has a troubled spirit.'

'Then good for him.'

She nodded. 'He has a gentle heart but he's weak-headed; there's no strength in him.' She looked up. 'I saw that woman of yours the other week. With the little boy.'

He lowered his eyes. 'My wife, you mean?'

'I'd rather not call her that. It was all I could do not to tell her what I thought of her.'

'I'm glad you didn't, Ma. Where did you see her?'

'Oh, in the town. Eric was taking me. There was something about a licence for a machine.' She looked at him shyly for a second. 'Is that why you're here, Ralph? For her and the boy?'

He shook his head. 'No, Ma. That's not it.'

She looked pleased, as if she had drawn him into a confidence. She lowered her voice. 'So where have you been, my love?'

He frowned, then looked up into her livid eyes. 'I went along the coast – a month here, a month there. I took digs through the winters and lived in the van the rest.'

'Like a gypsy,' she said, half admiring. 'Did you make some friends?'

'A few; not many.'

'Quality, not quantity . . .' She watched the cat nipping at the fur at the base of its tail. 'So are you here for a while, Ralphie?'

He heard Eric moving in the room upstairs, scraping the legs of something across the floor. 'A while,' he said. 'Just for a while.'

'But no more than that?'

He felt uncomfortable under her smile. He looked away and saw a tiny striped spider running across the bedcovers and then dropping from sight on an invisible thread.

Three

'I haven't got a gun but I could get one,' Jean said.

Cliff smiled and put the phone to his other ear. 'Talk like that helps no one: I don't even want to hear that kind of thing. If you see him you can phone me – I can be over to your place in five minutes.'

He heard her suck in her breath and pictured the exact expression she might have on her face. 'Look, I'm trying to get the kid's tea,' she complained, 'and you phone me with this.'

'You'd prefer ignorance?'

'Is he likely to turn up here, Cliff? Is that what he told you?'

'I told you – I haven't even spoken to him.'

'Is he staying, though?'

He looked at his watch. 'He might be. He might be on his way to somewhere else.'

She left the phone for a second to call to the little boy. When she picked up the receiver again, her voice was quieter, as if she'd managed to calm herself. 'I'm sorry, Cliff, but the thought of him walking about out there doesn't please me one bit.'

The edge of the desk was pressing into his belly and he turned in the swivel chair to ease himself. He looked through the open door. It was mid-afternoon but only a couple of customers were wandering, lost-seeming, among the rows of appliances. Colin was repairing something in the yard and he heard the shriek of a drill.

'Sorry, Cliff, but that's the truth,' Jean said.

'Look, I didn't want to frighten you; I just thought you ought to be told.'

'And *she* didn't?' she said, intuitive.

'Ma?'

'Who else would I mean?'

'She thought it might not be a good idea.'

'The last time I saw her, she gave us such a look!'

'You told me, yeah.'

16

'The sort that would freeze you over.'

'A look's just a look, Jean. You're getting as bad as she is.'

'I mean it, Cliff! I felt something. I had to grab hold of John and turn him away from her.'

He let that pass. The space of a breath. 'He's family for her as well, don't forget.'

'I think she has. Or she wishes he wasn't.'

He said nothing.

'Is he still drinking?'

'That depends what you mean.'

'Is he?'

'I don't know if he's drinking. Ma brought out a bottle of wine she'd been keeping.'

'He'll be drunk then; he'll start with that and continue.'

'Drink wasn't his problem, Jean. It was more than just the booze.'

'If you believe that, then you have my sympathy. That guy puts the fear of God into me, Cliff. Drunk or sober.'

Cliff could hear the boy now, calling from another room, it sounded like. Demanding attention.

'Wait!' Jean screamed. 'Wait one minute!'

He looked up and saw one of the customers hesitating at the office door: an elderly man in a yellowed tweed cap and overcoat.

'As far as I'm concerned, I owe you a lot,' Jean said. 'That's a personal thing between us, Cliff.'

'You owe me nothing. I mean that.' He swung the chair again, undecided. Struck by a spirit of indecision. 'Look, I'll have to go now, Jean. Are you sure you're OK?'

She gave a laugh like a dry cough. 'I'll need to be, won't I?'

For a second he didn't know what to say. The old man was still in the doorway, sending him a sad and baleful look. A little black and brown terrier was standing at his heel. 'That's the spirit, Jean. Ring me back if you're still worried.'

'If!' she said.

'So how is the lad?' he asked carefully.

'If I have to tell him anything about this, then I don't know what will happen.'

'Then leave it with me for a while.'

'Having a kid leaves you vulnerable,' Jean said. 'A kid is always your weakest point.'

* * *

17

'. . . fill it and then sand it down and then fill it again and sand it until it's right and then maybe three coats of the eggshell emulsion. It depends on the state of the surface how many coats you'll need: how the paint sinks in. But as you'll know, that old plasterwork is very porous.'

Ma nodded. 'Its pores are known to me.'

'Then I needn't have spoken.'

'*White,*' Ma insisted. 'But not a *glaring* white: the kind of white that doesn't shout for itself.'

He smiled, understanding her well. 'There's as many kinds of white as there are colours altogether. Then there's white with a hint or a tint of something: a kind of faint pastel, if you like.'

'I've never cared for pastels. They are colours that are ashamed of themselves.'

'So a quiet white in eggshell then?'

She moved so that a cushion slipped. He stepped forwards to reinstate it but she waved him away and pointed towards the glass fruit bowl. 'Fetch me a peach instead of fussing!'

He delved into the fruit. Apples and bananas, waxy-skinned satsumas. He rejected a peach with a blemish and picked out another.

'You'll decorate while Rome burns,' Ma told him, holding out her hand.

'Are we on fire, then?'

She turned the fruit, frowning. Any second she might fling it back. 'Well, what did you think of him?'

He went back to his chair, perching at the very edge because he was in his work clothes. 'Think? Why should I have thoughts in particular?'

She made a noise in her throat and struggled again. It was the time she usually napped but she was awake for excitement and restless as a tired child. Eric jumped up quickly and this time managed to arrange the cushions for her. It was so humble an act that it angered him he could not perform it for ever.

Ma sighed as she settled again. The whole side of her hip and thigh was aching. 'So you've no comments to make?'

'It isn't for me to comment. And whatever I'd say you'd turn it against me.'

'I'll only have to catch you once,' Ma warned. 'If I let slip, then your neck will be broken.'

He looked at the cat which was watching the rain from its spot against the window. 'So where is he now?'

Ma let her lids droop. 'On his way to his father, I expect.'

'Oh? He didn't ask for the keys to his van.'

'He said he'd walk. To see what changes there are.'

'I've given him dinner,' Eric said. 'He'll go for miles on that: he could walk and never stop.'

'Only I wouldn't allow him!'

He shook his head. 'You dote on him and that's your weakness.'

'Why a weakness?'

'It means you're left with nothing in reserve.'

'Well, you'll see what my reserves are . . . He only went away because of that bloody Abyssinian woman: anyone would try and distance himself from that.'

He stared, not knowing whether to laugh. 'Why Abyssinian? Why say that?'

'Because she has that darkness about her.'

He shook his head. 'I don't follow you sometimes, Marion.'

'You're too full of yourself, that's why.'

'He'll slip away again when he's got what he wants,' Eric said. 'Whatever the extent of that is.'

'You are viperish,' Ma told him. 'The next life you'll crawl on your belly.'

He laughed, blowing it between his lips. 'Then no change there . . .' He picked at the dried adhesive on the pads of his fingers, peeling it away in little strips. 'He's nothing like his father, you see: you can't rely on his good nature.'

She looked up, glaring. 'Are you the bloody expert?'

'I'm saying nothing, only that there's no comparison.'

'Then why should I compare them?'

Ralph walked through the streets as it became dark and the traffic wound down for the day, thinking about his father and then about Jean and the kid. About his wife and the child he felt nothing but curiosity.

The streetlamps passed through changes of colour before strengthening to yellow. He stood outside a café near the station without intending to enter. A woman was sitting at a table by the corner. She must have become aware of him on the other side of the glass because she looked towards him and then away. The fat

19

owner was leaning against the counter, talking to her and laughing, having made some joke.

He walked on for a mile or two, then stood out of the drizzle in a shop doorway. The wet tyres of the passing cars made a swishing sound which soothed him. The rain had released smells of oil and rubber from the dry roads. Starting to laugh, despite himself, he became short of breath and had to gulp in air. The laughter and the warm dampness of the air relieved a sore, tight feeling in his chest and throat. Sensing someone looking over his shoulder, he turned his head and saw a naked mannequin staring beyond him with painted pupils. He started to laugh again, couldn't help it now. A woman pushing a child under the plastic cover of a pushchair glanced at him and looked away. A bus went by with lit windows and slowed for the junction with a squeak of brakes. Still smiling, he felt his pockets and found his father's business card. He read it in the light of the window display.

Ma slept. She woke. She wasn't sure she had been asleep.

'You're still here then?' she asked.

'Still,' Eric said. 'We were talking about Cliff.'

She had no recollection. Her hands were cold on her lap, like cuts of meat. She gathered them together.

'He might have been a mouse,' she said.

Eric looked about the room, smiling at the cat dozing at its window.

'The way he was with that knocker,' Ma explained. 'Only scratching at the door.'

He nodded. 'So what are you saying? That he was timid?'

'He was never that, only deferential – a Barnardo's boy, as they are.'

'Other people can be just as fine,' Eric said.

She did not rise to him. 'He was in digs in Cintra Street. Mrs Bawdley, dead now. He'd come after work but not so late that it could count as evening. The place was hardware then, DIY.'

Eric sighed for the lost years. 'DIY. Don't I know it!'

A suit that was too tight for him and his brown shoes waxed. He'd lift the striker a fraction and let it fall, with less effect than the clearing of his throat on the step. She could see his dark shape through the pebbled glass as she went to the door.

'He'd always have some little thing with him. A present.'

For her or for Joyce. A set of handkerchiefs. A plant – one of those ferny things that wouldn't last but the fineness of their leaves expressed him. He'd never declare himself with colour. Ma would always take them, on behalf of . . . He would smile and blush as if he were courting the mother, the widow.

'I was five years a widow by then,' she said.

Eric shook his head. 'You never were: it wasn't your temperament.'

'He'd shiny-shoe into the hall with his little package of something. What would he have been?'

'Nineteen, twenty. A kid, anyway.'

'Did I ask you . . . ? They were shy at first.'

'You mean *he* was.'

After a chat over tea she would leave them in the room. She'd hear them in the hall when they went for their walk. They would not hold hands until they were out of sight of the house. When it was raining he would take the grey umbrella from the stand. On Sunday afternoons he brought her back before five.

'I almost had to do his work,' Ma admitted. 'Move things along for him.'

'Chivvy him up, say.'

'Foresee any obstacles. For instance, she was years older and he was frightened by that. He was so gentle with her that I thought he might let her slip.'

'Never come to the point of it.'

'And with his background he could never presume. I'd be playing cards with Mrs Foster.' She smiled towards the cat. 'Cribbage or gin rummy. "Your mind's elsewhere, Marion," she'd say. We'd hear them beyond the wall, their voices in the quiet parts of the wireless. Listen but not listen, if you understand—'

'Oh, I do that perfectly.'

'He'd never stay beyond nine thirty, when he'd tap on the door and look disappointed we'd not joined them. "*You and your friend.*" She'd walk to the stop and wait with him, come back on her own.'

Eric nodded. 'The streets were safer then but I'd watch them sometimes, keep an eye.'

'Follow, you mean.'

'If I happened to walk in the same way. The buses would pull in from the town then, come round that corner near to Hollises. You could wait for an hour at that time of night.'

*   *   *

21

The drizzle had stopped by the time Ralph reached the yard. A man was working at something under a lamp in the shelter of an awning: a small electric motor laid out on an enamel-topped table. A long silver estate car with a dented front wing was parked crosswise in the cobbled space and behind that was the white wall of a small caravan. The man looked up from his work. He had thin, puckered features and dark hair which fell across his forehead.

'Looking for Cliff?'

'That's right,' Ralph said. 'Cliff will do.'

The man stared as if he were thinking that over. He looked lost somewhere in his thirties, although he might have been older or even much younger. The bare lamp swung gently on its cord, changing the lines of his face. Then he made a decision and pointed over his shoulder to the caravan.

'He's in there?' Ralph asked.

The mechanic nodded and scraped back his greasy hair. His eyes wandered uneasily.

'So that's fair enough,' Ralph said.

A light was showing behind the caravan's steamed window. Another window was set in the narrow door and he saw a shadow behind it. When it moved it lost its shape in the dimpled glass. He crossed the yard, stepping over pools in the tarmac. It was still raining, hadn't stopped for a second. He saw that the yard was cluttered with the carcasses of washing machines, refrigerators, gas cookers. A building bulked to his right. It was set with dark, barred windows, narrow and arched.

The door of the caravan opened when he was still a yard away, swinging out and back.

'I see you but I don't believe it,' Cliff said. 'I don't believe it for a minute.'

He held out his hand. Ralph stared at it for a second, making some adjustment, then shook it. His father wore a tan shirt and white slacks. The shirt had a fancy tapered collar and little fringes below its yoke. The other man watched them from below his lamp.

'You can go home now, Colin,' Cliff said.

Colin wiped his hands on a rag, working it into the spaces between his fingers. He shifted his weight to his other leg but didn't move.

'Just go home!' Cliff said. 'Go on!'

Colin tossed down the rag and stepped softly away from the

22

light, his head down. Cliff watched him until he was out of the gates.

'He'd never leave unless I told him to,' Cliff said. 'This place is a refuge for him, you see.' He laughed, finding something ridiculous about himself standing in the narrow doorway, his back to the light. Mine host. 'Well, this is where I live,' he said.

Ralph nodded, looking about. His hair was shiny with wet and the shoulders of his jacket were dark and soaked.

'So come inside!'

He stepped back while Ralph climbed the metal steps and ducked through the low doorway. He brought the smell of rain into the warm air.

'You'll have to dry yourself,' Cliff said. 'What was the idea of walking?'

He didn't answer. He looked at a tiny TV buzzing on a tabletop at the far end. He had never seen one so small. His father leaned out to pull the door shut and then brought a dry towel from the rack outside the shower cubicle. Ralph considered it, then started to rub his face and the rat-tails of his hair. Cliff squatted to turn up the small gas fire. Almost at once the cabin felt uncomfortably hot.

'Like a gyppo,' Ralph said.

'It suits me: my bachelor existence. If you don't mind the mess . . .' He stared at his son in the mirror over the basin. The remains of his meal were still on the fold-down table. Wasn't expecting him until tomorrow, if at all. He danced about on his small feet, shifting his weight, not able for a second to stop himself. 'I don't think I could live in a house now,' he said. 'You get used to everything being close to hand.'

'Ever take it on the road?'

'I've no time for roads.'

'So what about the flat you had?'

'I bought this – I had to tow it from up-coast. Now it's in the yard it doesn't cost me a penny. And besides of that, I'm my own night security.'

'And you make a living from this place?'

'I make a living, yeah. I'll show you around when your clothes have dried.'

'They're drying now,' Ralph said.

The caravan was backed up against a tall brick wall, one end nosing into a corner of stacked fridges, washers and microwave ovens. A tarpaulin was draped part of the way over, tethered by ropes and weights.

'He might not look it but Colin's a genius with those things,' Cliff said. 'He'll put three together to make one that's a runner. Then we get rid of the leftovers . . .'

Ralph was looking up at the canopy. The lamp above the workbench showed the ironwork painted in red with the curling brackets picked out in green. Some of the glass panels looked new – a different glass to the old, thinner and without its mysterious cloudiness.

'You painted that yourself?'

'Eric gave me a hand when I moved into the place. It took a week just to chip away the scale.'

'Labour of love then.'

'You know what he's like.'

Cliff fiddled with his keys, dropped them and picked them off the cobbles, grunting as he bent. A pain swam upwards through his stomach. 'I wanted to talk but I thought you should rest first. And I feel a bit constrained with Ma around. No reason why I should but that's the fact of it.'

'That's Ma,' Ralph said.

He watched while his father unlocked the red double doors, then pushed at them until they released with a crack and hinged back.

'Why a station?'

'A couple of them came up when they closed the branch line.'

'You mean you've bought it?'

He nodded. 'I did my sums, then took out a loan.'

'A bank loan?'

'A loan's a loan.'

They stepped inside. There was a chill under the open spaces of the roof. The windows with their dusty, wired glass gave very little light. Ralph waited while he flicked at switches. Fluorescent tubes began to stutter into light. The main hall was taken up by rows of washers and fridges.

'White goods,' Cliff said. 'That's where the money is.'

'That's all you do now? Washing machines?'

Cliff stared down the hall to where one of the tubes was misfiring. 'My main line, yeah. I sell bits of furniture as well, anything I can turn a quid on.'

'So what about the other place? What happened there?'

He gestured, smoothing the air with his hands. 'Things were

going well and then they weren't . . . I decided I could use some larger premises.'

'It's larger, all right – it must have taken all you had.'

'More than that . . .' Feeling his son staring at him, he wondered what was showing on his face. He pointed to the broad door at the far end of the hall. 'There's more rooms behind – old waiting rooms, toilets, stationmaster's office . . . I use some for storage, junk that accumulates. Then a door opening to the street . . .'

Ralph laughed for some reason, just a little bark, a joke he wasn't about to explain. His father waited a second and then tapped him on the shoulder to show that they should go on. When he didn't move, he was sorry that he'd touched him.

'There's something else I'd like you to see,' Cliff said.

He led the way through the rows of machines, to the far wall where high windows overlooked the platform. There was a broad door with strap hinges branched into curlicues of painted iron, secured by a bar and a big galvanised padlock. He hunted among his keys.

'You're taking no chances,' Ralph said.

'No sense in that. No sense in chancing.'

He unfastened the padlock and pulled back the door, straining a little. They stepped outside, on to a narrow platform lit by a wired lamp on the wall above their heads. Shiny patches of rain were drying on its uneven paving. An old overstuffed chair stood with its back to the wall of the building, like an animal in a crouch.

'I like to sit out here,' Cliff said. 'A smoke and a beer when the day's over. To think things over.'

Ralph went to the edge to look at the place where the tracks had been. It was an overgrown gully, smelling ripely of something. The dark backs of houses stood on the far side – a lit window here and there, noise from a TV, the sudsy smell of washing. 'I can't say I'd like to myself.'

Cliff watched his back. 'Foxes wander down here. Have you ever heard a fox at night?'

'Plenty of 'em.'

Cliff nodded. 'You came here to see Jean?'

'Did I?'

'I'm asking you,' Cliff said.

Ralph shook his head. A light came on in one of the houses, shining on the tangle of brambles and saplings on the slope of the cutting. Cliff stepped closer and they stood like people waiting for a train.

'The boy then?'

'At some time I might like to see the boy,' he said with care.

Cliff nodded. 'You'd have to talk to her first. At least you should let her know you're here.'

His son turned to him, smiling. 'I thought you might have done that already.'

Someone opposite opened a window – kitchen or bathroom – and he looked up sharply, as if his train of thought had been disturbed.

'I don't know your plans,' Cliff said. 'That's the only reason I'm asking.'

'I wasn't aware of having any.'

'That's fair enough. If you're satisfied with that . . .' Cliff shifted, staring at the windows of the houses opposite. Sometimes he felt overlooked, sometimes he was doing the looking. 'If you're here for only a while, you'll need somewhere to stay.'

'The van will do.'

'There's somewhere more comfortable. This little flat I've got the keys of . . .'

Ralph grinned at him. He couldn't quite read his expression.

'In return you could help out, say. A few drives . . . There'll be a couple of quid on top, of course.'

'Do I look as though I'm short of cash?'

Cliff felt teased. 'Well, are you?'

'That's a question for my accountant. So you're offering me a job?'

'Not a job as such – this place doesn't run to employment. It'll be just bits and pieces, cash in hand. How's that van of yours fixed for paperwork?'

Ralph laughed, tucking back his shoulders.

'I could help you on that, as well. No point in asking for trouble, is there?'

'No, there isn't.'

Ralph walked a few yards up the platform. There was a worn white line marking its edge and he put his toes to it. The wind along the cutting carried the smell of something sweet.

'Call it flesh and blood if you like,' his father called after him.

Four

They followed the blank wall of the railway past a night café and then a glazier's with its iron shutters down. A man on a push-bike passed them, going in the same direction. Leaned over the handlebars, he gave them a warbling whistle.

'Recognise him?' Cliff asked.

'Should I?'

'You only went to school together.'

He shrugged. 'That's a while ago now.'

'You can't shrug away your life,' Cliff said. 'Even if you wanted.'

Ralph looked after the bike with its wavering backlight. 'Do you own this flat?' he asked eventually.

'I'm just the caretaker,' his father said. 'I haven't got the nose for property.'

'So whose is it?'

'You kept asking questions when you were a kid: who? when? why? No one could keep up with you. But then you seemed to lose interest . . .' Cliff stopped to watch a car backing into a tight space by the kerb, angling his head to look in at the driver. 'A feller by the name of Terry Wordsworth. He'll be away for a while. In fact I don't expect him back within a year.'

'I see.'

'You don't see – you're just jumping to conclusions.' Cliff shook his head and walked on. Ralph watched him for a second and then caught up, matching his father's rapid steps.

'So Ma can't climb the stairs now?'

'She can but sometimes it's better if she doesn't have to. That's why Eric installed the chair.'

'Eric installed it?'

'That's right.'

'And he stays there now?'

'He comes and goes – he's got a key. He rents a room somewhere but he can't see much of it.'

'So where does he sleep?'

Cliff laughed. 'You know he doesn't sleep.'

They had crossed the railway bridge and were going down its other slope, past the wire fence of a breaker's yard. The smell was of damp cinders and spilled oil. A dog started to yap. In an aisle between broken cars they watched it pedal the air at the end of its tether, snapping at nothing.

'I can't spare much time myself,' Cliff said. 'Too busy with the business. It's better if there's somebody with her.'

'It's like they were married or something.'

Cliff gave him sideways look, frowning. 'If she has a fall, say. Or the bastards who took her clock pay another visit . . .'

'Her clock?'

'A couple of months ago. They came in through the back and stole her perpetual clock. She was awake and heard them moving about. They tried the door of her bedroom. They must have seen her lying there and decided not to risk it.'

'Any idea who?'

'I'm still making enquiries. I'll turn them up one day – a timepiece like that doesn't just disappear.'

'No. Does she still meet her women?'

He pulled a face. 'The odd one still comes to visit. A few more have dropped off the twig.'

'So she still believes in that stuff of hers?'

'I'm not sure now. Maybe she doesn't. People think you need more to believe in when you get older but really you need less – like you need less sleep.'

He thought, He wants to know it all but he's tight with his own information.

'She still has the cat,' Ralph said. 'No change there.'

'*Mrs Foster*. Eric has his own thoughts on that . . . If he wasn't so scared of Ma, I think he'd throttle the thing.'

'I could do it for him,' Ralph said, smiling. 'I could throttle it myself.'

They turned the corner, walking on past the low redbrick blocks. The grass fronting the flats was overgrown and caught with scraps of paper.

'Is it one of these places?'

'Very similar,' Cliff said. 'A bit further on.'

He nodded at something ahead of them, close to one of the high yellow streetlamps. At first Ralph could see nothing but a

28

wire trolley piled with splitting plastic sacks parked against the low area wall of one of the courts. Then as they came up to it he saw an old man in a greasy coat standing close against its far side.

'Hello, Lester,' Cliff called.

The old man grinned at them, showing a yellow stump of tooth. Cliff started to feel the sides of the plastic sacks, like someone testing fruit for plumpness.

'Anything there for me?' he asked.

Lester held on to the side of the trolley as if mooring himself to it, grinning over the road towards the flats opposite and lifting one foot after the other, marking slow time. His fingers clasping the wire had the shine of old teak. A group of youths went by shouting on the other side of the road and he stared after them, more watchful then nervous. The whale hump of his back pushed under the shiny coat.

'Lester's the richest man around here,' Cliff said as they walked away. 'At least that's what people say.'

'He should be in hospital in that condition.'

'He'll outlive the rest of us. If you suffer enough, you live for ever.'

'Is that right? So, how old is he?'

'Somewhere between fifty and a hundred.'

'And how old is Ma now?'

Cliff stopped for a second. 'That's a hard one too . . . Is that why you came back – you were worried about Ma?'

'Who says I've come back?'

A young girl pedalling a bike with another kid perched on the crossbar dodged past them as they stepped off the kerb. Cliff called after her but she whooped back at them and went on, pushing at the pedals, standing up from the frame.

'The kids are buggers around here,' he said. 'You'll need to keep an eye on the kids.' He pointed across the road. 'How's that place strike you?'

It was a narrow three-storey block entered by a pair of glass doors. A couple of cars were parked on the square of tarmac to the side. A refrigerator with a trailing black lead stood door-first against the wall of the building. A path of tilting concrete slabs cut across the area of lank grass at the front. The name of the place stood in raised lettering above the glazed doors.

'Mossiman House,' Ralph read. 'So who the fuck was Mossiman?'

'Never made his acquaintance. I'll just show you where things are and then leave you to settle in. Is your luggage still at Ma's?'

'I've no luggage.'

'OK,' Cliff said.

He pushed back the sprung doors. The front hall was cool and narrow, the cement floor glossy with wear. A round ceiling lamp gave off a pale light. There was a flat-door with a frosted panel to their left. A staircase with an iron handrail led up to the landing and turned. There was a smell of disinfectant. A door at the back was wedged to let in the air.

'You'll have a bit of garden,' Cliff said.

'I'm not a gardener.'

'I know . . . It's the top flat.'

He led the way upstairs. Metal-framed windows looked out on the gardens and the lit-up blocks opposite. When they reached the second floor, he pushed a silver Yale into the lock.

'I'll bring you a few things tomorrow, if you like the place.'

'What things?'

'Curtains, a bit of rug to make the place look lived in. You'll meet your neighbours soon.'

'Friendly, are they?'

'Oh, you can't fault them on that . . .'

The hall light had a fringed paper shade, Japanese-style. He pushed back another door and flicked at the switch. A naked bulb made the few pieces of furniture seem isolated in the square area of the lounge. A teak-effect electric fire stood against one wall, topped by a narrow shelf carrying an upended matchbox and a single brass ornament. There was a smell of stale tobacco.

Cliff struggled with a latch and opened one of the metal casements, letting in damp air and the barking of a dog. He pointed to a phone on the low table by the couch. 'The bill's due about now but I'll pay that myself. Have you any friends long-distance?'

'Not that I'd want to phone.' Ralph stared at a dartboard fixed to the wall by brass brackets, halted in front of it as if it had stopped him in his tracks.

'There'll be a set of darts somewhere,' Cliff said. 'Did you play much when you were away?'

'Not a lot.'

'Kept your hand in, though?'

'Not even that.'

'Shame to let a talent like yours go to waste,' Cliff said. He opened more doors and leaned in to snap on the lights. 'Kitchen . . . Bathroom . . .' He stared into the bathroom and then closed the door. 'I wouldn't trust anything you find in the fridge but there's a takeaway around the corner.'

He stepped across the little hall and opened another door. Ralph peered over his shoulder. A narrow bed was covered with a faded red quilt, standing against the side wall with its head to the window.

'I'll try to find you some curtains,' Cliff repeated. He sighed and closed the door. 'The gas is on a slot meter; we'll have to work out something on the electric.'

Ralph stood at the window in the lounge, watching a man carrying a bicycle up the lit stairwell of the block opposite.

'Do you need anything for tonight?' Cliff asked. 'Money, I mean.'

He smiled at the man with the cycle negotiating the tight bends. 'I'll manage.'

'Take this anyway. Where's the point in managing?'

Ralph looked down at the note, then took it. He crumpled it and pushed it into his shirt pocket. 'Thanks.'

'You never were a saver,' Cliff said, staring. There was something wrong but he couldn't see it, couldn't put his finger. 'I tried to show you the value of money but you couldn't seem to grasp it.'

'No.'

Cliff stepped back from him, a yard or two. He found the distance more comfortable. There was a faint stale smell, sweetish. Something spilled on the rug and left there. He would have to speak to her about that, make an issue.

He pointed. 'I'd open more of those windows if I were you.'

The fridge was defrosted and dark, a box of something in the freezer compartment which Ralph didn't examine. He went through the wall cupboards and found a tin of beans and another of pear halves in syrup. He ate the beans cold from the can and then rinsed the spoon and ate half the tinned pears. The pears were good. He found tea bags in a caddy but no milk. Sitting in the living room he could hear the voices of the TV in the flat downstairs. His stomach was sensitive, odd chemicals churning. He thought about his father's story of the clock, picked up the phone and dialled his old number. The earpiece made a series of stutters and then a message came on to tell him it was no longer obtainable.

He took off his shirt, peeling it from his skin. There was a whisper from the new note. The bathroom was tiny with a handbasin tight in one corner and a bath with a shower fitting plumbed above. The plumbing was clumsy and amateurish, with rough drips of solder under the joints. The walls had been tiled in a pale-green glaze and some of the tiles were broken or missing altogether, leaving spots of dried adhesive on the plaster behind.

He undressed and out of curiosity slid back the mirrored door of the medicine cabinet. It was empty except for a box of Aspro and a small bottle with a rubber cap. He unscrewed the cap and sniffed at it carefully. He sneezed once and put it back on the shelf. As he turned away, he noticed a red toothbrush with its bristles worn to a wiry pad caught behind the cold tap of the handbasin.

He stepped inside the bath, careful how he placed his weight. A plastic curtain with a pattern of sailboats hung from the rail. He could still hear the TV from downstairs and a door opened and closed directly below him. Standing naked he thought he detected a warmth against his skin. As he turned the tap of the shower, he saw a clock spring of hair sticking to the side of the bath near his small toe. The water came with a gush and it was swept away. He looked for and found a damp sliver of soap in the bowl at the head of the bath.

Ralph woke during the night to a man's cracked voice yodelling into the dark. There was silence for a while after but it began again when he tried to settle. He kicked his legs clear and went to the open window. The breeze was damp against his chest and arms. The voice was a low mutter now, grumbling to itself in broken words which were nearly sobs. Then it started into the song again, the tune of it gathering in the throat before being released, lifting. Not loud but with a penetrating tone.

'Blood . . . Jesus . . . saved . . .'

Ralph leaned out, resting his breastbone against the chilly edge of the frame. He could see nothing at first but the lit windows on the stairs of the flats opposite. The sky was reddened above the roofline – the belly of a low raft of clouds lit by the lights of the town. The well of space between the blocks was in darkness but when he looked down further he could see the white smudge of a face below, a puncture of a mouth.

'Jesus' blood never . . . never . . .'

A crash of stems. The man cackled, pushing himself back to his feet. A light snapped on, swinging over the plot. There was the crack and creak of an opening window.

'Jesus' blood . . .' he sang, swaying like a weighted doll, the black gash of his mouth vibrating. 'Jesus' blood never failed me yet, never failed me yet, never failed me yet. Jesus' blood never failed me—'

'*Sammy!*' a woman's strong voice shouted.

He grinned up, straddle-legged, adjusting himself to the shifting of the ground, standing in a trodden space in the tall weeds.

'You drunken old bugger,' she called down, more in sorrow than in anger. 'You noisy old sot!'

A light came on in the block opposite. Ralph looked at his watch but the luminous face was too faint to read.

'You get to bed now, Sammy!'

He slowly shook his head. 'I just want to sing you this, Alma. A little song for you before I go—'

Ralph saw the dark outline of the woman's head directly below. She pointed. 'Sing to me in the morning! Get yourself to bed before someone calls the police!'

The man shook his head again, desperate, pushing out his arms. 'Fuck the police! Fuck the bastards! I've been quiet for long enough.' He squared himself to sing, planting his feet.

'Sammy!' she hissed before he could draw a proper breath. 'I've got one of the kids staying over. She wakes up and I'll break your neck.'

'A hymn would never wake an innocent babe—'

'Go to sleep, Sammy! Now!'

Her window closed with a bang, as if she had settled the matter. There was silence for half a minute. Ralph was turning away when he heard the man's complaining grumble start up again. The words were low and broken and seemed to stutter to an end of their own accord. He looked out again and in the second before the light snapped off downstairs he saw the man lying at his full stretch among the weeds, his eyes and mouth open, one arm spread, the other folded across his chest.

I'll sleep when I'm dead, Cliff thought.

He sat in the easy chair and listened to the crying of the foxes, not like babes tonight so much as mad old men sobbing in the dark

33

beyond the railway tunnel. After a while the Dobermann bitch from the scrap yard joined in, then another dog or a couple from the windy balconies of the blocks to the west. A stir of animal grief in the early hours.

He lay back in the narrow bunk with his eyes closed, listening and not listening. When I'm dead but not before. The racket subsided until it was one stray dog and then the phone began to burl inside the station.

Not at this time of night. No!

It stopped as the answering machine in the office clicked in. Cliff listened to the silence as his own message played. Have to get that changed. A civil tone invites all kinds of cranks. The bleep sounded and then the message must have been reeling on to the cassette. Silence again, but for the yapping of the one dog.

He sat up in the chair. They get you down, they walk over you. Feeling for his tin on the low table, he encountered a cold spill of coffee, cigarette lighter, glass ashtray. He put his hand on the flat tin and brought it close to his chest. He worked at the top with his thumbnail.

He assembled the makings in the dark, then cooked the pea-size of shit in the flame of his lighter, rotating it between his thumb and finger. He'd taught himself or learned from example, this craft or trade. Tiny grains of it then, hard as gravel, working by feel on the hard edge of the mattress. And nowhere darker than there. The other men would wake at the cooking smell of it, perking like dogs.

He drew some in, listening to the little crackles of the burning paper. He felt his body lengthening, the little hooks of it unfastening. The dog stopped and he could still hear the faint singing of the fox. They know my habits, whoever is calling. He started to think about his son, and then by a slip of the mind about his wife.

Wayne Crowley had shown him how to smoke. Not this stuff but the other, the plain. To draw it into your lungs and not to swallow. Hair like liquorice and that snaky way of moving. Serpent. They worked for Davidsons the movers, jolting around in the back of the big van, lumping and lifting. Wayne was a few months younger but had an older way with him. All mouth and clever fingers.

Cliff thought, No one to model on. Feeling my way.

Sitting on a front-yard wall together. Wayne had a Vespa which never seemed to run. A basin underneath to catch the drips of oil. Shared it with his older brother. Army later and then dead. Stepped on a dog turd and it blew off one leg, both bollocks. Or vice versa? His shirt off a skinny chest and a fresh tattoo where a bicep might be. Then that other mate of his – scab-faced but better than the company he kept, and the only one with a working vehicle.

They lit up, drawing the stuff into their lungs. The bro was tinkering with the Vespa, explaining the finer points. He glanced up suddenly and stood up with shims in hand, greasy-knuckled. From the set of his pigeon chest they knew that a girl was coming their way.

Cliff didn't turn. Squatting down with a bare inch of fag between his fingers, he stared at the bike's carburettor and felt a blush starting as he followed with his eyes the ins and outs of pipes, valves, linkages. A black oil drip was getting heavy below a perished seal.

'Joyce!' the brother called. He grinned but then let his mouth hang slack in the pantomime of a drool. His friend watched her, too, with this idiot smile, the blackheads in different stages of scab and weep around the folds of his gills. As she came closer, he dropped his eyes.

Cliff stood up, the dead cig in his fingers. She was walking past on her way to the shops, a green bag folded under her arm. She could have crossed over but she chose not to, approaching in the busy smooth way she had of walking.

Seven years older – woman with a woman's fat walk – she looked not at his face but at the inch of fag he'd forgotten, nodded at the rest of them. A jerk of her round chin for them all. Dark hair in a bob and pale skin, tiny freckles like pinpricks of soot. The brother stared at her as she passed, not looking away once, staring at her back and then down at the push of her hips and the space between her legs under the print skirt, pointing his face at it, gathering it to a snout of attention. He pursed his lips and made a damp mewling noise, calling it to him as you would a kitten.

She stopped as if she'd realised she'd forgotten something. When she turned around to face them, she had a frown which gave her a look of calm thought.

'Going somewhere?' the brother asked – already windy you could see, regretting it but now he had to play the part. Took a step back as she came towards them and knocked his hip against the bike, which shuddered on its stand. He giggled and glanced sideways at the others. Pissing his pants already.

Except that she ignored him. She glanced at the others and stopped in front of Cliff, standing square before him. Her face was set but not frowning now, looking at him less than level because he was an inch the smaller. A small nineteen. The terror of her made his stomach turn.

He didn't see her hand move, only felt the sting. It was more across the mouth than the cheek, numbing his lips and teeth and drawing a ringing sound from the air.

She took one step back. Her bag had fallen to the pavement and she leaned to scoop it up, then turned her back on him and the rest. They were silent anyway. He watched her walk away through his watering eyes. The plates of his skull were still vibrating. He had some inkling he'd been chosen, victimised. He could feel grief behind his teeth. Salt tears and phlegm.

Five

Cliff walked through the market. The air was still muggy after the rain. He had no memory of driving. He caught himself in the windscreen of a car and saw he was wearing a pale straw hat with a curling brim, its crown frayed into wisps and spikes. He snatched it off but after a second replaced it.

He stared into the back of a van. A fridge and a tumble dryer were tied with linen ropes to the frame.

'The dryer needs attention but the fridge is hundred-per.'

'Bring 'em along tomorrow. Early if you can.'

'I need the cash today.'

A hand on the man's arm. 'You can do that for me. You can be patient.'

He walked away, crossing the road. Somebody called after him. 'Cliff!'

He waved his hand without turning, walking through a drizzle of music from radios and limping cassette decks. The streets were lopsided with sunshine. The smell of burgers and frying onions made him hungry and nauseous. He lifted the hat to smooth his hair. It slipped his mind why he wore the thing. The crowd was dense suddenly, pushing against him. A woman passed some comment to her friend and he smilingly touched the brim of the hat to her and then squeezed edgeways between two stalls to the far pavement. A man was lying half in a doorway, legs thrusting out and his face flattened against the stained tiles of the entry. Gnats buzzed above a splash of vomit. Cliff stood still for a minute, taking his bearings, then turned into a street where fly-pitchers stood against a nine-foot wall of glazed brick. Sheets of cloth or weighted newspaper were spread to mark the limits of their premises, petering from half-legit to some oldster holding out a wristwatch without a strap.

'Keeps great time, it's the cold that's stopped it.'

'Cold?' he laughed.

'When you get to my age . . .'

37

He took the watch, squinting at the face through the rubbed glass.

'A quid would be all right,' the man said.

'Gold, is it?'

The old man nodded, stepping closer. His eyes were yellow and confidential. 'Half the sods nowadays wouldn't know a good watch if they shat it.' He stared up the road, frowning as if his enemy would come from that quarter. A smell like pickled walnuts lifted from the folds of his clothes.

Cliff thumbed him a pound piece and dropped the dead mechanism into his pocket. Something heavy was already resting against his hip. He found a paper bag and drew out a peach. At the same time as he bit into it, he spotted Alison on the other side of the road, her back to him and her head down as she sorted through a box of items.

The peach was sweet and soft. He finished it in three bites, threw away the stone and wiped the juice from his chin. He adjusted the hat again, glancing in a car window. She was walking by him, holding something tight in her fist which he thought she might have stolen. He noticed that she had a man in tow.

No business of mine now.

He thought he was safe under the hat but maybe it was the opposite because her eyes turned to him straight away. She waved with a look of pleasure on her face which made him half pleased, half disgusted.

'Your eyes!' she said, peering under the straw brim.

'What's wrong with them?'

'Nothing's wrong – they're only bloodshot.'

'Nothing wrong with blood,' the character put in.

He chose to ignore that, judging it below comment. He stared into Alison's face, which looked plumper and fresher than he recalled, her skin holding the light.

'That's the reason for the hat?' she asked.

'I must have picked it up somewhere. I forget.'

She laughed, tilting back her head. 'It suits you.'

He smiled but she was talking to her friend now, her shoulder turned. The man had an accent he couldn't locate, a buzz to the edges of his words as if another voice were speaking below it and just a fraction behind. She turned back to Cliff and opened her palm to show a tiny diamanté brooch in the shape of a bird. She closed her fist over it again.

'Like it?' she asked.

'These people aren't idiots,' Cliff said. 'He's probably missing it already.'

She shrugged. 'If he comes chasing after me I'll throw it half a mile.'

They stared at one another a second. The companion was smirking. He was short but broad-bodied. Cliff's height or a fraction smaller. The shoulders of his jacket were too tight, the arms an inch short of his wrists. Dead man's trousers.

'Look, Alison,' Cliff told her. 'Thing is, it turns out I need that key back after all. A friend of mine's turned up and needs somewhere to stay.'

'Well, that's fair,' she said.

Cliff took the brown bag from his pocket and offered her a peach. The bag was saturated with juice. 'Go on. Take a couple.' He held them out to the man-friend.

'This is Frank,' Alison said. 'This is Cliff who I've told you about.'

The other man nodded, biting into his peach. He held it in his mouth while they shook hands. His eyes were a shade of very pale blue so that for a second they gave the effect of blindness. When he blinked one lagged behind, like a limp in his face. His red hair was cropped so close to the skull that it was a shadow. The hand Cliff held was sticky from the peach.

Young anyway. A bit of youth for her.

Alison was squatting down now to look through the leather shoulder bag she carried, dragging out various things and putting them close to her feet for safekeeping. She wore a dark square-shouldered jacket and slacks – in the likeness of the man, as if they were a pair, say. Her black hair was decorated with a comb Cliff thought was new. Had she stolen that? He noticed that the brooch was no longer in her hand. There was a trail of something across the shoulder of her jacket which she could not have seen. Snail trail. Baby drool. He didn't want to think.

Frank said, 'She can never find a thing in that bag.'

'Then what's this?' She held up the Yale key, started piling things back with her other hand. 'So no more baths?'

'You can always use the shower in the caravan,' Cliff said.

She pushed home the clasp of her bag and stood up. 'I like to soak, you see. That's the whole point for me.'

'He might be gone after a couple of days. I'm not sure.'

'Anyone I know?' she asked.

He felt a smile crossing his face, couldn't stop it. 'No, you don't know him. It's Ralph that's back for a while.'

She was looking around her, interested in the comings and goings of the crowd. 'Ralph?'

'My son, that is.'

'Ah!' The crooked set of her teeth powered her smile. Months ago he'd wanted them put in order, even offered to make a gift of the money. 'That's good news,' she said.

He couldn't answer. She watched him too closely for a second. He thought of how her eyes went slantwise when she was on the track of something. The companion was taking an interest also, grinning in their direction.

'It is good news, isn't it, Cliff?'

He crumpled the paper bag around the broken peach and threw it underarm below a parked van. 'It is, Alison, 'course it is.'

He ate in the Bengal Café. Fat ladies on the wall in see-through trousers. Fountains and nightingales. The waiter in a grubby white jacket, yawning because of no rest from the night before when they put out linen to make a restaurant. The place had a licence but it wasn't time yet and he thought even a medicinal brandy would be out of range. He ordered the special breakfast anyway and then two cups of coffee to lay a ghost.

He dozed in a corner booth and woke to a finger prodding his chest. Eleven thirty by the wall clock. He tried the phone with his third coffee balanced on the shelf. He rang the flat first and listened to the ringing tone for a full minute before he pressed the button for redial.

He swallowed half the coffee and then tried Ma's number. Someone picked up the receiver at the fourth or fifth ring.

'Hello?'

'You're some kind of secretary now, Eric?' Cliff asked. 'You answer all her calls?'

'She didn't sleep much last night and so she's taking a little nap.'

'Seen the rest of the family lately?'

'You mean Ralph, I take it?'

'Any sign of him?'

'Not today.'

'What about last night?'

'He picked up that van of his. It must have been in the early

40

hours, otherwise I'd have heard that engine start. Have you tried him at that place he's staying?'

'Tried him there, yeah.'

'Maybe he's gone for a walk.'

'I don't think so.'

'What, then? I mean, what's your worry?'

'You know what my worry is,' Cliff said.

Eric laughed. 'So? If he's gone, then it's good riddance.'

'You don't mean that, Eric.'

'Don't I? I don't want her upset, that's all. Not in her state of health.'

'He hasn't done that yet.'

'He'll soon work his way round to it.'

'Give him a chance first. A dog you take in from the street gets a chance to behave.'

He could hear the old man fussing with something next to the phone. Restless hands. That habit he had of picking things up and examining them for flaws – ornaments, fruit, a cup on a saucer.

'Eric?' he asked.

'I won't do that, Cliff; I won't give him rope.'

He paid and went outside. The sleep had made him forget where he'd parked the car and he stamped about for twenty minutes. The main market was over and the stalls were being dismantled and stacked on vans. Mounds of cardboard and packing were knee-high in the gutters. The chill and the hard shine of the morning were tempering and the pubs were already packed, spilling out into the street with thickset men in trader's aprons, the jukeboxes leaking their tunes and empty glasses already lined up in the angles of the walls.

He found it with a scrape along the driver's side. Trader's van, maybe. Dustcart. He had some trouble starting and ran the engine for a while before he put it into gear.

A kid's trike lay on its side across the front path of Mossiman House. The refrigerator was still standing against the side wall, its length of black rubberised flex trailing across the concrete. When he went inside he saw the door of the first-floor flat wedged open with a chair and heard the drone of a Hoover from inside. He climbed the next flight and rang the bell, waited. He slipped the key Alison had given him into the Yale. It was a poor copy and he struggled with it before it worked the latch. The hall light was burning behind its paper shade. The door was open to the living room.

'Ralph?'

There was no one in the lounge. The effort of climbing the stairs had left him feeling dizzy. He thought about taking a pill but decided to leave it. The bedroom was on the block's shady side but when he opened the door he could see bright sunshine opposite the bare window.

He made one coffee and took it in. He laughed when Ralph sat up and stared at the mug. 'Just drink that.'

He went back into the lounge. The gardens were filled with sunshine. He saw how the long grass of the garden below had been trampled, then looked at the trimmed lawn next door to it and saw one of Alma's daughters, he thought the younger, sitting on a plaid rug spread over the lawn. She was breast-feeding her baby.

He thought that Ralph had fallen asleep again but then he came in from the other room.

'I'll go if you want,' Cliff said. 'If you're still feeling tired.'

Ralph went into the bathroom and came out looking even paler.

'You didn't sleep well?'

'I was up half the night. Some lunatic was caterwauling outside the window.'

'Which lunatic? You'll need to be more specific.'

'Some old guy – the woman downstairs gave him an earful.'

'Alma,' Cliff said.

'If that's her name . . .'

'Good. Another thing is I don't suppose you've eaten?'

Cliff watched his son shave, talking to him from the doorway, seeing the way he looked through the mirror as if he didn't recognise himself, moving his face under the blade.

'Ma will be expecting you.'

'When?'

'Some time today. She takes her nap between three and five so any time after that.'

'How long has she been taking naps?'

'The doctor says she needs her rest. She had a little stroke, you know.'

Ralph stopped the razor with his face half-shaved. 'I didn't know, because no one told me.'

'I'm telling you now.'

42

He went back to shaving but nicked himself at the corner of the lip and had to stanch the blood with a cold flannel. Cliff wandered away and then came back to the door. 'I wanted to tell you last night but I couldn't find a space to put it in.'

'No?'

'No. That's the truth.'

The kid's bike was gone from the path. Cliff glanced up at Alma Drean's flat. She must have still been cleaning because every window was standing open.

'Think of Alma,' he said. 'If you're in a situation.'

Ralph looked up also. 'What kind of situation?'

'I mean that she knows her way around here. She knows the faces.'

The big estate car was parked at an angle to the kerb. A cooker lay in the back, half covered by a dustsheet.

'I've been around the market,' Cliff said.

'That's all you bought?'

Cliff pulled a face. 'It isn't really worth my while any more but it pays to keep yourself known. You can't afford to drop out of sight in this line of business . . .' He fiddled with his keys. 'Somebody clipped it while it was parked up today. I'll get Colin to take a look at it later.'

Ralph nodded, waiting patiently beside the car.

'Is your van parked near here?' Cliff asked.

Ralph pointed to the black hump of it across the road, behind a line of cars.

'Do you mind if we take that instead? I might have some business to put to you later.'

Ralph led the way over the road. The van's door wasn't locked and he slid it back against its stop with a crash. He swung himself into the driver's seat, leaned over and pushed back the passenger door. Cliff hauled himself inside. He felt his heart struggling. He glanced into the back.

'Is this where you used to live?'

'I still do,' Ralph said.

Out of cardboard boxes, then. A plastic barrel in one corner over a basin. A striped mug on its side; gutted glossy mag spilling tits. A sour smell of fruit gone bad. 'Home, sweet home, ay?'

'That's right.'

Cliff settled himself on the torn upholstery. The pads of the

43

pedals were worn through to bare, smooth metal. His son had to coax with the choke to start the engine and then it hammered away with a lopsided rhythm. There was a throaty stuttering sound as they drew away from the kerb.

'Needs a new exhaust,' Cliff said.

'I know.'

'I'll give you an address later. I use them a lot so I've got an account.'

'Thanks.'

As he turned the corner, Ralph saw the man who had woken him sitting on the low wall of the court opposite, as if waiting for the day to start. He pointed.

'That's him. The singer.'

Cliff leaned across to look, nodded.

'You know him?'

'He's known to me, yes.'

They sat in Murdo's while Ralph put away a full breakfast and then a pile of toast and marmalade. When the woman came to clear the plates, Cliff tipped her and beckoned the owner.

'Murdo, this is my boy Ralph.'

'I can see that,' Murdo said.

Ralph put his mug down and they shook hands.

'You get an eye for faces in this business,' Murdo said.

Cliff paid for the meal and put the change in the blind box. He'd swallowed a pill in the narrow toilet and it left him feeling sleepy and content.

'I have to pick something up,' he said when they were back in the van. 'Then there's someone I want to introduce you to.'

The layout of the roads was different from how Ralph recalled it, with some of the main routes turned one-way. The engine laboured on the long inclines, shaking against its mountings in lopsided spasms. He drove behind a trundling yellow digger until it turned right. Space started to open around them, the houses and small shops turning to broken frontages with brick piles in between. The light had turned yellow now, midday. They could taste the smoke of a fire from somewhere – woodsmoke with an oily edge. A gull catapulted towards them, veered and missed by an inch.

'Those things can break a windscreen,' Cliff said.

Ralph grunted. 'So what's happening here?'

'Supposed to be a new ring road. They started the thing and

then the money got tight. Someone's swung for it already. Some small-fry councillor.'

'Pity.'

They crossed an empty junction. A yellow chemical closet was set like a sentry box a few yards from the road, beside two Portakabins erected one above the other. A man leaned in the doorway of the lower cabin. Ralph watched the digger navigate the broken ground with its shovel held high. He heard the drone of something above the racket of the motor.

'Look out!' his father warned.

He flattened the pedal. A middle-aged woman in a dusty white raincoat was crossing the road, holding the big hoop of a tambourine above her head like a threat. She stared at them, affronted. Her wire spectacles shone. The rest of the band was marking time behind her, the front rank waiting at the edge of the road and the others trailing back across the margin of the vacant site, their feet stamping the ground, raising the dust. They were mostly children of early school age with a few older kids among them. Their line had telescoped so that those in the middle could hardly lift their feet but still kept their comb harmonicas to their lips, humming out the march. A small elderly man towards the rear was carrying the baton with its silver knob.

Ralph shook his head, breathing again. 'Are those things still around?'

Cliff laughed. 'You've been away four years, not forty.'

As if she'd been delayed for long enough, the leader brought down her tambourine and started to strike it with the heel of her hand, setting out the slow pace. Giving the van another stern look, she positioned herself on the other pavement and the children began to file past her, fifteen or twenty of them. The man brought up the rear, leaning on the baton as if it were a staff. One of his feet was dragging, splayed out at an angle to the other. Ralph restarted the engine, which had stalled. There was a small queue of traffic behind them now. He drew away slowly.

'I used to be a bandsman when I was a kid,' Cliff said. 'I wouldn't claim it did me any good.'

'I can't see you with a comb and paper.'

Cliff turned in his seat to watch them as they filed out of sight. He leaned back, feeling the weight of himself. 'No, maybe you can't.'

*   *   *

45

He had to stand with a hand against the side of the cab after he'd climbed down. His face had turned pale and a patch between his eyebrows stood out as white as bone.

'Something wrong?' his son asked.

He righted himself without answering and tugged at the ends of his jacket. He nodded across the road, at a row of pebble-dashed houses behind thin hedges.

'See the one with the chicken?' Cliff asked.

The corner of one of the hedges had at some time been trimmed into the shape of a bird. Stems were pushing out from the sides now so that the outline was nearly lost. A low iron gate was held closed by a loop of string. Cliff carefully opened it. The narrow front garden was taken up by rubber-lidded dustbins. A pair of stone temple dogs guarded the front step. Cliff sounded the chimes and positioned himself in front of the spy lens. Ralph placed his hand on the head of one of the dogs.

The door was opened by a small, stout woman with glossy curls of chestnut hair. She must have been Ma's age or a couple of years younger. Ralph stared at her hair.

'This is my son Ralph,' Cliff said. 'This is Mrs Cromer.'

'I was waiting to meet you,' Mrs Cromer said. 'I'm glad it's sooner rather than later.'

She turned her cheek to him. Ralph glanced at his father, then put his lips to it.

'I see you've made friends with my dogs,' Mrs Cromer said.

She laughed and turned abruptly away, passing out of sight through a doorway. Cliff made a noise in his throat and held out his arm to show that they should follow. They stepped across the hall and then into a long room with drawn curtains. Dark furniture emerged from the dimness.

'And how is Marion?' Mrs Cromer said. 'It must be more than a month since I saw her. Because of my commitments I can hardly leave the house. As you'll realise.'

'She knows well how you're situated,' Cliff said.

When his eyes had adjusted a little, Ralph saw that an old man sat in one of the low armchairs, turned towards them but bent over his own lap as if he were nursing a pain in his middle. Mrs Cromer stepped around him and offered them the couch. They sat down. The upholstery had a smell of medicine. The old man did not lift his head to them. His long hands hung limp between his knees.

46

'Will you take some tea or refreshment?' she asked, standing before them.

'Unfortunately we're behind in our calls today,' Cliff said.

She waved a finger at him. 'There's such a thing as being too busy, you know. The boy is hardly arrived and you're working him already!'

Cliff ducked his head. 'I've just a few things to show him. As it happens.'

She smiled down at them. 'I'm sure that's the case.'

She turned to the old man, as if she'd only just recalled him and bent to prod at his chest. He looked up, staring open-mouthed at her.

'Cliff has arrived,' she said. 'And Ralph, Marion's grandson!'

He gave no sign that he'd heard.

'He maintains that he's deaf sometimes,' Mrs Cromer told them. 'Really he can hear a pin drop.'

'He's a good age, anyway,' Cliff said.

She gave her head a little shake. 'It's the deceit of it that hurts me.'

An alarm went off somewhere in the house but she ignored it. After a while it stopped.

'No sign of Colin?' Cliff asked.

Mrs Cromer lifted her hands. 'I hardly see him except when he comes in to sleep. He can't even make an appearance for Sunday dinner.'

'That might be my fault for keeping him so busy.'

She shook her head. 'Your influence is only to the good, Cliff. As I remarked to Marion the last time I saw her.'

'She'll have her own ideas on that,' Cliff said.

Mrs Cromer nodded and smiled down at Ralph, rubbing her hands. 'It must be marvellous to be home after your travels. I know you were never far from her thoughts.'

The old man flinched in his seat and made a smothered cry. 'Well, if I could see this TV . . .' Cliff said.

'That's right. You'll see his face light up when that's put to rights.' She turned back to Ralph. 'If this young man would do me the honours.'

Ralph followed her up a steep flight of stairs into a room full of the vapour of aromatic linctus. A dressing table with a three-way mirror blocked the light from the window. Mrs Cromer flicked at a switch. 'Here it is.'

The lamp seemed only to colour the dimness. The TV stood with its screen against the wall, a deep veneered cabinet with a black cable looped around, then secured by a knot of black insulating tape.

'He seemed to think it was all my doing,' Mrs Cromer explained. 'When it finally gave up the ghost.'

Ralph squatted and picked up the set. It had the dead-iron smell of fused circuitry. He carried it down into the hall and stood it near the door. It was immensely heavy.

'Are you positive I can't offer you something?' Mrs Cromer asked in the lounge. 'A glass of wine, for example? Wine is a sacrament.'

'Best not,' Cliff said.

Mrs Cromer put her hands together with a soft clap. 'Well, give my regards to Marion. I hope she understands my difficulties.'

'Oh, she's full of understanding.'

Six

They drove through scrappy Sunday-afternoon traffic along one of the long arterials, passing discount stores, bingo palaces, the yards of small builders, used-car lots. Cliff smoked one of his squat little cheroots, dotting the ash through the wound-down window with a backhand flip – quiet for a while and content with his own thoughts, composing himself around the centimetre of glowing ash. As they slowed for a junction, he tapped Ralph on the arm and pointed to a skip parked by the kerb.

'Do a favour for me?'

'The TV, you mean?'

Ralph drew into the kerb and took the set from the back of the van. It wasn't any lighter. He lugged it crook-backed across the road, his arms around the big teak-effect cabinet. At the edge of the skip he managed to get a hand below and tipped it over. The skip was nearly empty and it fell with an iron crash.

'I'll get her another,' Cliff said when he climbed back into the cab. 'She'll never see the difference and if she does, why should she care?'

'The old feller might but I don't think he'll put up a struggle.'

'That's right.'

'And she's Colin's mother?'

'That's one of her faces,' Cliff said.

'I don't know about Ma's friends. I'm not sure I like the company she keeps.'

'They seek her out. She's no heart to refuse them . . .'

A row of shops – laundrette, café, a plant-hire with mixers and scaffolding on the pavement. A pub at the corner. He found a space down a side street and they walked back. It was after closing time but a side door was open with a chair across the threshold. His father scuffed it to one side and they went in.

Tobacco smoke was solidifying against the ceiling. The coloured lights of the games machines chased their tails in silence. A man sat at the end of the bar with his eyes on the TV.

'Bar's closed.' Just glancing their way.

'I can see that,' Cliff said. 'Is Charlie at home?'

The barman looked them over, then pointed towards the other side of the bar, behind the screen with its mirrors and optics. He looked back to the TV, which was showing a black-and-white film.

'On his own?' Cliff asked.

He twisted on his stool again. The seat of his trousers squeaked against the leatherette. 'Pardon?'

'Is he on his own?' Cliff asked more slowly.

He stared at them for another second, his mouth half open. 'I think so.'

'I'm glad that's cleared up,' Cliff said.

Ralph looked about the room. There were booths and secluded corners where someone might have sat in private but there was no one else. A dartboard hung in a deep recess protected by a bench and a corner seat. Half a dozen mismatched darts were already sticking in the pocked face as if someone had scattered them from his fist. He felt his father nudge his elbow.

'Feel like a game?'

'With those things? You might as well throw that ashtray.'

'Not them. Wait for me a second?'

He nodded to the barman and went through a door in the screen to the other bar. Ralph heard him talking but not what was said because of the noise of the TV. He watched the old film, which he thought he'd seen before. It troubled him that he couldn't recall the title.

'What's it called?' he asked the barman.

'No idea.'

Cliff came back after a couple of minutes, a slim black leather case in one hand.

'My friend Charlie lent us these.'

Ralph took it from him. It opened like a spectacle case. He drew out one of the thin metal barrels. The flights were folded behind a spring clip.

'Charlie likes the best in life,' Cliff said, watching.

'I'll bet he does.'

He walked over to the board and stripped out the house darts two and three at a time, dropping them with a clatter on the copper surface of a table. The barman turned his head at the noise.

'Some light, if you please!' Cliff called.

The barman watched the film for another few seconds and then got down from his stool and walked the length of the bar to flick a switch. A swan-necked lamp came on above the board.

'We could put a fiver on it,' Cliff said. 'No point in playing cold.'

Ralph assembled the darts, smoothing back the flights. The barrels were made of some dull, dense material he hadn't come across before. They had an expensive machined look. 'I've hardly played in four years,' he said. 'Besides, I've no money. Or only what you gave me.'

'That's yours now.'

He shook his head. 'No.'

'No harm in a fiver,' Cliff said. He took off his jacket and laid it on the seat of the bench. The lining behind one of the pockets was torn. 'So let's see you.'

Ralph stood just under the influence of the lamp. There was some crisis on the TV with a roll of music. The barman did something that caused the volume to drop. Ralph dropped a dart on the rubber mat and picked it up. His father leaned forward.

'Why is it you're playing left-handed?'

Ralph stared at the dart in his hand, pursing his lips. A smile started to creep, as if he'd been caught out at something.

'So why's that?' Cliff persisted.

'Does it worry you?'

'Worry? No, it's only puzzling me.'

'Why is it? I scratched my arse one morning and wondered the same thing.'

A wild throw to the dead wood at the right of the board. It struck nearly side on and rebounded. It skittered along the ridged mat.

'Take your time,' Cliff said. 'Warm up first.'

He went forwards to collect the dud and Ralph threw past his head and took the twenty a shade below the wire of the double. He threw again quickly and hit the meat of it.

'Those things aim themselves, you see,' Cliff said, stepping forwards.

He was stiff-elbowed, feeling the strain of the day a little. He contested the first few throws and then settled to watch, left standing in the two-hundreds. The boy was left with a ninety-six finish and took it with treble seventeen, double eighteen, double nine.

51

He went to retrieve but his father was there before him, wiping the score and taking up the darts again. The barman had turned off the TV and in the silence Ralph heard the scrape of a fork from the other bar.

'Well, mugs away . . .'

Cliff threw and fluked a straight-off double but his next dart bounced from the wire and bedded itself in the rubber mat. His next attempt peeled off into the five.

He passed the darts over. Ralph settled himself at the mark and threw rapidly, tearing them from the board just as his father chalked the score. A couple of throws after and he was on to a finish. He heard his father snap the chalk.

'I'll give you that one as well, I think.'

'Thanks.'

'Say that like you mean it,' Cliff said. 'Now come and meet a friend of mine.'

A man was sitting on a corner bench in a place from which he would have a view of the full length of the bar. He smiled at them and held up a gravy-ended fork.

'This is Charlie,' Cliff said. 'Charlie Sanderson.'

'Charlie Muggins,' the other man said, laughing. He had finished his meal and the knife and fork were laid crosswise on the plate, over the skin and gristle of a chicken.

'Charlie, meet my son,' Cliff said. 'My boy Ralph.'

Charlie pushed out a hand but then withdrew it. He tried again with his left. 'Sorry, I didn't know you were a southpaw.'

He pressed Ralph's hand, then held it loosely gripped between his finger and thumb, detaining him. He wore a limp jacket of fine grey check, turned yellow at the lapels. His thinning hair was a pale straw. The effort of eating had left a shine of sweat over his face. His eyes were humid-looking and sore. He stared at Ralph for what seemed too long for politeness, then drew him on to the bench beside him, smiling at him as if he were a woman. Cliff sat down opposite.

'A southpaw is as rare as a two-yolked egg,' Charlie said.

Cliff nodded. 'That's right. And both are supposed to bring luck.'

Charlie dropped his grip as if he were only then satisfied that contact had been made. 'Excuse me if I didn't come through, Ralph. Only I believe in making time for a proper meal.'

'We managed to divert ourselves,' Cliff said.

'So I noticed.'

Cliff took the darts from his pocket. 'Well, thanks for the lend.'

He passed them over the table but Charlie fended them off with his palm, pushing them towards Ralph.

'Those are yours.'

'Sorry?'

Charlie blinked and smiled. '*Here.* Don't look a gift horse.' He picked the case out of Cliff's fingers and laid it on the table. 'I know you'll make good use of them.'

'The lad doesn't know what to say,' Cliff said.

'He doesn't even need to say thank you,' Charlie said. He laughed and pushed the remains of his meal further from him. 'Eaten yourselves?'

'A little while ago,' Cliff said.

Charlie Sanderson leaned over the table and pushed at his arm. 'You should have eaten here, Cliff. You're welcome at whatever hour.'

'You know me, Charlie. I don't like to presume.'

Charlie sat back, nodding to himself. He touched his nose at the side with his thumb. 'So this is the famous Ralph? Is it good to be home, Ralph?'

'Ask me in another week,' Ralph said. 'If I'm still here.'

Charlie laughed. Cliff laughed as well and then cleared his throat and looked serious. 'He isn't clear about it himself, Charlie. Ask him why he's here and he can't tell you.'

'It's the same the world over, Cliff. My own lad couldn't tell you what day it is.'

'That's something different there,' Cliff said in a soft voice. 'You can't talk about that in the same way.'

Charlie stared in the direction of the barman, who was hovering as though he required a word. 'I saw your driver,' he said. 'The queer feller. He's another one that isn't quite right.'

'He has just enough to get by,' Cliff said. 'If Ralph decides to stay, he might be doing some driving for me himself.'

'That right?' Charlie flicked a scrap of food from the front of his jacket. 'Well, don't spoil those hands lumping and lifting, son. There could be money in them, from what I've seen.' He nodded to himself. 'I've got boys of my own in that line. All good lads but some better than others.'

Ralph looked at the wreckage of Charlie's dinner, waiting for the jellified gravy and scraps of glazed skin to begin to disgust him.

'What Charlie means is you've a lot of potential going begging,' Cliff said.

The barman came over to the table. 'All right if I go now, Mr Sanderson?'

Charlie nodded and held his hand out for the keys.

'We ought to be getting along too,' Cliff said. 'Now you've given us something to think about.'

Charlie laid the bunch of keys on the table and stared misty-eyed at Ralph. 'I was ready for anything at your age . . . A drink before you go?'

'Ralph here is teetotal,' Cliff said.

Charlie put his head on one side. There was a white scar just below his temple. 'Well, you need to respect him for that.'

'You could have been more gracious,' Cliff said.

'*Gracious?*'

'You could have behaved as if his kindness was appreciated.'

'He's just a fuckhead.'

'No one's just anything.'

'And that business you'd cooked up between you . . .'

'What business?'

'That lark with the darts. Do you think I don't see?'

Cliff shook his head, going in front of him now, head down and holding an inch of cigar inside his cupped hand, trailing a thin lash of smoke. He turned when they came up to the van.

'OK, he jumped the boat, that's all. That's the sort he is – short on timing.'

'So who is he? Some fucking entrepreneur?'

'Then you know the type,' Cliff said. He offered a note backhanded.

'What's that for?'

'We had a bet, didn't we? Don't make an issue of everything.'

'I'm not.'

'That's exactly what you're doing.'

He stared at his son, out of breath now from the pace of his trot. He made a spill of the note between his finger and thumb and pushed it towards him. A determination in the set of his head made Ralph take it. Then he had to thank him.

*   *   *

54

The arcade was open, dark inside except for the flashes of the machines. The display windows flanking the door were crowded with glitter – pottery clowns with gilded grins, top-hatted drunks draped around lampstands, potbellied china saints. None of the punters looked up when Ralph entered. He crossed to the glass booth where a fat man was counting change.

'Is Eric around?'

The man laughed, squeezing the coins between thumb and forefinger. 'He is if he cares to be.'

'Can I go upstairs?'

He shook his head, paying attention to the cash. When he looked up, one of his eyes was covered by a thin film of something. He blinked it away. He had the thin, neat beard favoured by doormen. 'Sorry. But who are you?'

'You could ask him. He'd know.'

The big man turned his back to him, moving in a slow and insolent way. He wore a pale-blue shirt of some shiny material. His shoulders were heavy and sloped and rolls of fat had gathered above his waistband. He spoke into the phone and then replaced it. He resumed his counting, feeding the money into small plastic bags and folding over the ends. Ralph waited. The connecting door opened and Eric beckoned, as if it was urgent that he came quickly.

'She'll be *tired*. Those crows exhaust her.'

'Crows?'

Eric nodded, following him upstairs. 'Vultures, I could say: those women of hers. A couple of them called. You'll see the state they've left her.'

He made a noise of distaste in his throat. He was dressed in his faded brown suit, his tie knotted tightly so that it crimped the collar at his thin throat. Sunday best. He put his hand on the greased rail of the chair lift and then pulled it quickly away. Glancing upstairs, he lowered his voice.

'They were in a panic about that fox in the road.'

'Which fox?'

'A fox that was run over. Its guts were spilled and they saw some significance in it.'

'I didn't notice.'

'Because you're wrapped up in yourself,' Eric said. 'And so was the fox.'

'Very funny.' Ralph reached the middle landing and looked back to see the old man standing outside the armoured door of the office. 'You're not coming up?'

'Not me.' Eric fingered the knot of his tie and eased it away from his throat, as if that part of the day had been gone through. 'Cliff was looking for you this morning.'

'Then he found me.'

Ma sat among the cushions of her high chair talking to a pale woman with permed white hair. The woman turned to stare when Ralph stepped into the room. Fat Mrs Foster was sitting upright on Ma's lap, purring as she teased the thick fur of its throat.

'Stranger!' Ma said.

The other woman turned away from him, gazing towards Ma with heavy, sentimental eyes. Sunlight was angling in and he could see the fumes of incense in the air. A dark lump of it was burning in a brass bowl set on a low stool behind Ma's chair. His eyes were already starting to prickle.

'Eric said you were tired.'

She stared at the door as if she suspected he might be standing behind it. 'I'm tired for him, always have been. Other people might see a different side to me.'

She lifted her eyes. The cat stared at him also. Its throat vibrated with joy at her fingers.

'This will be your grandson?' the other woman asked.

Ma frowned as if it was too close a question. Then she gave a short nod, relenting. 'He's the one, yes.' She turned in the chair, dislodging a cushion from below her arm. When the woman started forwards, she put out a hand to stop her. 'I think we're finished now, if you please, Mrs Ferguson.'

Mrs Ferguson withdrew. Before closing the door she silently placed a sealed brown envelope on the octagonal table. Ma gave it a look and then closed her eyes. She remained like that until they heard the rattle of the front door. The cat jumped from her lap. Ma seemed to sink a fraction and then drew herself up again.

'Are you OK, Ma?' Ralph asked.

'What's OK? What condition's that?'

He laughed back at the look she gave him. 'I was only asking.'

She sighed. 'People want answers straight away nowadays. They think it's the same as shopping.'

'They pester you, Ma?'

'Oh, there's never a shortage.'

'Shall I make you tea?'

She considered that, weighing pros and cons. He saw that a crimson sash had been hung about the frame of the photograph of her and Mrs Foster. Ma stood behind the chair with a ringed hand resting on the back. Her hair was heavy and glossy, the same tone as the carved wood. Alice Foster was already frail-looking. Her right ankle showed the folds of a surgical stocking. Her blind left eye was a blank space in the emulsion.

Ma saw him looking. 'It was her birthday last week, you see.'

'How long's she been gone now, Ma?'

She sighed, annoyed with him suddenly. 'What does that matter?' She cast around and pointed to the brass bowl. 'What you could do is douse that stink for me.'

The dark ember was still leaking smoke. He found the heavy brass cap and laid it over the bowl, sealing it. Then he retrieved the cushion that had fallen and drew one of the chairs closer. Ma brushed cat hairs from her lap.

'Not your style this, Ralphie?'

'No. Not my style, Ma.'

'That's right – some of us can find our way without this palaver.' She stared at him, smiling. 'But you're not cheerful today.'

'Maybe not.'

She lifted a finger. 'When you're in my position, the last thing you want is long faces.'

'I'll remember that, Ma.'

'Take your father, for instance. When I first saw him, he had a shine to him. You could see your face in his, if you understand me.'

'I'm not sure that I do.'

She nodded, accepting his limitations. 'Plenty of water under the bridge since then. More than you'd believe . . . And you're in that place he found you?'

'That's right, Ma. Very nice too.'

'I won't ask you how long you'll be staying, though you could volunteer.'

'I don't know, Ma. I'm not sure myself.'

She half closed her eyes. Her hand trembled in her lap. 'I've never seen the place myself. That part of his life I take no interest in. Was there any sign of that trollop he had installed?'

He recalled the little clockspring of hair sticking to the side of the bath. 'I think she left her toothbrush,' he said.

Ma scowled and then laughed. She put her hand to her chest to control her shaking. 'Poor Cliff! I think he gave her money.'

'He told me nothing,' Ralph said.

'He's only sheepish about it: he was old enough to be her father.'

'She's my age then?'

'Oh, a bit older than you. No spring chicken.' She shut her eyes for a second, as if a thought had offended her. Then she looked up quickly. 'May she rot in hell, for taking advantage of him.'

He drove to Mossiman House in the early evening. The lamp in the stairwell wasn't working and he climbed the stairs by the light from the windows overlooking the court. The door on the first floor was open and light and a lump of shadow tilted through it on to the landing. He looked inside. A woman stood with her back to him in the small hall, close against a man who had his arms about her. The woman made a little growl in the back of her throat as the man hung against her, one leg with its black shoes splayed beyond the line of her body. The grip of his arms was loosening, slipping lower. Ralph went to the door and tapped with a knuckle against the glass panel. The woman glanced over her shoulder.

'Help me with him!'

She wrenched herself around so that he was able to catch hold of the man around his waist and take his weight from her. He sagged into Ralph's arms, swearing softly. The woman shrugged herself free and stepped away from them, as if she were divesting herself of a heavy coat.

'Are you all right?' he asked.

She stared at him, supporting herself against the wall. She was breathing heavily, as if she'd been holding it back before. She lifted her free hand to her face, covering it for a second.

'I'll take him downstairs,' Ralph said. 'Move him into the air.'

She shook her head. She had a soft, lined face. Her pale hair was pinned back but escaping from its grips. 'Bring him inside.'

'Sure?'

She turned her back and pushed open a door into the flat. He saw that she had lost a shoe and then saw it on its side against the skirting – an off-white sling-back sandal. At the same time the drunk's head lolled back and he recognised the old man who had sung mournfully in the garden. His lids were open on the whites of his eyes and his breath was rancid. His feet slipped against the rug. As they struggled into the room, he tried to stand upright. Ralph felt the edge of a sole scrape against his ankle.

The woman was helping now, taking some of the weight. He caught her scent as their heads came together, above another smell he had just recognised.

'Put him down on the bed,' she ordered.

There was a single bed in the corner with a blue quilted cover. The man's feet scuffed the rug as they dragged him towards it. They sat him down on the edge and he seemed to come half to consciousness, staring up at them from one to the other with his mouth open and a child's trusting look on his face. The woman bent down towards him and laid her hand on his shoulder. He looked towards her again, murmured something and then suddenly closed his eyes and slipped over sideways.

'He's arseholed,' the woman said.

'I can see that.'

She nodded. 'The reason I'm telling you is because he's pissed himself and I need you to do the honours.' She waited for a second, looking down at the sleeping man. 'But if you're feeling squeamish, then I can do it myself.'

'It's OK.'

She nodded to him and went out, closing the door behind her. Ralph sat down on the chair beside the bed. The curtains were open at the window; he reached over and whisked one half closed. Then he went down on one knee and began to unlace the other man's shoes.

The drunk moved on the bed, brushing something away from his face. 'It isn't even raining,' he said as if he were continuing a conversation.

'That's right,' Ralph said. 'It isn't raining.'

The woman was waiting for him in the hall, holding a pair of kitchen scissors as if they were a knife.

'You're wondering why I let him in,' she said.

'It's not my business.'

'The fact is I didn't. I only opened the door and he fell through it.'

'Then that's the sort he is.'

'Oh, there's worse than him. A lot worse.'

Ralph nodded at the scissors. 'You're expecting more trouble?'

She stared at her own hand, then laughed. She looked very tired despite the laughter. 'Sorry, only it calms me down to have

59

something in my hand.' She laid the scissors on a side table with a glass top, beside an open letter held there by a stone. 'My name's Alma Drean,' she said. 'The one in there is Sammy.'

'Drean's an unusual name.'

'Not in my family.'

'I'm Ralph. I won't shake hands.'

'You can take a wash if you like.'

He shook his head. She was looking at him calmly, as if he interested but did not impress her. The flat door was still open a couple of inches and he took a step towards it. He heard Sammy murmur to himself in the other room.

'You're Cliff's son?' she asked.

He stopped. 'That's right.'

'He told me. So that I wouldn't worry. I'm on my own most of the time and I need to know who belongs and who doesn't. He had a friend of his upstairs before. A woman. There was a little bit of trouble between them and she left.'

'What sort of trouble?'

'Trouble's too strong a word, really.'

'What was her name?'

Alma shook her head. 'I never found that out. She kept herself to herself, as they say. She wouldn't socialise.'

'Not like me,' Ralph said.

She laughed, lifting her face. 'I'd offer you tea,' she said. 'But one man in the place is enough.'

She put a finger to her lips and they listened together. There wasn't a sound from the other room.

7

Her skirts, her dresses, her intimate garments. Mistrusting the thermostat, Eric spat on the iron to test the heat. Steam began to spout from the vents on its underside. He stood it heel down on the asbestos pad and picked a glass-green blouse from the basket, arranged it on the board, paying attention to the narrow pleats and frills, carefully forming the collar against the shaped padding at the front. He waited for the moment, the iron clicking and gushing little jets. He heard a gull squeal. The first bus on the road gave a rubberised sigh of brakes. One eye on the window, he reached for the iron. A faint bar of light was already showing between the curtains.

'I thought you were asleep,' he said.

'I do that with one eye open – besides, who could rest with that racket you're making?'

'And I thought I was keeping you company.'

'Persecuting is a better word.'

He shook his head. 'A bitter word.'

She stared at the light between the curtains and then eased herself against the tormenting mattress, shifting painfully on to her back.

'So your boyfriend was here,' he said.

'Are you talking to me?'

'Is there a third party?'

'I wouldn't tell you if there was.'

He worked the iron again, pleating the finicky garment. He almost trembled with concentration. When he'd finished he replaced the iron on its rest. 'It's only a fact that you adore him. You've doted on him since he was a scrap.'

Ma could hear the sluggish beat of her own pulse. 'There isn't much in this world to excite that feeling.'

'Not me, certainly,' Eric said. 'You love money first and then your own flesh.'

She held up her hand. The little finger was crooked. Fifty years ago it had been broken and badly reset. 'You'll go too far soon. And then you'll never find your way back. I could send you away with a word, remember.'

'So what word is that?'

He could see it on her lips but she only shook her head. 'Your comeuppance is coming: it'll stride in here and tap you on the shoulder.'

He looked at the picture of Mrs Foster with its dark drape. For protection against the evil eye he touched the top of a pencil nesting in his pocket. Ma gave a groan. He turned to her, concerned for a second, but she was only easing her back.

'And the other was looking for him,' Eric said.

'Cliff? You never told me.'

'You were sleeping when he phoned. And then your ladies arrived.'

'That doesn't matter: you should keep me informed. God knows what will happen to that one.'

'He's in a shade of trouble, I know,' Eric said. 'Let's say more than a shade.'

'Say what you like.'

'He takes from one to pay back the other and every week he's deeper in the shite.'

'You have a vulgar mouth.'

He nodded, relishing the times they could agree. 'With your money you could buy and sell him: you could take that place and make him a present of it.'

'My outgoings would make your hair fall out.'

He laughed. 'Mine maybe, sweetheart: not yours.'

Ma blushed a little and smiled at how he could be charming suddenly, like some types of animal.

'But your cash is earmarked?' he said.

'It'll go where I want it.'

'To the waster,' he said, nodding.

'Everything you say only proves your ignorance.'

He laughed at himself, folding one of her skirts against his lap. 'And it's the lad you care most for.'

'What of it?'

'Because he's like his mother.'

'And you had to mention that,' Ma said. 'To put your grimy finger there.'

* * *

62

That hair Joyce could never train. Ma had to wet it or it wouldn't lie still. She'd say she'd bought her from the gypsies, and she'd start to sob. That veering of children between laughter and fear. And in the end she was too old for him, too much life gathered in her already.

He must have known that from the first, when he shuffled on the step, a suit on him like sombre cardboard. 'Is Joyce in?'

'Is who?' She could tell from his tone he knew the name only through others.

'Is Joyce in, missis?'

She damned herself. 'I'm sorry, she isn't.'

He stared past her with his damp, white face.

'It's no use peering over my shoulder, young man.'

The second she told the lie, Joyce must have shown herself, having listened from the turn in the stairs. She took her coat and went out, still in her own shoes. So Ma could only step aside.

The flightiness of nearly thirty.

'And where did they go?'

'You know,' he said.

'Tell me; I'm sure you must have followed them.'

'Am I invisible, then?'

'Only insignificant.'

He smiled. 'You'll tease that nonsense out of me like it was a tapeworm.'

'What else have I to do, lying here?'

'You sit sometimes.'

'That's right: I sit.'

They walked side by side. When there was no traffic Cliff could hear the brushing noise her stockings made. Though they didn't touch, he felt sometimes a pressure against his thigh and he'd glance down at the space between them. She wore a blue skirt and a short green jacket. A tiny gold arrow was set in her lapel. One of her heels was scraping.

'These shoes are about worn out,' Joyce complained. 'I wouldn't be wearing them, only they're so comfortable.'

He liked the idea of a woman who wore comfortable old shoes. 'I'll buy you some,' he said. 'I'll buy you some more shoes.'

She stopped and then started to walk again, smiling. 'You've more nerve than the rest of them.'

63

'Have I then? So who's the rest?'

'The friends I saw you with.'

'Only one of them's a friend.'

'They make noises at me,' she said, 'because they daren't speak. Do they tell you things?'

'No,' he said quietly.

She shook her head. 'You wouldn't say. They must have told you where I lived?'

'Only because I asked them.'

She smiled again and took his arm. 'Shall we walk like this?'

'OK,' he whispered. His mouth was dry.

'What was that?

He could feel her fingers through the cloth. 'I said OK.'

The tone of her footsteps changed as she leaned on his arm. Wrappers from the fruit market were blowing along the ground, little cups of tissue. He wondered if he should try to kiss her there or wait. The possibility of it made him shiver.

'Are you scared of me?' she asked.

He looked down. 'No.'

Her fingers soothed his sleeve. 'So where shall we go?'

'We could just walk.'

She laughed. 'There's no such thing as just walking!'

They reached the place where the street doglegged. There was a pub on the bend, its hubbub welling through the hooked-back doors. A man sat on the lowest step, crooning to himself, holding his head between his hands. The dimness inside was layered with cigarette smoke. Someone lifted his arm and threw a dart into the light of a lamp. It struck with a noise like a soft wooden bell. It must have been on target because a cheer went up.

'Do you play?' he asked.

She stared at him, surprised. 'That game? I should think not. Do you?'

'Sometimes.'

'It's an old man's game.'

He shook his head. 'There's a youth league. Even a women's.'

She didn't answer but slipped her hand to his wrist. They took the hollow gravel path between the buildings. It was shadowy for a second and then they were smitten by sunshine. Cliff perspired in his stiff suit. The pub had a yard set with iron tables and a man in a white apron was sluicing the floor with a hosepipe. He cleared his throat and spat as they passed. Then they were crossing the fly-buzzing half-acre where people walked their dogs. There was already the smell of the river and they could see the propped hull of a boat on the small boatyard on the creek.

'Take that jacket off or you'll expire,' she warned.

He smiled at her, just as a boy on a cycle burst out of the bushes, brushing past them so that they had to step from the gravel path. The wheels left a cloud of dust behind. Cliff gripped her hand very gently. She was an inch taller so that she had to bend her face to him. His mouth was clumsy until he found a fit. She had eaten something to sweeten her breath.

Another couple of kids pedalled by. He felt the tip of her tongue and then she stepped back from him. She tucked the front of her cream blouse into the waistband of her skirt.

'I'm years older than you.'

'Just a few.'

'A few is it?' She laughed. 'Well, then . . .'

She leaned against him again. A boy walked by leading a dog on a frayed length of string. The dog sniffed at their feet. A woman who followed made a clicking noise with her tongue.

'You old bat!' Joyce called after her. 'You only want some for yourself!'

The woman did not turn. She shook her shoulders as if she were expelling a chill.

'You shouldn't have said that,' Cliff said as they walked on. 'Now she'll tell people we were doing something.'

She blew between her lips. 'Her husband gassed himself. He found her in bed with the lodger.'

'Is that true?'

She took his arm again. 'So what did they say?' she asked.

'Who?'

'What did your friends say about me?'

'Nothing.'

'Did they tell you I was easy?'

He didn't answer and she looked away after a second. They walked in silence and came to a spot from which they could see the water through the trees. The sun turned it into little points of light. He let go of her hand and slipped off his jacket. There was a wooded slope and they could hear the shouts of kids. The tide was on the ebb, leaving a trail of slack water behind Wilson's Island. A couple were sitting nearer to the water, kissing. He turned away and saw how she was leaning forwards, peering, her mouth half open.

'You shouldn't be looking,' he told her.

'Are you my husband or something?'

'No.'

'And what's wrong with looking? Isn't there anything you'd like to see?'

'Of course there is.'

'Then what's that?'

'Lots of things.'

'But nothing special?' She rolled her eyes, impatient with him. 'I'm only curious. What's this thing you'd like to see?'

When he didn't answer she caught his arm, just above the wrist so that he felt tethered by her. He was light-headed suddenly. He felt the laughter lifting in his throat.

'You'll have to lose that shyness,' she said.

'I'll try.'

Her fingers slipped into his hand again. She was taller but her hand was smaller than his and cooler. The underside of her wrist where it left the cuff of her jacket was white as crockery with a pale crazing of veins. The sight of it made his heart hammer. He could smell the warm mud at the margins of the water now, the sourness of the brine against the chalk boulders. The island stood out from the water with its topping of bushes. The couple in front of them stood up, smoothing their clothes.

'A friend of my mother's saw a man naked once,' Joyce said.

'Here, you mean?'

She nodded over the water. 'Standing on the island. He'd taken everything off.'

He stared over at it. A ruined building stood among the stunted trees and you could see the sky through the timbers of the roof. There might have been a fire. 'Maybe he was sunbathing.'

She nodded. 'She swore he had a big erection.'

He said nothing. He could feel her hand warming in his, and the slight awkwardness of her grip as if their palms would never quite match.

'You know what an erection is?' she asked.

'I know that, yeah.' The wind was making his eyes water but he didn't take them from the island. 'Your mother will be waiting,' he said.

She laughed and tugged down at his arm, sending a pain

66

shooting from the socket. 'Oh, she'll have sent someone to keep an eye.'

'Who's that?' He glanced over his shoulder. He could see no one but the light was going and the rise of the beach might have hidden them.

She made a noise between her lips. 'Oh, you'll never catch a sight of him! It's only her little slave I mean.'

Eight

Rain fell but almost at once it stopped. The pavement was visibly drying as Ralph walked to the van. The firing of the engine was ragged and lumpy. He drove as far as the main road but then the racket was too much and he found a space and parked with the nearside wheels over the kerb. A trapped car hooted from behind and he saw the passenger's lifted finger as it drew away. He took out his wallet and riffled the folds, hunting for the little creased card his father had pressed on him:

IDEAL EXHAUST
Exhaust and tyre-balancing specialists
Our object is satisfaction

The office was divided from the workshops by a glazed partition. There was a counter and then an admin area behind a screen. A red-faced man in ragged orange overalls followed him in through the door. On the other side of the screen a pair of mechanics were working under a raised Volvo. The flare of an acetylene torch made him look away. He saw his wife standing at a copier in the other part of the room, bending over it to align papers on the screen.

'What kind of vehicle, sir?' the red-faced man asked.

'Sorry?' He looked away from her.

'What vehicle is it?'

He told him.

'Year?'

He was punching at a keyboard. Lists of makes and models came up on the screen. Little diagrams. He looked up.

'Which year, sir?'

Jean left the copier and sat behind her desk. For a second it suited him to doubt that it was her but he knew that was nonsense. She wouldn't look his way and because of that he knew that she'd seen him. The mechanic had a dent in his forehead which could have been a birthmark or from an accident. He waited with his finger hooked above the keyboard. Out of his eye-corner Ralph saw his wife standing up again, gathering herself from behind the desk, stepping around the partition.

'Did Cliff send you?' she asked.

'I'm sorry?'

'I asked, did Cliff send you?'

He thought she was thinner. She wore her hair in tight little plaits instead of straight and shoulder-length. Her face was brown and shiny from some kind of sun-ray treatment. She'd always had trouble with her skin – spots and dry little patches she took too seriously.

'As good as,' he told her. 'As good as.'

The mechanic leaned over his keyboard, looking from one of them to the other. 'Something the matter, Jeanie?'

She shook her head and went back to her desk. Her plaits bobbed as she sat down and Ralph saw that some were threaded with little coloured beads. She wore a tailored suit and white cork-heeled shoes. He was certain now that she'd lost weight. The mechanic touched something that made the screen go blank.

'Seventy-four,' Ralph said.

'What?'

'It's a seventy-four model.'

The man stared at him. His cheeks had an inflamed look. A draught made the door swing back an inch against its spring and a sour smell of flux drifted in from outside.

'There's another place about five minutes from here,' he said. 'You'll find one place is as good as another.'

Jean looked up from her desk, and said something he didn't quite catch because of a noise outside. He was absorbed and even frightened by the expression on her face.

'I have to listen to the boy grinding his teeth,' she said. 'In his sleep, you know.' She put her hands to both her temples.

'Don't upset yourself, Jean,' the man told her. He turned back to Ralph. 'Look, I think you'd better vanish.'

The men on the floor had stopped working. He watched them through the glass partition – a heavy bodied character of about fifty and one who was smaller and younger. The older one switched off the torch and at the same time a dark, balding man in a boiler suit, joined them from somewhere at the back of the shop.

Ralph pulled back the office door and stepped outside. The sour smell was still in the air. The mechanics watched him but didn't move, except for the little one who caught up and then followed until he reached the entrance.

'You're that bugger?' he asked, in a hissing whisper.

'What bugger?'

'Her old man, I mean.' He had an accent. Cypriot, say, or Maltese. 'The one that hit her kid?' he asked again, quietly.

Ralph stopped just as he was on the pavement. He wanted to answer but only shook his head. He had all kinds of reply but that was the best. Not to deny it but a sad shake of the head.

The little man kicked him. Ralph had known it was coming from the quiet way he'd spoken. Always a bad sign. Because he was short, the kick landed high up on the back of Ralph's right leg. For a second he didn't feel anything, but then the leg went numb and folded up. He had to go down on his other knee and rub at it for a while. A pigeon landed near him and flew off again.

He lost himself, lost himself again. You wouldn't think it was the same place. What was left of the traffic was behind him, over his shoulder. Glass burst under the tyres. He tried to recall what she'd said, the order of it. Had he answered her at all? The houses folded back into scruffy space.

He needed to stop. The pain hadn't seemed so much but now it was coming at a gallop, an express train of a pain. He parked at a stretch of broken pavement with rain in its angles. The engine jarred into fuming silence when he turned off the ignition. A sigh of lost compression.

Gulls were making noises like a knife on glass. He got down and leaned against the wheel arch. A car went by slowly, its wheels crackling. A woman pushed a buggy, crossing the empty space towards him, the wheels splashing through pools. A dog started to yap and he saw it on the roof of a building some distance up the road – a skinny hound, tilting its head to croon. He thought from the way it trotted to one side, then the other, that it was restrained by a chain. The blank side of the building – pub, was it? – was buttressed with heavy beams of timber. Half a dozen cars were parked outside.

He rubbed his leg, digging his fingers into the big muscle. The place where the kick had landed was too sore to touch. He spat at the pavement, a white wad of phlegm. The woman pushing the buggy was staring at him.

'Something the matter?' Ralph asked.

She smiled. One side of her mouth was higher than the other, an enquiry suspended in the air. Her face had a look of having been broken at some time and then reassembled almost as it had been. Instead of a child, the buggy carried a black refuse sack, bulging with something and rolled over at the top. 'I was going to ask you that.'

He shrugged her away. Rain was sliding down again. Its cold drops were in his hair. He heard a hacking cough and saw a big slope-shouldered man with bushy grey hair and beard frowning at him from twenty feet away.

'Stare at him and he'll stare back,' the woman said.

'He can stare till he's blind.'

She leaned against the handle of the pushchair. Her dark hair was flecked with grey, thick and matt, making him think of the hair of an animal. Her teeth were uneven but she showed them boldly, drawing back her lips. 'He just likes to keep an eye on things. All this is his back yard.'

The big old man was still staring – shrewdly but without understanding, as a cat might. The collar of his shirt was open on a froth of hair which seemed continuous with the hair of his beard. After a few seconds he must have reached a conclusion because he began to walk away from them, stepping with heavy daintiness towards the other side of the cleared area. The back of his old suit was wrinkled and dusty.

'Know him?' Ralph asked.

She seemed pleased that he'd asked. 'Oh yeah. He's a friend of mine.'

He felt a twinge from his leg and put his hand there. He must have flinched.

'Something the matter?'

'Nothing's the matter – touch of cramp only.'

'You should take a stroll: nobody walks enough nowadays.'

Ralph looked after the greybeard but couldn't see him now, as if he'd quickly hidden himself. An area of a couple of blocks had been scraped to dusty bare earth, the houses bulldozed to piles of bricks which stood out as little hillocks in the flatness. Someone slammed a car door in front of the pub.

'Is Cliff about?' the woman asked.

He stared at her, not prepared. 'Excuse me?'

She quirked her mouth. He didn't like the knowing look for a second. 'Your dad, I meant,' she said, pointing. 'That's his hat, isn't it?'

He looked up at the windscreen and saw the hat with its crow feather pushed against the glass. He laughed. 'Is it? It's been there for a while.'

'I was only guessing,' she said. 'He told me you were around. You're about as I expected you to be.'

'Ah.'

Her look was forceful because of her angled nose. It tilted the horizon of her face and then the straight look of the eyes pushed it back.

'You're a friend of his?' he asked.

'Don't know . . . He might describe me as that.' She gazed at him for a second, looked away again. 'He's not about, I take it?'

'Only his hat.'

'You're Ralph, then,' she said.

'That's it.'

'Alison. He showed me a photo of you once. From years ago.'

'It would need to be.'

She smiled as if this line wasn't worth following. Her brown eyes were quick and full of something – a slyness that wouldn't hide itself properly.

'You shouldn't drive if there's a problem with your leg,' she said.

'No condition to walk, you see.'

She put out her hand and he shook it. The gesture felt more personal then it needed to be. The dog began to whimper on the roof of the pub.

'Do you ever use that place?' Ralph asked.

'Now and again. Why?'

'I just wondered.' He let go of her hand.

'You can tell Cliff we've got some things,' she said.

'Oh?'

'Some things he might be interested in or not.'

'Then I'll tell him.'

She was already walking away. He had the sense that she'd forgotten him at once, had taken a decision not to hold him in her mind. Instead of continuing along the pavement as he'd expected, she struck off across the waste ground, in the direction taken by the bearded citizen. He saw how bricks and broken masonry had been pushed into a long mound near the far side of the cleared ground. Behind were the roofs of a terrace of four or five houses.

One had already been stripped of its slates and daylight showed between the bare timbers.

'Hey!' he called. He pushed himself away from the cab, struggling for a second to balance. There'd been no feeling in his leg until he'd tried to move it. 'You were his girl?'

'Too old to be a girl,' she said. She waited, one hand on the buggy.

'His woman then?'

'I don't like "woman" either.'

He opened his hands. 'Then we're stymied . . .'

He found a garage and had the exhaust patched. He watched the mechanic working with his mask and torch. The flame of the torch was an intense white as if all the light in the place had been condensed and liquefied. The mechanic saw him through the tinted shield and switched off the torch.

'You'll damage your eyes like that.'

'It isn't your worry if I do.'

The man stared at him. Ralph walked away, humming to himself. The torch was switched back on behind him and he saw his shadow fall across the stained concrete. A pair of overlapping orange discs, each with a black core, floated before his eyes. He wondered if it was a permanent condition. There was a dartboard against the back wall, hung from a silver masonry nail hammered into the breezeblock. A fire door was open to the yard outside and he heard the scuffing of a ball, shouts.

Nine

His father drove the big estate, hand resting on the crown of the wheel, an inch of panatella between fore and index. 'Power steering, you see. Easy as pie.'

'Does Charlie know I haven't played in five years?'

'He saw you that afternoon – he knows you'll give good value. And if you lose, his man wins.'

'So who's he to you?'

'Charlie? Now and again we perform some business.'

'I see.'

'You don't see.'

'Does he play himself?'

His father blew out his breath. 'Charlie plays money – that's his interest. The sport's on the up and he's positioned himself at the start. You might not know but some of the big matches are being shown on TV.'

'So who's the opposition?' Ralph asked.

Cliff laughed again, windily. 'I've told you I don't know him.'

'Is he local?'

'He lives local but he isn't from around here. Charlie says he's from over the water.'

'I didn't know they played.'

'They'll tell you they invented the game.'

'Any good?'

'He's good but no more than that. Though I'm only going by what Charlie said.'

'Charlie strikes me as a bullshit-artist.'

Cliff turned to stare at him. 'I'd appreciate your keeping those thoughts to yourself tonight. While we're in company, say. That sort of statement would worry some people.'

Ralph nodded but sat quiet. The wipers made a scraping sound on the windscreen. His father switched them off.

'You don't mind me saying that, do you?'

He shook his head. 'No.'

'Sure?'

'No.'

The venue was a large pub standing in its own grounds, its front decorated with scrolls of purple neon, a new name over the old. He knew it vaguely but he couldn't recall ever having been inside. His father drove around the side and then reversed against a chain-link fence guarding dark spaces of allotment. When he stopped the engine it was quiet except for the contained thump of music. About a dozen cars squatted on their shadows under yellow security lights.

'Feeling nervous?' Cliff asked.

'No.'

'A little nerves beforehand is normal.'

They entered through a side door into an atmosphere of smoke stirred by overhead fans. The Friday-night whoosh of talk. A man and a couple of women serviced the long lounge bar.

'I've never liked it much as a pub,' Cliff said.

He looked awkward and off his patch, but he lifted his chin and led the way to the bar. Ralph looked over to the other side of the room and saw a dartboard set at the back of a recess, the rubber mat unrolled over a cleared space where the rug had been cut back and edged by brass strips. The area beyond was crowded with tables and chairs.

Ralph found a space at the bar and settled to watch the play while his father waved a note. A tall, slope-shouldered character in a navy polo shirt looked handy; he had a slick throw mainly from the elbow and a smooth follow-through. Ralph squinted to see through smoke but thought he set two in the bed of the twenty, trebles or near, then the last one off to the left, the wrong side of the wire but close. He shook his head as he retrieved.

Cliff was having a word with the barman, leaning towards him but being careful of the sleeves of his suit in the spillage. The barman nodded and raised his hand. He called a name into the crush. They waited without talking while Charlie Sanderson pushed through the crowd in his lumpy brown suit.

'Here's the real opposition,' Cliff said out loud.

He and Charlie shook hands. An arm around the waist for old acquaintance, fingers digging near the spine. Ralph watched them, leaning back against the bar. Charlie's shirt had a stain on the collar – blood or brown sauce. The barman had lined up his father's Pilsner and his own spa water. Charlie caught Cliff's wrist when he tried to pay and folded the money back on itself with his other hand.

'My treat tonight, Cliff.'

Cliff nodded. 'That's kind of you, Charlie. But then you always are.'

Charlie smiled at them blandly, then leaned closer, wary of being overheard even in the racket of music and chat. 'You see that man over there?'

He nodded towards a fat, middle-aged man with heavy-framed spectacles lounging in an open doorway at the back of the bar. He was taking no visible part in the running of the bar but watched the staff in their toing and froing. He had the same disappearing fair hair as Charlie but was otherwise not similar.

'That's my brother or near enough,' Charlie said. 'And when I use the word "brother" it's only standing for something else I'm really trying to say.'

Cliff laid a hand on his arm. 'You don't have to explain that to me, Charlie.'

They started to laugh, a joke between them. Ralph took a mouthful of the tepid water. They began to talk a yard away along the bar, out of his hearing in that noise. The man who might have been Charlie's brother glanced at him and then away. Ralph looked towards the board again. There was a new set of players. After a minute he felt a soft breath against his ear.

'Come and meet my boy, Ralph.'

A stocky man with cropped red hair sat with his back to them at one of the tables close to the boards, talking to an elderly woman. The woman's hair had a silvery rinse and her face was pale with powder. When Charlie laid a hand on his shoulder, the man glanced round but then seemed to disregard them. He leaned closer to the woman and began to talk rapidly into her ear, touching her on her bare upper arm with just the tips of his fingers. Ralph saw his father look around the bar, staring into its crowded corners and checking the swing of the entrance doors through their eddies of smoke. He looked down at his watch: nearly nine thirty. A ballad was coming from the jukebox.

They waited, Charlie with a strained smile now as his man ignored them, his fingertips still on the woman's elderly flesh. Finally he kissed her softly on the cheek and stood up, scraping back his stool. He turned towards them, his eyes half-closed and a lazy smile on his lips.

'This is Francis,' Charlie said. 'Or Frank if you like.'

The other player nodded. He might have been giving permission. His face was smooth and wedge-shaped, with a jaw too narrow for the width of the forehead. He wore a dark suit of some nubbly material with a metallic thread. He was short for a player, about five foot six. When Ralph took his hand it was flat and chilly, the cold collected in the tips of the fingers. His eyes slid away, came back, slipped away again.

Charlie made the rest of the introductions. Ralph noticed that Frank did not shake his father's hand but nodded and clapped him on the arm.

'Frank's one of my best soldiers,' Charlie said. 'Or he could be if he made the effort.'

Frank laughed. His eyes were still fidgety. 'Never excel, I say. Do the job but never excel.'

'You'll find he has his own sense of things,' Charlie said. He turned away with a little sigh.

'One drink would steady your nerves,' Cliff said.

'Now that I've seen him I haven't any nerves.'

'Never underestimate your opponent.'

'Who said that? Napoleon?'

Ralph looked up and located the other player in the mirror behind the optics. Charlie was talking to him as the MC opened up the match board. A couple of bar staff were setting up tables and chairs at the back, well away from the mat. The MC signalled to the bar and the board lamp came on. A fine cloud of chalk dust swam in the white light.

'We're starting early,' Ralph said.

'You're only the taster, remember. The main event is due at ten. I think you could piss on them as well but it's best if we start slowly.'

Ralph set down his glass on the bar and took out the darts, slipping the thin bodies from the pouch and starting to fix the flights. Only when he'd finished all three did he look up to see that his opponent was standing on the edge of the playing area, not looking at the activity around him. His arms were folded high across his chest and his head was lowered so that he could have been studying the toes of his shoes.

'They're waiting,' Cliff said.

The MC was making announcements through a cordless mike.

Ralph caught his own name, nothing else. A couple of people started to clap but no one took it up. There was hardly a drop in the level of chat.

'People like that disgust me,' Cliff said.

'Like what?'

He shrugged. 'The sort of attitude they have. They might as well stay at home.' He nodded towards the board under its light. 'You've a few throws each to loosen up.'

'I don't need it.'

His father looked irritated. 'Don't you? Then do it for the look of the thing.'

The MC lifted his arm and stepped back sharply from the line of fire. He wore a velvet waistcoat and trousers. His florid face looked as if it had been polished with a cloth. Ralph glanced round and saw Frank taking his seat at one of the tables. He set a small glass of something before him and settled back, sinking his chin on his chest. A southpaw like himself, Ralph noted.

One of the barmen had taken up position beside the scoreboard. Ralph stepped up to the mark and took a few throws, keeping his aim loose and giving nothing away. He grouped the bull and then retrieved and sent a few throws towards the top of the board, getting the feel of it. The lamp was set so that its light glanced off the wires on the top half, making the coloured segments seem to recede. It had been rotated for the game so that the worn patch usually under the twenty was at four o'clock between the two and the fifteen. Ralph took another pot at the top and then finished with a throw at the double seven, firing across his own grain towards that quarter of the board in which he found most difficulty. He removed his darts and stepped back from the mark.

'Any problems?' Cliff asked.

He shook his head.

'I have to ask you these things, as it seems I'm your manager.' He reached out and picked a loose thread from the front of Ralph's new shirt.

The MC made another announcement and there was laughter at something he said. Frank was sitting placidly but at that he stood up and took off his shabby cabaret singer's jacket. He folded it carefully as if the lining were precious and laid it on the empty seat beside him. He wore a pale-green shirt which bagged above the waistband of his trousers. The sleeves were short and his bare arms were as pale as a child's. Without the jacket there was a disproportion between his body and his bowed legs. The darts were in his hand suddenly, as if he'd palmed them at some point and just then brought them to light. The music and the lights slipped down together, leaving a muddy thrum and dimness except for the lamp over the board.

Ralph was the first to throw. He sank one below the treble but found the mark with the other pair: 140. Charlie's man scored a couple of plain twenties but then wasted the last dart, letting it drift sideways into the one. He took time to wipe his hands on a towel, then favoured Ralph with a thoughtful look.

Another couple of throws each, the scorer striking through the previous results and chalking up the new. Frank switched to the nineteens and found the treble with his first dart but sank the next into the margin. His last throw hit the wire and he retrieved it from the mat with a swoop of his hand. He straightened the flight with a small smile, glancing towards Charlie, who was sitting with friends near the back of the bar. Charlie's face was set, a shine of sweat on his forehead.

Ralph easily took the first game and the next. The Irishman won the third while he was stuck on the jinxy double one. But by then he was feeling too confident to be shaken and he took the fourth and fifth to almost a whitewash. There were a few cheers and whistles and the lights came up. He turned away from the board and saw Cliff standing with his back to the bar. His father made the O-sign between thumb and finger. Charlie Sanderson's fat brother stood behind him, not smiling.

Cliff counted money in the car, folding back the notes with his face wrinkled, as if they had a slight smell.

'You did well,' Ralph said, watching.

He twitched one shoulder. 'A couple of side bets. For some reason that beats me, they didn't expect him to lose.'

'Maybe he shouldn't have.'

Cliff didn't look up but his fingers stopped. 'You're not the only one with that thought.'

'It's his business now.'

'But not only his.'

'I got the impression he knew you,' Ralph said.

Cliff nodded gravely, as if it were an uncomfortable fact. 'We met once before – recently, as it happens.'

There was still a crowd outside the side door, talking, finishing off their drinks. A reversing car threatened their front wing and Cliff sounded the horn. A few faces turned. The other player came through the swing door, stepping out quickly as if he had no business there now. He wore his dragging silver-flecked jacket and a high-crowned cap of multicoloured wool. He made his way through the crowd with a brown bottle in one hand, looking as if he felt the eyes on his back.

'Charlie told me he was disappointed in him,' Cliff said.

'As bad as that?'

'You may laugh.'

'You told me that Charlie won either way.'

'That's right. But it's not a good idea to make things that obvious. People start to feel cheated.' Cliff separated an amount from the bundle. 'Here, this is yours.'

'I don't need that much.'

'You spend the stuff, don't you?'

'When I can't avoid it.'

'It's shite but everyone loves it,' Cliff said.

Ralph took the notes and compacted them in his palm. He let the wad fall into his jacket pocket. 'It's only a bloody darts game.'

'That's all it is.' Cliff pushed the rest of the money into his inside pocket. 'Did you notice the old dear our friend was chatting up?'

'Difficult not to.'

'That old girl was once Lord Mayor of Stockport.'

'She's a long way from Stockport.'

Ten

Eric stood on the lawn, holding his breath for a second, his fingers hooked around the shaft of the putter, thumbs in line. He took a minimum backswing and then carefully stroked the ball. It hung on the rim of the hole for a second and then rolled in. A four-foot putt. He was pleased. He breathed again and at the same time heard the tinkle of Ma's little porcelain bell from the room overlooking the green.

If my ears were not so attuned, he thought.

He went upstairs, forgetful of the club tucked under his arm. It was only on the landing that he recollected himself and leaned it in an angle of the wall. She did not answer when he rapped on the door but he took silence as permission and went inside. She was sitting up in the bed with her back to a couple of pillows. She pointed to the mahogany dressing table in front of the window.

'Sorry?' He was puzzled. The club's damp leather grip had left a sticky deposit on his palms.

'You haven't turned the calendar,' Ma said.

He sighed. 'How do you know I haven't turned it? How do you know time doesn't stand still?'

She looked away as if the question were beneath her. He went over and rotated the little drum. Her various jars and bottles were arranged on the embroidered cloth. There was a smell of face powder. He saw himself for a second in the angled mirror.

Dry old bastard. Did she say that?

'He's been here a week now, a fortnight nearly,' she said.

'Are you keeping count then?'

'And why shouldn't I? He's working with his father as he's every right to.'

'Lumping and lifting. That kind of thing won't detain him for long.'

'Cliff has him playing that game again.'

'Oh, he'll settle for that. If the pickings are there—'

'You might keep a civil tongue,' Ma said.

He laughed. 'Anyway it won't last. Blood will out, you see.'

'Oh? Which blood is that?'

He turned defensive under her look. He despised himself for the craven feel it gave him. 'I'm only warning you, Marion: I don't want to see him disappoint you.'

'As you did.'

That cat was on her bed again. You didn't have to look, only breathe the air. He had a mind to leave but instead he made a pretence that something claimed his attention through the window nets. He could see a white circle of sky in the neat hole in the centre of the lawn.

'I made my offer and that was enough,' he said. 'It's not a thing that bears repetition.'

'When? When was that?' Her hand was on the neck of the animal. The swollen joints she had. She wanted the last ounce of his humiliation.

'You know,' he said. 'You know exactly.'

Ralph closed his eyes and opened them again. It was still very early because the light in the room had a submarine look – clear brown water. The bare window was full of shadows. There wasn't a sound in the building and even the birds were quiet.

He left the flat at about seven. The sky was crossed by ribs of cloud like soft pink stone. Specks of birds were circling very high. He walked to the corner and saw the man he had undressed and put to bed sitting on the low wall in front of one of the courts, at a point from which he would have a view of the street and the main road. He wore a thin shirt and was hugging himself against the early air, his knees drawn up sharply. When Ralph stopped before him, he looked up with a calm smile.

'I thought it was you.'

'That makes both of us,' Ralph said.

'That's the sort of a comment your old man would make. You didn't tell me you were Cliff's boy.'

'I didn't think you knew him.'

He leaned his chin against his forearm. There was a length of yellow shin between the hems of his trousers and his scuffed brown shoes. 'Oh, I know your dad all right – I was best man at his wedding.'

Ralph didn't answer. He felt it was important to have nothing to say to that. The other man watched him and then squinted up the road.

'Sammy's my name. Sammy Curl.'

'Ralph.'

'Oh, I know your name . . . I'm waiting here for my money.'

'The sort that walks by?'

'That's right, the kind that walks.' He pushed out his lower lip so that it undershot the other. 'You won your match the other night, I heard. Your old man must think you're a chip off the block.'

'I don't care what he thinks.'

Sammy nodded at that, mulling it over. Then he extended his long hand. 'I wish you many more, son. Good luck with it.'

When Ralph let go, he had the feeling that he was taking away soft flakes of skin. He was a few yards away when he heard the other man's shuffling walk. He turned and saw him coming urgently forwards, one leg swinging stiffly to the side. Sammy caught up and took hold of his arm, leaning his weight on it. He was flushed and smirking to himself, as if there was some secret he wanted to spill.

He pushed his face close. His lips were trembling. 'I'd have killed for your old man . . .'

'What?'

'I said I'd have killed for him.'

'But you didn't have to?'

Sammy stared up at him, his jaw working. Then he straightened himself with a struggle and took a step backwards. 'Now don't get smart with me, son! Or I might forget whose kid you are. What I'm saying is that your dad only needed to give the word and I was there. People used to pass comment on how we were always together. And do you know something?'

'What's that?'

'Nothing's changed between us, nothing at all. We might not be bloody Siamese twins any longer but I'd still put my head in a noose. That's how I feel about Cliff.' He squared himself for another handshake, taking Ralph's hand in both of his and squeezing it between his palms. ''Course I wouldn't be the same use to him nowadays – it's this bastard leg that keeps me back. It took me two years to learn how to walk without a stick.'

'You should take it easy,' Ralph said.

Sammy let go of his hand. 'For what? What's this thing I'm saving myself for?' He laughed and let his head drop. The cup of

83

his ear was filled with white hairs. He mumbled something Ralph didn't catch.

'What's that?'

'I said your old man's nearly a saint,' Sammy said.

'There's a bit of that in him.'

'More than a bit, son. The only reason I say "nearly" is that it's not possible for us – people like us . . . We're too busy with this and that, with just keeping going. They keep us at it from the cradle to the grave.'

'That's right,' Ralph said.

'And what I mean is that given half a chance he'd be up there with the rest of them – St Peter, St Luke, St Mark.'

'I know them.'

Sammy nodded sulkily and stared along the road again. Ralph saw that his teeth were starting to chatter.

'Feeling OK?' he asked.

Sammy shook his head. 'It's the alcohol, sonny – it's poison to my system.'

A car came round the corner, sloppy on its tyres – a white saloon with rusting wings. A couple of kids in the front, another behind. As they went by, the driver sounded a two-tone horn. The kid at the back pushed his hand out of the open window, palm open.

'Know them?' Ralph asked.

Sammy watched the car until it was out of sight. 'Used to know their mothers. A set of whores, they were.' He came closer, making a scooping step with his gammy leg. 'Got a ciggy on you?'

'I don't smoke.'

'I remember now you didn't . . .' He looked anxiously into Ralph's face. 'You couldn't loan me a couple, could you? Anyone around here will tell you that I pay my debts.'

'I'll see what I've got.'

He looked into his wallet and pulled out a five.

'You shouldn't mention this to your dad,' Sammy Curl said.

'OK. It's just between us.'

'He'd feel he had to step in if he thought I was having a hard time and I don't want that. I know he's got problems of his own.'

'So what are they?'

Sammy looked cagey suddenly, his face livening with tiny quivers. 'No doubt he'll tell you himself in good time.'

'When the time is good,' Ralph said.

*   *   *

84

Cliff stood for a while in the street door to take the breeze there and then walked back through the bedroom furniture and the electrical goods. A woman with a child asleep in a buggy was looking at a microwave oven.

He smiled down at the child. 'Little boy, is it?'

'Girl,' she said.

There was something about the way her nose passed into her forehead. Strange, the features that you find attractive, Cliff thought. 'Handy for them,' he said. 'Makes a hot snack in a couple of minutes.'

She looked away from him. The buggy's wheels squeaked on the cement floor. 'I like her to have proper meals.'

'Just the thing for those as well. Cuts out the element of drudgery.'

'What?'

'*Drudgery*,' he repeated. He saw he'd been wrong about the nose; when she turned her head it looked only lumpish.

'Is it guaranteed?' she asked. Still looking.

'It has our personal guarantee.'

'And what's that?'

'It means if you're not fully satisfied, then I'll refund your money in full.'

She sucked at her cheek. 'Maybe I'd be better off buying new.'

He nodded, both hands clutching the top of a tumble dryer. Gentleman in defeat. He watched as she pushed the child away, passing into the main hall with its bedroom suites and leaning rolls of carpets. Just as she vanished, his heart lurched heavily against his ribcage.

Was he this minute dying? He felt the blood in his face, pressure in his ears. He thought about calling out, to the woman or anyone else among the white goods or in the yard. There was some barrier in his throat which he pictured as tough, flexible and transparent. Like a caul. He began to walk towards the office, through the double doors. An old lady with a stick was sitting on one of the easy chairs. She stared and made some noise but he ignored her. What help would she be? He saw a rat cross the floor and then realised it was a scrap of paper, driven by the breeze from outside.

The phone was sounding in the office, penetrating the congested hum in his ears. He reached for it just as the answering machine clicked in, then stayed his hand, resting the tips of his fingers on the receiver as the message tape unspooled. The tone sounded. As if it were a signal, he could feel everything in his body starting to return to normal, the adverse chemistry slackening.

'Cliff?' the voice came through the machine.

He took up the receiver. 'Jeanie?'

'You're a sod, you are,' she said.

He laughed. 'I am. I'll own to that, Jeanie. I take it you've seen him?'

'What were you playing at?'

'I'm not playing, not at all.' He waited for her to speak. 'It still makes sense to me that you two have to meet.'

She wouldn't answer. He pictured her smoothing her forehead with her fingertips, pressing back a little pain.

'Jeanie?'

'I'm here, Cliff.'

'So what happened?' He was irritated by her suddenly, because she hadn't begun with that.

'Do you deserve to know?'

'For Chrissake!'

'One of the fellers went a bit too far,' she said.

'What?'

'He got a bit wild.'

'Wild? Like an animal?'

'He had a go, I think. At Ralph. I don't know what he did exactly because I didn't see it. I don't think it was anything serious. Maybe a bit of pushing and shoving.'

'Was he hurt?'

'I don't think so.'

'But you don't know that he wasn't?'

'I didn't bring this about, Cliff.'

'No.'

'Have you seen him yourself lately?'

'I see him every day now. Nearly every day.'

'Don't give him my number, will you? Not my home number.'

'I wouldn't do that.'

'Good. But I wanted to make sure.'

His legs were twitching. He stood up from the desk. He could see through the office door along the length of the hall. The old girl was still sitting in her chair, her knotty hands clasped on the handle of her stick.

'You think everyone can be happy, Cliff. That's your mistake.'

'I'd ask, why not?'

'Because it's not always possible. Sometimes it's better to forget about it.'

'I won't believe that.'

'Then you're pathetic.'

'OK. Do I need to apologise?'

'I'd appreciate that as a beginning.'

'Sorry,' he said. 'Sorry.'

Ralph ate in Murdo's, methodically putting back the full breakfast. There was an alcove of cab drivers and an old girl sitting on her own by the counter. Murdo came to stand by his table, wiping his hands on the ends of his apron.

'Your dad was here a couple of hours past.'

Ralph dabbed at his mouth with a slice of bread. 'That so?'

Murdo smiled at him awkwardly. 'I thought you might want to find him.'

'If I do, then I know where to look.'

The old girl started to laugh to herself, shaking with it suddenly. The cab drivers stopped their conversation and turned to stare at her.

'I have to tolerate these people,' Murdo whispered. 'Just for the price of a tea.'

He walked into the shop without meeting his father. The phone started to ring as he crossed the showroom floor. He stepped over a splash of spilled tea at the entrance to the office. The top drawer of the filing cabinet was open on a jumble of papers, nearly barring his path. He pushed it back and picked up the receiver.

'Hello?'

He listened. There was a movement behind him and he turned. Cliff snatched the phone. 'You have no right at all!'

Ralph was smiling – a look of amusement at the old feller's ways. Cliff put the phone to his ear and then gently replaced it.

'You must have crept in here,' he said.

Ralph shrugged. 'You know the way I walk.'

'All kinds of people leave messages – people who rely on confidentiality,' Cliff said.

'I thought that something might be urgent.'

A fat fly was settling and Cliff flicked at it with his hand. 'A man about a dog, say?'

'With a dog's breath,' Ralph said.

'No business of yours what breath he has.'

'Has he rung before?'

Cliff shrugged. 'A dog, as you said . . . Any more questions or is that the end?'

Ralph didn't answer but walked out. A couple were standing against the row of fridge-freezers – the woman in a white ribbed sweater, the man with combed-back hair and a thin moustache. As he watched, the man leaned forward and planted a kiss on the woman's lowered head.

Cliff caught him by the arm. 'Did you take care of that exhaust?'

Ralph stared down at his hand.

'I was enquiring about the exhaust,' Cliff said more slowly. 'Remember I asked you to get it fixed?'

'I had it patched,' Ralph said.

'Patched?'

'It was just the tube that had gone so I had a patch made.'

'I wanted you to get a new exhaust. I told you where I had an account.'

'I thought I'd try somewhere else.'

'Any particular reason?'

He wouldn't answer, just gave that twitch of a smile in explanation.

'You'll be doing work for me,' Cliff said. 'That was why I wanted it sorted.'

'I'm not sure about work,' Ralph said.

'What d'you mean?'

'Working for you, I mean.'

'Then why are you here?'

'Because I'd finished over there.'

'Or they were finished with you,' Cliff said. 'I know these resort towns.' He looked towards the double doors hooked back, sunshine in the yard. He felt gentler now. 'Look, go out today. Make a few drops for me. You don't have to commit yourself.'

Ralph looked up at him.

'And don't think about that business on the phone. Promise me you won't think about it.'

'OK.'

'So, a friend of mine called,' Cliff said. 'She has some things to look at. She said she'd already spoken to you about it.'

'Did she? She might have, yeah.'

Cliff looked over to where the couple were examining the

interior of a fridge-freezer. 'I'll give you the address then. I'd like you to pick up Colin on the way.'

Mrs Cromer opened the door, holding a wooden-backed brush. Ralph could see long stands of grey hair among the bristles.

'I'm giving him his grooming,' she said.

'Colin?'

She shook her head. 'Colin is a lost cause as far as that's concerned. I was talking about my husband.'

She held the door open. The hall was as dim as before. The frames of the holy prints held rectangles of felty grey.

'It's Colin that I'm looking for,' Ralph said.

She laughed at that, a string of gasps from the site of her breastbone. 'This is the last place you should try.'

'Is there somewhere else he might be?'

She waved her hand. 'Oh, he never tells me ·where he goes. I only feel safe when I know he's with your father.'

She looked behind her, listening as if she had heard a sound and was waiting for a repetition. Ralph listened too and heard a faint slither, like something rubbing against a wall. He glanced past her and saw Mr Cromer's heavy head pushing at knee-level around the front-room door. Mrs Cromer spun around, shaking a finger at him. She smiled back at Ralph but then seemed suddenly beside herself and ran towards her husband, who had half emerged from the room. She began to bundle him backwards, pushing at him with both hands. The old man shook his head and protested with a soundless shudder of his throat. The hall carpet had come loose beneath him and was lifting in a stiff fold between his struggling knees.

Ralph pulled the door closed. The leaded panel rattled. A tight wedge of children ran screaming past the gate. He walked quickly along the street. A group of older kids had gathered near the back of the van and as he approached they began to distance themselves from it with long strides of exaggerated slowness, as if they were carrying something fragile in their bunched jackets. He called out. A couple of them stopped and turned, little smiles on their faces.

'You know Colin?' he asked.

One of them made a phlegmy noise in his throat. The other watched Ralph's face for a reaction. Then the first one giggled. They were about twelve or thirteen.

'Colin's nuts,' the taller one said. 'So's his old woman.'

89

'Have you seen him today?'

The boy laughed.

'This your van?' the other one asked.

'Have you been touching it?'

The boy turned and began to walk away. When Ralph took a step towards him, he started to run, bounding lightly on his rubber soles. He reached the end of the street in seconds and then turned around, watching with his hands pushed deep in the pockets of his jacket.

The other kid was still a few feet away. He lifted his arm and pointed. 'You want Colin?'

Colin was walking towards them, pushing an ancient-looking moped along the crown of the road, leaving a thin trail of black oil. Some part of the mechanism was making a broken rasping noise. He spotted Ralph and stopped the bike's progress, pulling back on its handlebars.

'Hello, Colin.'

Colin pushed the bike towards the kerb. He kicked out a stand. His hands and clothes were filthy with oil. He nodded to Ralph, knelt beside the bike and began to poke at the little pipes and linkages with his fingertips.

Ralph went to stand behind him, staring at the engine over his shoulder. 'You'll never resurrect that thing.'

Colin was still immersed. He stood up finally and wiped his hands on his front.

'Somebody dumped it. I'll strip it down and rebuild it. If Cliff'll let me use a corner of the yard . . .'

There was a whoop from the end of the road. The kids had re-formed and were gesturing towards them. The one who had run away was pointing and jerking his hips obscenely. Colin stared at them mildly and then looked back towards the bike.

'I saw your mother,' Ralph said.

Colin didn't take his eyes from the bike but a cautious expression came over his face.

'Cliff wants us to look at a few things.'

He nodded and started to turn away. Ralph noticed that his knuckles were scraped and bloody.

'Don't you want to take a wash first?'

Colin shook his head. The kids were still jeering. A scorched smell hung over the bike.

He stayed silent as they were driving away, and leaned towards the noises from the back of the van.

'I've had a patch made on the exhaust pipe,' Ralph told him.

'It's no good – you can still hear it fluffing.'

Ralph changed down. The engine sounded throaty and congested. 'Your mother sounded worried about you,' he said.

Colin didn't answer but settled further into the collapsed seat.

'Did you hear what I said?' Ralph could feel the other man watching him but kept his eyes on the road. 'Respect your father and mother, that's what the Bible tells us.'

'Is it?'

'Oh yeah. And your mother must have known mine, I think.'

'Might have done.'

'I reckon it's stronger than that. Stronger than might have done.'

'She did, then,' Colin said. 'She did know her.'

'Has she talked to you about her?' Ralph asked.

'Not much.'

'She said something, though? There must be something you can repeat?'

Colin didn't answer. Ralph glanced towards him and saw him picking at a patch of loose skin on his palm. He stopped the van in the middle of the road. The tyres squealed and a car behind bulleted into the other lane, its horn blaring. Colin wasn't wearing a seat belt and was thrown almost into the windscreen.

'Sorry,' Ralph told him.

Colin climbed back into his seat, wiping spittle from his chin with the edge of his wrist.

'Sorry,' Ralph repeated. 'I wasn't concentrating.'

The engine had stalled. He waited for a few seconds before turning the key. The smell of petrol was very strong. When it was running, he turned back to his passenger.

'Well?'

'Only that she died,' Colin said. 'She'd only tell me that she died.'

Eleven

'I asked you into the garden,' Eric reminded her.

Ma shook her head. 'Only I wouldn't have gone.'

'Are you making me a liar then?'

'I'm only saying your memory is at fault. I would never have responded to a summons.'

Eric laughed, a creak of a laugh. 'Oh, it was never a summons, only a request. It had your refusal already in it like the fly in the ointment.'

She put a hand to her throat, catching the pulse there. 'I want sense from you and you talk about flies.'

'You'll have it out of me – you've only to wait ... I'd put some lights in that tree of yours – little bulbs I'd bought, like Christmas lights except that they weren't coloured. More tasteful, I considered. If you'll recall.'

'Lights in the tree?' she asked, incredulous.

Eric nodded. 'The night they were wed, if you remember. That was the reason I raised the subject.'

'I remember nothing, that's the only reason I ask.'

She had put her cake down on its plate and stood it carefully on the sill of the kitchen window. She wore no make-up but was Romany-looking in her dark-crimson dress. The brown of her eyes was so dense it seemed black. There were grey streaks in her heavy hair. Why would she never dye it? The sight of her made him proud and troubled.

'I was never one for wedding cake,' she told him. 'It was all I could do to stomach my own.'

'Then you're cursed with a delicate stomach – or is it blessed?'

She sipped her sherry from a tiny glass. It was getting dark and birds were racketing in the tree – heavy-bodied, thick-winged birds that plagued the town in certain seasons. When it was full night they'd pipe down and fly off quickly.

'You should have made a toast,' he said.

'I didn't know what to wish them.'

Eric laughed. He wanted to touch her dress somewhere, say in the small of her back where her build was most delicate. 'Why, Marion, you wish them well.'

'We'll have to see,' she said. 'It's no use wishing them well when we can only wait and see.'

'You should try a glass of something else,' he told her. 'Something more livening.'

He had rigged electric lights in the lilac tree and when it was darker he'd throw the switch. The back door behind them was open to the hall and they could hear Mrs Foster playing the borrowed piano in the front room of the shop. 'Lay Down Your Arms', with a heavy military rhythm. A couple were sitting at the foot of the stairs, just visible to them. During a fall in the music he listened to the woman make a murmur of half protest, half pleasure.

Hand up her skirt.

'She makes everything sound like a march,' he complained.

'What?'

'Your friend. She has only the one tempo.'

She stared into the garden without answering. Not deigning to, she would have said. He wondered if it was dark enough for the lights.

'He seems steady,' he ventured. 'As far as I can judge.'

Ma sniffed. 'No man is steady. Even when they intend it.'

'I reckon misfortune has soured your outlook, Marion.'

She considered that and nodded. 'That would be true to an extent.'

'And you should look to yourself more. Where your future lies now that she is off your hands.'

She looked away. He was impertinent but didn't he have the right? Eric thought of his friend in the hospital. Her husband, it had to be said. The tall, narrow bed with the covers reaching nearly to the floor. That pale cream paint they used for everything: death pigment. Rubber wheels and someone said they'd slip a body underneath, wheel it away under people's noses.

'I was his best friend. Best man, as well.'

'I'm not denying that.'

'I walked past him twice before I knew him,' Eric recalled. 'I wasn't expecting it, not at all. They tell you fuck-all in those places: the less you know the better, that's their motto.'

Told him I was waiting to be fitted with specs but he wasn't compos anyway and the lie was wasted on him. 'Eric,' he said, 'be sure you look after Mags. You are the one to do it.' He didn't say anything except for noises in his throat. Little sighs and clearings. This clear fluid going in through a tube and then another tube of yellow stuff leading from under the covers to this sack thing below the bed. Clear wrinkled sack that held about a gallon and they changed it three times a day. Pissing himself away. Then the nurses came to bathe him – Irish lasses with big freckled arms who'd flick him over like a pancake. They whisked closed the curtains on hissing rings.

'I'm still light-headed from all that smoke,' Ma told him. 'I could never understand the attraction of cigarettes.'

Eric flicked the butt of his own roll-up towards the dustbins, hearing the couple on the stairs laugh. 'She'll find she's up the spout,' he predicted. 'And then they won't be so humorous.'

Mrs Foster had finished at the piano and the record player was sounding some creaking tune. He imagined the slow turning of the dancers through the smug, red curtains blocking the view from the street. The newly weds sat in pride of place on the embroidered covers of the couch. Her hand in his, a fine sweat on Cliff's face despite loosening his tie. When you looked at them they were the same height sitting down.

A short-arse, anyway.

'I said I'd look after you,' Eric said. 'I made that a solemn promise, an oath.'

'You'd no right to be promising. Not concerning me.'

He took his half-pint glass of Guinness from the windowsill and swallowed some. His throat was dry and it went down like a stone.

'Now Joyce's leaving, you'll be in this place on your own.'

'I would relish that,' Ma said. 'And there's always my work.'

'That mumbo? Carry on with that and they'll be putting you away.'

He was the only one who could speak to her like that. The knowledge made him roughen his words.

'Then maybe I'll take a job,' she said to tease him.

'In some factory, or behind a counter? That'd be a waste of a woman like you.'

He glanced behind as the noise of the party welled and saw Mrs Foster leaving the front room. She frowned, first at him and then at the couple on the stairs. They parted to let her through. He watched the blunt tips of her fingers against the polished rail as she climbed to the landing.

Emptying her tank. 'I think you know what I'm suggesting,' he said.

'Do I?' She shook her head. 'Then I couldn't countenance that.'

He nodded towards the yellow light the doorway cast on the lawn. 'I would dig that up and re-seed it.'

'My husband's bit of grass, is it?' She watched him fidget. Like a man on a bike, he had to stay in motion to keep his balance.

'He wasn't a practical man,' Eric said. 'He didn't know the value of consistent effort.'

'Not like you,' Ma said.

He stared at her but couldn't see enough of her face to make a guess at her expression. He swallowed. 'Give me the word and I'd grub up that tree and cut those shrubs right back. A small garden needs a firm hand.'

She was silent, the big, dark shape of her beside him, swaying slightly. Or was it his own movement? He shuffled his feet again. 'I'm only saying, Marion, now that you are free to make decisions. He as good as told me, you know. As good as cleared the way—'

She shook her head. 'He wouldn't do that: he had more respect.'

'It wasn't so much in words,' Eric said.

'In what then? Which way did he communicate?'

'The impression he gave: his demeanour.'

'And I thought they'd taken that out as well,' Ma said.

She snorted in that vulgar way she had of signalling through her nose. He fell quiet, the words sucked back into his throat as if his powers of expression had been thrown into reverse. The music from the front of the house was louder and the birds were leaving the tree, flying soundlessly above them and over the roof.

Twelve

A shuttered cinema on one corner and then a dragging hill past a parade of ground-floor enterprises – retread tyres, café, laundrette, doner and shish.

'You know this place, Colin?'

He mightn't have heard.

'Colin?'

'You take a left,' Colin said.

The street was narrowed by an overloaded skip, a mound of builder's sand at the kerb. Tall houses of corroded brick were fronted by scaffolding. Colin tapped his shoulder and he turned down another side street, a tight terrace which opened out suddenly into waste ground punctured by the concrete columns of streetlamps.

They parked and walked back along the street. Some of the ground-floor windows were boarded with rain-soaked plywood. Others showed leaning curtains. Rain fell quietly. Tall weeds were growing on the margin of the cleared ground.

They crossed the road towards a row of half a dozen houses which looked lived-in or livable. A van and a couple of cars were parked at the kerb. Thick red paint had been applied to one of the doors. Its front steps were bridged by a slope of three scaffolding boards.

'This the place?' Ralph asked.

'Think so. Think it is.'

Colin squinted along the street at something, wiping one hand against his thigh. There was nothing but the shell of a washer-dryer, canted against the kerb. One of the door's glazed panels was blanked by a sheet of painted board. There was an iron knocker, a rusty swag of something unrecognisable. Ralph lifted it and let it fall. He looked into the front yard and saw shapes under a sodden rug. He knocked again and felt Colin tug at his sleeve.

Someone was staring at them from the dusty bay window on the house to the right. A thin white face above a dark suit. Ralph lifted his hand but the old man stepped back and disappeared.

Ralph knocked again, louder this time, setting up an echo.

'No one there,' Colin said.

'We'll give it a couple of minutes. You can sit in the van if you like.'

'I'll stay here.'

'Please yourself.'

Ralph heard a faint clicking now. He turned from the door and saw a woman in a wheelchair being pushed across the road towards them. She was holding a dark bundle and when it squirmed he saw the bright face of a child. A tall man with a lopsided bush of fair hair was behind the chair, bending over close to talk into the woman's ear. When he looked up he saw them waiting at the house and stopped.

They stared at one another for a second. The child made an O of her mouth. Then the woman said something and the man frowned and levered the chair forwards over the kerb. The child's feet pushed out in red wellingtons. She was clutching a scuffed white ball.

'Looking for someone?' the woman called.

'Is Alison in?' Ralph asked. Assuming it was the place.

He went down the steps towards them. The woman was in her mid-thirties with long pale-red hair. Her cheeks were rough and pitted, but her eyes shone strongly. A line of black was drawn on their upper lids. Ralph saw now that one of her hands was angled back from the wrist with the fingers curled. He looked back at her face.

'Is Alison expecting you?' she asked.

'I think she'll want to see us.'

She took thought for a second, glancing behind him at Colin still standing in the doorway. The little girl was wriggling about, wanting to be let down, but she held her with a forearm across the waist.

'Alison's been working and she may be asleep,' she said.

She turned to make some remark to the man and at the same second the child lost her grip on the ball. It rolled from her lap and along the pavement. She began to wail but Colin stepped down quickly and stopped it with his foot. He scooped it up and spun it in his hand. The little girl laughed, trilling it out.

'My name's Rose,' the woman said. She held out her crippled

right hand. There were silver rings on three of the fingers and on the wrist a loose weave of silver bangles. Ralph shook it.

'Ralph. That one's Colin.'

Colin had returned the ball to the little girl, who caught it with a smack of her hands.

'Say thank you,' Rose ordered.

The child lisped shyly, leaning over the ball and circling her feet in their boots. Rose tutted and held out her hand again. Colin took it carefully, as if it were a new category of object. She laughed at the expression on his face.

'Face-ache here is Lizzie.' She pointed behind her. 'And Tony.'

The man nodded at them, not smiling. The child started to sing under her breath. Rose released her with a kiss on the back of her head and she slipped down, holding the ball tight to her chest and then bouncing it and running after it down the slope of the street, catching it before it could gather speed. Tony turned the chair through the empty gate and started to push it up the ramp. At the top he reached past to shove at the door. It jarred back. Lizzie squeezed past her mother's chair and ran inside.

'You'll have to excuse me if I go next,' Rose said.

Leaning his weight, Tony manoeuvred her over the step. A door was open to the right and he turned the chair in the narrow space and eased it through. Its wheels cleared by a fraction. The little girl had gone before and they heard her ball cannoning from the walls.

Rose called after her, 'Lizzie!'

The front door was still open and Ralph turned to shut it. It resisted for a second but he managed to wedge it into the frame. Colin was standing to one side but away from the wall as if careful not to bring himself into contact with it. The little girl shot back out into the hall and started to call up the stairs. 'Alison! Alison!'

She waited with her head on one side and then made a funnel with her hands. *'Alison!'*

Rose appeared in the doorway, her ringed hands on the wheels of her chair. 'Be quieter, tadpole!' She smiled at them.

'She's coming! She's coming!' the little girl cried. She stamped her feet in their red boots.

Rose listened doubtfully. 'You'd wake the dead but I don't think so.'

Light filtered down from above, barely enough to see by. Lizzie was a flight ahead and they could hear her scrambling on her hands and feet. Ralph flicked a switch as they reached the landing but nothing happened except for the tingle of a shock. He snatched back his hand.

'Shit!'

Colin was silent, following behind. A floor above them the girl's sharp little knuckles rapped at a panel. She knocked again, this time with the sides of her little fists, shaking the door. 'Ali! Alison!'

Ralph heard a woman's voice – a protest and then clear laughter.

They reached the top of the house as Alison stepped from her room. She was holding the little girl by her arms, swinging her over the uncarpeted floor. The child's face was shining. Alison swung her again and then lowered her to the floor, touching her down gently. One of her boots had disappeared from a bare foot.

'You've brought me visitors, Lizzie!' She smiled at Ralph and then nodded over his shoulder. 'Colin.'

'Hello, Alison,' Colin mumbled.

The child still hung from her hand, pivoting on her feet with the bare one on top of the booted. The rubber sole squeaked on the boards.

'I'd given up on you, to tell the truth,' Alison said. She wore a man's blue V-necked sweater over black leggings. There was a look of sleep in her face. She stroked the child's cheek. 'You go down now, Lizard. I need to talk to these gentlemen.'

The child set off glumly. Alison watched for a moment from the top of the stairs and then nodded them into her room. Curtains were half-drawn over a window overlooking the back. There was a blue rug and a narrow bed, its covers pushed to the wall. Cardboard boxes cluttered the hearth. Colin was staring and she watched him for a second.

'You don't think much of this, do you, Colin?'

'Not much,' Colin said.

She nodded and turned to Ralph. 'So how's the leg nowadays?'

Ralph thought of the expression on the little mechanic's face as he let go with the kick. 'Just a touch of cramp.'

Alison crossed the room. A frameless square of mirror leaned against the wall above the empty fireplace. She reached into the space behind it and took out a little book with a pale-yellow cover.

'A friend of mine thought this would interest you.'

'Why doesn't he show me himself?' Ralph asked.

'He's shy. He's got plenty more to show you. Rooms of the stuff.'

Ralph looked about. There was nothing but bareness. 'Is this his place?'

'No, it's not.'

A lamp stood on the floor beside the bed. She crouched to switch it on and held the book in its light. She beckoned and Ralph leaned forward. Sleep hung like a gas over the bed. The thing she held was not a book but a creamy tablet carved with tiny figures and fragments of windows and gables and the overhanging bows of trees. The carving extended into the depth of the panel. The figures gazed out from the windows and climbed little outside staircases.

'What is it?'

'Take a closer look,' she offered.

It was unexpectedly light, as if most of its substance had been lost in the carving. A crack ingrained with dark matter extended from the top edge and lost itself among the detail. The material held the light with a waxy yellow glow.

'Stare long enough and they'll start to move,' she said.

'I believe you. Now where did you find this?'

'Not me. The friend.'

'He was lucky.'

'Not luck – he just goes further than most people.'

Ralph turned the plaque to examine its back. She watched the way he handled it.

'I've a feeling it might turn into bad luck,' she said.

'That's possible.'

He made as if to hand it back to her but she nodded across the room. 'Let Colin take a look.'

Colin shook his head. 'I can see enough from here.'

'I'd like to take it with me,' Ralph said. 'Get another opinion.'

'Cliff, you mean?' Alison asked.

'It's his money we'll be spending.'

'So take it then. If it's worth nothing you can throw it in a bin.'

'I don't think it will come to that,' Ralph said.

She smiled and turned towards the window. There was a rattling noise from the back. 'He's calling the cats,' she said.

'Who is?'

'The old guy next door – old man Fishburn. He feeds them.'

'I've never liked cats.'

'No? Do you remember my friend of the other day?'

He thought back. 'The old guy with the chin weed?'

She nodded. 'That's his father downstairs.'

'He looked too old to need a father,' Ralph said.

He glanced through the bare panes of the window but could see only a corner of overgrown garden, a piece of broken wall at its back and then the waste ground. He looked down at the plaque again.

'I can take it with me and give you something on account.'

'If you like.'

She turned away when he took out his wallet. The money his father had given him was in a different compartment to his own. He separated a twenty.

'I'll live in hope,' Alison said, taking it.

He looked towards Colin but Colin was avoiding his eyes, preoccupied with something. He took out another ten.

'What about her hand?' Colin asked in the van.

'Whose hand?'

'The woman with the kid. What was that trouble with her hand?'

'I suppose the same thing that put her in that chair,' Ralph said.

Colin considered this. When they stopped before lights he made a noise in his throat, almost a purr.

'Something wrong?' Ralph asked.

'I'm still thinking about it: the hand she had.'

'What about it?'

Colin was working his face around to something, shifting himself in the seat.

'So what about it, Colin?'

He managed to free his lips. 'I wanted to kiss it.'

Thirteen

Cliff turned his new wife through the cigarette smoke and the drowsy dancers, smiling with his mouth in her hair, his hands on her slippery waist. She gripped his shoulder through his thin shirt. The sharpness of her nails made him gasp. He had taken off the jacket of his mohair suit.

'So what's that for?'

She smiled into his face, a little bit the taller. 'To keep you on your toes.'

'We're married now, aren't we?'

'That doesn't mean you can relax.'

He laughed, turning her again, pushing his belly against hers where the baby hung in its fluid. Then the music ended with a chord and he felt miserable for a second. He looked about the room. The smoke was making his eyes heavy. A fat woman was asleep on the sofa, her drink still in her hand.

'Where's your ma?' Cliff asked.

She smiled and nodded to someone. She'd changed out of the dress she'd worn at the registry office. 'Downstairs with Eric. They're talking in the garden.'

'Only talking?'

'That's what I said.'

'Is he her bloke?'

'Eric?' She might have laughed but she closed her eyes instead. 'Don't be ridiculous.'

'He's always here.'

'That doesn't mean anything.'

'It must mean something.'

'Only that he's the sort you can't get rid of.'

The one-eyed woman at the piano turned the page of her music with a wet finger. She set her hands on the keys and struck up a rhythm, ham-fisted. He held out his arms but Joyce protested. 'My legs are giving out. Let's sit for a while.'

'All right.'

When he cupped her waist she didn't move, resisting him. She nodded over at the pianist. 'That's the woman I was telling you about – my mother's friend. The one that saw the man on Wilson's Island.'

He stared at the woman's thin back in her lace blouse. Her sharp shoulder blades were working to the music. A deep hollow at the back of her neck looked like a healed-over wound. 'You mean the one the man exposed himself to?'

'He wasn't that sort . . . Don't let her see you staring.'

He turned away. He felt primed with drink and prodded his toe at a balloon trailing its ribbon. 'She can't play that piano, anyway. She's a bloody disgrace on the thing.'

She pinched his arm. 'Quiet!'

He calculated her expression. 'You're frightened of her?'

'No, but I think I should be.'

They sat down on the studio couch. The sleeping woman leaned against him, breathing out crème de menthe. Cliff listened to Mrs Foster pressing out the tune. Too much pedal, he thought. There was an upright in storage at work and he had lately started to play himself, vamping a few chords, singing below his breath.

'So what was he then? Somebody starting up a nudist camp?'

'How should I know? It was years ago – just after the war.'

'All sorts of things happened then. It turned people's minds, you see.'

'Not hers,' she said.

He watched Eric come back into the room, dragging his feet so that he tripped on a fold in the rug and nearly fell. The shiny wave of his hair hung like a cowlick over his forehead.

'The old feller's plastered.'

'He isn't, and he isn't old.'

Cliff leaned closer to her, whispering below the hammered chords of the music. 'And he had his thing upright? This feller on the island?'

'I think you've drunk too much yourself,' she said. 'Remember we're going away tonight.'

He stared at the woman leaned over the keys. A small glass of sherry stood on a doily on the piano top. 'We're not going far and we'll be taking a cab. Did anyone else ever see this man?'

'Not through the want of trying.'

'What do you mean?'

'They go back on the day it happened. They have a picnic on the foreshore.'

'Who does?'

'She and her friends. Mrs Foster and my mother.'

He started to laugh but then felt drowsy. The sleeping woman shifted against him, threatening to slide into his lap. He looked up and saw his wife's mother crossing the rug towards them.

'Hello, Mrs Orr.' The wine was hot in his cheeks.

'Hello, Cliff.' She gave him a placid little smile out of scale with her face. He noticed that a bird had left its mark down her sleeve and wondered if he should tell her. 'You can call me Mother now,' she said.

Racing from Wincanton. At the end of one race, when the riders were leading their mounts to the enclosure, Cliff heard someone come into the shop. He killed the sound. The quiet tread of feet.

'Can I help you?'

A blond-haired kid of about nineteen or twenty, even-featured and with pumped-up shoulders. Well-laundered casual clothes and a slight cast in one eye. He was hiding something small in his right palm. There was a crucifix tattooed on the first joint of the index finger.

They looked at one another for about half a minute. 'Can I help?' Cliff had to repeat.

The boy shook his head.

'Take a look around,' Cliff said. 'Call if you need me.'

He didn't answer but lifted his hand. He held a brown egg between his thumb and his forefinger. From where he was sitting, Cliff could see a hairline crack.

'Well, it's better than that business with the phone,' Cliff told him. 'More the personal touch.'

The kid looked blank for a second. Then he cleared his throat and tossed the egg with a straight sweep of his arm. It came like a dead weight through the air.

Cliff showered in the caravan and then trawled through his wardrobe for clean clothes. When he heard the van enter the yard, he collected the soiled ones and stuffed them deep into the laundry basket. He was watching the midget TV when Ralph swung back the door.

'You should knock,' Cliff told him. 'I might have been entertaining.'

His son squinted towards the little screen. He had a sharp-jawed look to him, as though he'd lost weight in just the last couple of days. 'Why's the shop closed?'

'I had an accident,' Cliff said.

Ralph leaned into the cabin, sniffing.

'I had an accident with a rotten egg,' Cliff told him.

He saw that Ralph was holding a soapy yellow slab of something against his belly. The phone extension began to chirrup. Cliff willed it to stop and to his surprise it did.

His son was still watching him. 'You're not going to tell me, are you?'

'Tell you what, exactly?'

He tilted his head in the direction of the shop. 'What just happened in there.'

'I don't think I can,' Cliff said. 'I don't think it would serve any purpose.' He took off his glasses and stood them open on the table. The lenses cast little spools of light. He massaged his eyes and nose with his fingers and then put the glasses on again. He looked at whatever his son was holding. 'What's that?'

Ralph dropped it on the table. Cliff touched the TV and the picture collapsed with a snap.

'Colin says it's ivory.'

'Does he?' Cliff picked it up. 'It's damaged anyway.'

'I can see that.'

Cliff leaned into the light from the lamp, bending closer over the desk until his shadow interfered, a hand to each side of the plaque and his thumbs pressing. 'The carving's very fine.'

Ralph watched the deep creases at the back of his neck. 'Chinese, is it?'

Cliff nodded. 'But Hong Kong or mainland?'

'Does it matter?'

'Makes all the difference. It's modern, I'd say.'

'Doesn't look modern to me.'

His father laughed. He reached to turn off the lamp. Without it the cabin seemed as dim as a pit. 'Is it hers? Alison's?'

'It belongs to some bloke she knows.'

'And he didn't show his face?'

'No.'

'She lives with him, though?'

'How should I know if she lives with him?'

Cliff glanced up at him. Despite the shower there were little beads of sweat on his upper lip.

Ralph shrugged. 'She's in a place where he stores his bits and pieces. It didn't look like he stayed there himself.'

'It isn't important,' Cliff said. 'I just wanted an idea of her situation.' He sighed and stood the ivory on its base on the surface of the desk, his fingers resting on its top edge. 'So how much are we into this already?'

'Thirty quid,' Ralph told him.

'You had the neck to offer her thirty quid?'

'I told you – I wasn't sure about it.'

'I suppose it's better to keep on the low side with a first bit of business, anyway. Show them who's the beggar and who the chooser . . . I think I'll let you develop this one, though.'

'What do you mean?'

Cliff pushed the plaque towards him. 'Here, take it home. You could do with an ornament or two.'

Ralph took it up. 'Thanks. They've got more to show us – a houseful, according to her.'

'She has, or he?'

'I think it comes to the same.'

'Who else lives there?'

'Dunno. A young guy I saw. A woman in a wheelchair with a kid.'

Cliff nodded. 'At least she has a choice of company.' He turned the TV on again: snooker. He watched it for a while with distaste. 'I hope you're keeping your hand in,' he said.

'What?'

'The darts: I hope you're putting in some practice.'

Fourteen

Ma was in her chair, her big round back against the light cast by her desk magnifier. She must have heard Cliff coming up the stairs or recognised the sound of the car earlier because she turned her head and gave him one of her unsurprised smiles – a shared joke between them he couldn't fathom, which never changed.

She sat back and rubbed her eyes. The bed table was on her lap and the braided cord of the magnifier trailed towards the skirting. Mrs Foster was curled close to the socket as if it gave off some extra warmth.

He went over and kissed her on the cheek.

'Any news?' she asked, her eyes still closed.

That put him on the defensive. 'Not to my knowledge, Ma.'

She sighed and eased herself in the chair, pressing her hands against the arms.

'Shall I move your cushion?' Cliff asked.

She shook her head. 'You can move that spyglass if you like: my eyes are that tired.'

He switched off the lamp and moved the heavy viewer. An empty mug stood on the small table. The plaid rug was slipping from her lap and she pulled a face when he tucked it tighter. It was after nine but Eric was still busy upstairs. Cliff listened to the light placing of his feet on the bare floor overhead.

'Why doesn't the boy come?' Ma asked. A simple enough question.

Cliff laughed. 'If he was a boy I'd drag him here by the ear.'

'I'm sure you're keeping him too busy,' Ma said with a glance of mischief.

'I make no demands on him – just a spot of paid work when he feels the mood, which hasn't been often.'

'And you have him playing that game again.' She made the motion with her hand.

'That'll do him no harm. And there's a few quid in it nowadays.'

'That's true,' Ma said reflectively. 'Money never hurt a soul.'

She marked the page of her book with a fringed marker and closed it.

'What's that you're reading?' Cliff asked.

She smiled at him without caring to answer. He looked away. Sometimes her smiles had the effect of violence.

'You know what I want when I'm gone, Cliff?'

'Why talk about that?'

'I have to tell you because I can't rely on that one upstairs.'

'But not while you're in health,' he said. 'Why discuss it then?'

She blew between her lips. 'It might be too late otherwise.'

He leaned towards her. 'Are you feeling ill?'

'Not yet. But you know when these things are coming – it's like waiting for a train.'

Cliff looked at the pampered tabby and saw crippled Mrs Foster. 'Then we won't talk about trains, either.'

But he must have been standing too close to her because she reached out and caught his wrist. 'Don't be clever, Cliff. Just give me an answer.'

'The river's so polluted now, Ma. It's full of nothing else but mercury.'

'A little mercury won't hurt me. You know the spot I'm talking about?'

He nodded. 'That place.'

'That place, yes. Only not in that tone.'

She closed her grip until he could feel the sharp edges of her bones. He stared to pull against her but then couldn't. It was weakness or respect – same sodding difference. She spoke to him without lifting her voice.

'I'll always be stronger than you while I'm here, Cliff – so don't defy me.'

'All right, Ma.'

She let him go, as if she had no further interest. Cliff watched the cat padding across the room. He had an impulse to kick it.

'Touch that animal and it will finish you,' Ma said. He saw her glance past him and lower her heavy lids for a second. 'Besides, your friend's here.'

Eric was standing against one side of the door as if he'd been there for a while. He wore his loose blue overalls with the coloured tops of pens in the breast pocket.

'Aren't I *your* friend, Marion?' he asked.

Ma was casting about among the folds of her plaid, looking for something – a pen, a key, the slide which had fallen from her hair. She was forgetful of them and then surprised to find them still waiting. She looked up, scornful of them both. 'So what's this – a bloody delegation?'

In the room upstairs the furniture was still under covers in one corner but the paraphernalia of decorating had vanished and the floor was clear of dustsheets. The boards had been carefully swept and sanded free of paint specks. The bare wood was studded with the polished heads of nails.

'The carpet's coming in the week,' Eric told him. 'A sort of ash grey she has her eyes on.'

'Ash grey?' Cliff looked about the room. 'You've surpassed yourself this time, Eric.'

'Had to, son – had to be my best. It's the last time I'll take on anything like this, you see. The old joints are getting stiff now and the ladder work gives me trouble. I'm still fine on the flat, though . . .' He glanced up at the ceiling, wistful. 'If you could bring everything down to that level, then I could carry on indefinitely.'

'I'm sure you could, Eric. I'm certain of that.'

Eric smiled but then stepped frowning towards the blank space of wall between the windows, as if he could see some fault there not visible to others. He began to look puzzled, staring at the white surface which was harsh after a while in the unshaded light. He gave a hiccup, a gasp of air.

'You OK, Eric?'

Eric worked his shoulders, a small man in a big overall. 'Has she been talking to you about dying? Did she mention that at all?'

Cliff looked at the same point on the wall.

'Did you hear me?' Eric asked.

'She did mention it in passing.' He saw the joke he'd made.

Eric nodded. 'She'll give the place to him, you know.'

'Who's that, Eric?'

'I'm sure you know. That lad of yours.'

'She's just saying that, Eric. She likes to see you squirm.'

He laughed. 'Don't I know it.'

'When did she come out with that?'

Eric shrugged, sniffed. 'Oh, it's been several occasions. It's always been her intention . . .' He looked suspiciously towards Cliff. 'Are you trying to tell me you didn't know?'

'She says one thing and means another. She should have been on the stage.'

Eric brushed some of the soft white dust from his front. He looked as though he was still gagging on something – gristle in his throat. 'Stage, yeah,' he whispered.

'And you know she'll see both of us out,' Cliff said. 'You can kick my arse if she doesn't.'

Ralph set the plaque in a place against the wall where it caught the light. He threw darts at the board in the alcove until his palms began to sweat and then went into the bathroom. Having washed his face and hands, he looked for a while at the indentation left by the darts at the tip of his left index finger.

The door chimes sounded. The thought of playing dead crossed his mind but the thought occurred to him that it might be Alma Drean and that she would have heard him from below.

She stood back when he opened the door, her arms folded. She wore a green jersey dress. His eye was caught by a coloured pin in the collar.

'What's the stone?' he asked.

'Carnelian. It was my mother's.'

'Very nice.'

'I won't come in,' Alma said. 'I only came to thank you for dealing with Sammy the other night.'

'That's all right.'

'I should have thanked you before this but you never seem to be in.'

'I walk a lot.' He noticed that she was wearing slippers, the blue of which clashed with the dress.

'You shouldn't think anything bad of him,' Alma said.

'I won't then.'

She looked beyond him. He looked as well and saw the board under its lamp. He leaned forward and kissed her on the cheek just below the ear. Her skin tasted of some sort of bitter lotion.

'You're like a bull in a china shop,' she said.

He felt his erection folding before he'd been aware it was there. 'Am I?'

'Excuse me,' she said. 'I only mean that you don't know how to judge a situation.'

110

'I might be guilty of that.'

'I'm an old friend of your father's,' she said.

'How friendly?'

'Since we were kids. We have respect for one another.' She smiled, showing small teeth. 'I'll show you my old photos one day.'

'I'll look forward to that.'

She stared up at him, as if a thought had crossed her mind. 'How long is it since you were with a woman?'

'What time is it now?'

'No, seriously.'

'It's not a thing I can be serious about.'

'Then that's your loss . . . Well,' she said. 'I've done what I meant to.'

'Then thanks for that.'

'You're not half as nice as your dad,' she said.

'People often tell me that. You have to be philosophical.'

'Right . . .' She half turned and then turned back, frowning with what looked for a second like venom. 'I wouldn't treat a dog like you treat Cliff, you know.'

Fifteen

The demolition men had dragged a couch from one of the houses and were sitting along it drinking mugs of tea. Alison was standing before them in a dusty black coat and high boots. She must have heard the engine because she glanced towards the van and then back to the crew. One of them jumped up from the couch and started to talk excitedly to her, holding his mug and leaning towards her in his yellow hat. He jerked a finger at the surviving terrace at the foot of the street.

Ralph stopped the van and climbed down. She had finished her conversation and was walking towards him. Laughter went on behind her back.

'No Colin today?' she asked.

He shook his head.

'Does Cliff trust you out on your own?'

He didn't answer. Alison stared back at the men on the couch. The one who had spoken with her raised his mug to them and then hefted his balls with his other hand.

'That one's a cheeky sod especially,' she said.

'You're having problems with them?'

'Frank is.'

'Your friend?' Ralph asked.

She closed her eyes for a second. 'One of my friends. They don't like him taking things from the houses around here – that's their perk.'

'I can see their side of it,' Ralph said.

'Can you?' Her hair blew into her eyes and she pushed it back. He noticed that her lips were trembling. 'I'd say they've got a wage while he has to scratch around for a living.'

'I can see that as well.'

'Then you're an understanding person.'

She walked quickly away, her heels scudding on the broken paving. He looked after her for a second and then followed, down the hill towards the terrace. The wall of the first house

112

had been breached and he could see the papered walls of an upstairs room.

He caught up with her. 'They're making progress, anyway.'

She looked at him more kindly. 'They can't go much further while the Fishburns are still in their house. There's a demolition-purchase order on it but even they wouldn't knock the place down with them still inside.'

'There's nowhere for them to go?'

'The housing department make them offers but they turn everything down. They want to stay here, you see. And they can't see why they shouldn't.'

'These places will fall down unless they're pushed.'

'I know that.'

'So maybe it's best if they leave.'

She looked disgusted. 'The old guy will end up in a home. Walter will finish on the streets unless they think he's right for another kind of home—'

'Walter?'

'Is there something funny about that?'

'Nothing,' he said quickly.

A yellow Commer van with a flat front tyre was parked outside the house. A circular hole had been roughly cut in its side. Ralph could see the shiny edges of raw metal. The timber had been moved to the side of the front steps.

'Rose is out,' Alison said. 'She spends a lot of time at her friend's house.' She searched the pockets of her coat and produced a stubby key. 'We've had to start locking the place since the last disagreement. We don't want them walking in and compensating themselves.'

'Things are as bad as that?'

'Not yet. But you don't know which way it will go.'

The house was dark after the breezy sunshine outside. A yellow bulb burned in the kitchen at the end of the narrow hall. It dimmed suddenly and then grew slowly again in strength.

'There's a problem with the power supply,' Alison said, leading him along the hall. In the kitchen she hunted for matches and lit a ring of the stove. She filled a black kettle at the tap.

'Is this where you cook?' Ralph asked.

'Cooking's usually done in a kitchen.'

He looked around. There was a smell of stagnant water and the bottom half of the window was covered by a piece of board.

Sloping shelves beside the cooker were filled with packets and cans of food, stacked crockery and pans with blackened undersides.

'Cook much yourself?' Alison asked.

He shook his head. 'No.'

'If you feel up to watching the kettle, I'll tell Frank you're here.'

He sat down at the table and waited. There was a faint smell of gas. He could hear the digger working on the site. Alison came downstairs as the kettle boiled and set out three mismatched mugs. She had removed her coat and wore a thin grey cardigan over a loose print dress. Her bare legs looked very pale against the red leather of the boots.

'So how's your dad?' she asked with her back to him.

'Cliff is fine.'

'Why do you call him that when he's your father?'

'He went away when I was a young kid. When he came back I called him that.'

'Doesn't he mind?'

'If he does, he doesn't say so.'

'Will you do me a favour and tell him I'm thinking about him? Say he's in my thoughts a lot. Do you want me to write it down?'

'I think I can remember that.'

'I don't want to embarrass you.'

'It won't be embarrassing.'

She nodded and turned her head. There was a clanging and grinding from outside in the street. 'That's a new skip arriving. They fill about three of the things a day: you wouldn't believe there was so much rubbish in the world.'

'No.'

She filled the mugs and put an open sugar bag on the table. 'Frank's is the Cancer mug.'

'Is that his sign?'

She shook her head. 'Just his mug.' She smiled as if she were considering something. 'He's full of shite, you know, Ralph. Up to his eyeballs in it. This is just a quiet word of warning.'

Frank came down to the noise of the toilet flushing. He wore the greasy dark suit and Ralph wondered if he had slept in it. His face was stubbly and blear. He picked up the zodiac mug and leaned against the front of the sink, his stocky legs braced. He gave Ralph a wan smile.

'I could say it's a small world but then it isn't. You'll know how exactly big it is,' he said.

'You'll go crazy if you listen to him,' Alison warned.

Frank made the pantomime of a little bow to her, then turned to Ralph again. 'Still competing, are you?' He shaped his free hand as if for a throw. He clicked his tongue and flighted the phantom towards the wall above their heads.

'I'm persisting with it,' Ralph admitted. 'What about you?'

'Other things demand my time.'

'Like lying in his bed,' Alison added.

Frank lifted a finger as if he'd recalled something. 'Forgive the late appearance. I've been awake half the night, as it happens. A pain. *Here.*'

His voice had a changing brogue to it – sometimes gruff and at others falsetto, as if there were two voices in there, struggling. He pressed his fingers into the soft cushion of his belly, then turned to Alison, winking one eye like a camera shutter. When he opened it again, his face still seemed lopsided. 'Will you massage me there later? I've been told that your fingers are magical.'

'No one told you that,' Alison said quietly. 'And you can't avoid people for ever.'

He smiled at her. 'Those arseholes from the site, you mean? I'll take a stroll over there later, see if we can come to an accommodation.'

'You'll be lucky,' she said.

'But I am lucky.'

The light began to falter again, fading almost to nothing and then recovering in a flickering way.

'They know that time is money and money is flesh,' Frank said, staring up at it. He sniffed and turned to Ralph. 'Well, did you take to our little treasure, Ralph? Was it to your taste?'

'I'm still looking into it.'

He gave a short laugh. 'You've reached no conclusions at all? There's such a thing as theft, you know.'

'Frank!' Alison warned.

Ralph took out his wallet and gave him another three fresh notes. Twenties. Frank's face turned blank for a second, as if the possession of the money had wiped every feeling.

'So that's the size of it?' he asked.

'With a thing like that we usually like some kind of provenance,' Ralph told him.

'What's that in English?'

'I mean we like to know where it came from. Otherwise there might be trouble when we want to move it on.'

'You mean you think I might have taken it from somewhere? Some old girl with bad eyesight?'

'It's been known.'

Frank stared at the notes and then kissed them with an audible smack before slipping them into his shirt pocket. 'I'll introduce you to the men responsible. Because one good turn deserves another.'

He leaned over the sink to look out of the window.

'They're in if you want to know,' Alison said. 'Only that woman from social services was around earlier and they've been lying low.'

Frank clicked his tongue. 'Have you met our neighbours, Ralph?'

'I've seen them from a distance.'

He laughed. 'You have to meet them face to face for the full effect.'

'They won't be in the mood for visitors,' Alison warned.

'But moods can be changed . . .'

A door led out to the back. Frank bent to work at the bolts and opened it into the yard, which was at a lower level. He grinned back at them both and stepped down, whistling to himself.

'You don't have to go with him,' Alison said.

'He has me interested now.'

'Oh, he's as interesting as hell.'

The yard was a paved channel between the house and a tall dividing wall. The wall was so weathered that daylight showed between the brickwork in places. A cat jumped up almost at their feet and glided away.

'The Fishbones encourage the curs,' Frank said. 'There's enough shite around here to start a manure mill, so watch where you're putting your feet.'

The square of garden was choked by thickets of weed and thistle. A broken-down part of the back wall allowed a view of the site showing one of the Portakabins and the white sentry box of a chemical toilet.

Frank waved his arm towards it. 'I'll talk them round. Cheeky bastards think they own these places!'

'Alison thinks they might do you harm,' Ralph said.

'That's because she's frightened of men. Women always fear

what they don't understand.' Frank smiled sideways. 'I'm only telling you this for your own good.'

They stepped over a length of barbed wire guarding a gap in the fence. The other garden seemed bigger, losing itself in tall weeds and thistles. The cat smell was much stronger and Ralph saw melting scraps of fat set on a patterned plate. Frank kicked at it, spilling the food.

'I'd poison the brutes myself. Then the world would be rid of them.'

'My grandmother took in a stray,' Ralph told him. 'She named it after a friend of hers. A woman who died.'

Frank spat into the weeds. 'That kind of thing just makes me laugh.' He looked up, smiling towards the house. Walter Fishburn was standing behind the dusty window of a back room, looking out at them with his mouth open. He was naked and his body looked pale and cloudlike through the smudged glass. His beard and the hair on his chest was a froth of grey.

'Up to his tricks again,' Frank said.

'He does that a lot?'

'For years, I've been told. Since he was a youngster. People let him get away with it. One phone call to the police and he'd be committed.' He grinned. 'But then he has his uses so why take the trouble?'

More plates of food were set on the fractured slabs of the yard. The smell was sour and overpowering. A mangle with heavy wooden rollers stood against the side of the house. Walter was gone from the window and instead an oval mirror shone at them from the back of the room. The kitchen door was open but Frank knocked and waited. He tried again with the side of his fist, making the panels shake.

'Makes raising the dead seem like child's play,' he said.

Ralph watched a thin black cat creep timidly up to one of the plates and sit before it.

'That means the old boy's on his way,' Frank told him. 'They can sense him or smell him.'

A soft tapping came from inside the house and the elder Fishburn emerged into the doorway, making slow three-point progress with a rubber-tipped stick. He was smaller then his son and thin, dressed in tweeds and collapsing woollens. He had a smell of tobacco and disinfectant. His skin was the colour of old soap.

117

'Mr Fishbone,' Frank said with an ingratiating smile. 'I heard your friends were asking for you again.'

Fishburn pursed his lips as if puzzling over the words. He stared at Ralph as if that might refer to him.

'The bloody Social!' Frank reminded.

Mr Fishburn turned to stare painfully over his shoulder, to where maybe his son was standing.

'They're persistent, you see,' Frank said. 'They'll promise you everything but watch out!'

Fishburn hung in the doorway. There were broad empty shelves and an ancient gas cooker with bracket feet. Spent matches littered the floor.

'So won't you ask us in?' Frank asked sweetly.

Fishburn stared at his lips for a second and then stepped back from the door, placing his feet with maddening slowness. He wore carpet slippers below the sagging turn-ups of his trousers.

'This is a friend of mine,' Frank said, stepping smartly inside. 'He might be interested in some of your possessions.'

Mr Fishburn turned his face towards Ralph and then looked away again almost shyly. A long tabby was stretched sleeping on the top of the table below the window. He gave it a soft look and gently drew the tip of his finger through the short fur below its ear.

'A marvellous way he has with them,' Frank said. 'He should be on those telly shows: where they save endangered species.'

Fishburn made a noise in his throat. 'Hnn.'

'Ralph here's a businessman. He'll be able to tell you what's worth money and what's just trash,' Frank said.

The cat had woken and was cleaning itself, leaving a glistening trail of saliva along its side. Its teeth clicked as it searched for lice. There wasn't a sign of food in the room except for a row of cans. Their tops were dark with rust.

'You can see they never eat,' Frank said. He smiled through the connecting door into the hall. Walter Fishburn was standing, still naked, near the foot of the stairs. 'Oh, your other half is here, Mr Fishbone.'

Fishburn cleared his throat.

'Ralph here is interested in all sorts of things,' Frank said. 'But you can never predict just what might catch his eye.'

The old man began to turn ponderously around the swivel of his stick. Frank grinned at his fragile back and then raised his hand. As if it had suddenly realised its danger, the cat uncoiled and scooted from the table into the yard.

Walter retreated up the stairs as they approached, his big pale fingers curling around the rail above their heads. The room from which he had watched them was filled almost to the ceiling with heavy, dark furniture. A narrow path had been left through it for access.

Fishburn led them past the door. Ralph was surprised to hear him speak. The old man's voice was thin but clear. 'Nothing in there – nothing worth its weight in firewood.'

'You have to let the man decide,' Frank put in with a touch of irritation. 'What might be nothing to you could mean thousands to an expert.'

The front room was crowded with the same solid items but looked more domestic, with a couch and a couple of the chairs left free to sit on. Through a bare bay window they could see the yellow digger moving in sunshine on the other side of the street. Fishburn pointed to the couch and then lowered himself by stiff movements into an armchair.

Ralph sat down. The seat of the couch felt slightly damp. Frank perched beside him on the arm and took out a tin with a top polished to a mirrorlike shine. He flicked it open and stripped out cigarette papers.

'Where's the boy gone?' he asked. 'Is he playing shy with us?'

'I never know where I'll find him,' Mr Fishburn grumbled. 'He'll lose himself for good one day.'

Frank frowned. 'Let's hope not.'

He finished his cigarette, taking care over it. Fishburn was nodding to himself, his stick leaning against the arm of the chair. There was a noise about him which was hard to place: a little pneumatic creaking which might have been his breath. Ralph watched the digger doing its business across the road.

'I don't know why they don't come through the wall with that thing,' Frank said. 'It's only lack of imagination that stops them.'

Fishburn rubbed his hands with a chafing sound. 'Let them come and I wouldn't move from this chair. They can grind my bones any day of the week.'

'That's what I like to hear,' Frank said.

He handed the lit cigarette to the old man, who drew on it suspiciously. He coughed over it and took it out of his mouth to look at its burning end.

119

'My friend here would like to see upstairs,' Frank told him. 'I could save you the trouble if you like and show him about myself.'

Mr Fishburn had dropped ash on the front of his cardigan. Frank leaned forwards to brush it away with the tips of his fingers. Fishburn stared at him, then turned smiling as his son came quietly into the room, sliding his sagging, dimpled bulk through the tight spaces. There was a rash across his bare chest and shoulders. He reached for his father's hand and the old man took it gently.

'You're blocking the gentlemen's light, Walter,' he said softly.

Walter watched from the doorway as they went upstairs. He frowned and looked troubled, as though their presence had left him at a loss. He turned away as they reached the landing and a second later Ralph heard a high, childish crooning.

'That's him singing,' Frank said. 'You'd think a brute that size would have a decent voice.'

'So why does he walk about like that?' Ralph asked.

'It comes over him now and again, the need for it. It's a sort of melancholia.'

'I hope he never steps out the house.'

'Only into the garden. I like to think the sun on him might cure his scabs.'

Upstairs a huge broken bed was piled with soiled rags. There was a Turkish rug worn through to the boards and then bulky ebonised furniture. An off-white cat slept curled on a chair. Frank bent to tap it on the skull with the tip of his finger and it gazed at him mildly for a second and then uncoiled and fled with a scrabble of claws.

'His room,' Frank said. 'The youngster's.'

'He sleeps on that thing?'

'If either of them needs to,' Frank said. 'Which I have reason to doubt.'

'I know someone else who doesn't,' Ralph told him. 'Maybe they're related.'

Frank nodded. 'There's too much relation nowadays.' He dusted the seat of the chair and then tipped it forward so that Ralph could see the worn embroidery of vines and trellis. He caught it by its back rail and held it up with a hand. 'There! That's balance for you! And look at the carving – crisp as the day it was made.'

'Very nice,' Ralph said.

'Nice? I can see you're not a furniture man.' He laughed and let the chair fall with a jarring clack. 'There's pictures if you like. Mirrors. Even an upright piano if you're feeling musical.'

'Washer-dryers are more our line.'

Frank gave an open-mouthed grin, tipping back his head. It made Ralph think of a dog clowning for a biscuit. Then he closed his jaws with a snap and turned serious. 'There's money in this place, though: I'm sure you've realised that by now.'

He crooked his finger. Ralph followed. They climbed a shorter, steeper flight of stairs. Whenever he breathed he could smell the sweet cakeish smell of cat.

'Do you still see much of Charlie?' he asked as they reached the top of the house.

Frank stopped, as if the question had surprised him. 'Why should I have anything to do with that old fraud?'

'Charlie's supposed to look after his boys.'

He nodded, letting his lip curl. 'That's right. His involvement doesn't end with the dartboard.'

'What do you mean?'

Frank looked sly. 'Maybe he was being too much of a father to me.'

He opened another door. The narrow windows were hung with velvet drapes gone colourless with age and dust. The ends were feathered with moth. The light from the door was caught in a mirror.

'They're the sort who like to hang on to things,' Ralph said.

Frank shook his head, grinning. 'The old feller is willing. He wants money for some reason. Maybe he's opening a cat sanctuary.'

'Half this stuff's rotten, you know.'

'I know. The other half's enough to fund him.'

They crossed the landing. There was a room with a high bed against one wall. The fireplace was filled with soot and waste paper. Ralph looked out of the single window, down through dusty glass into the garden. From above he could see the narrow paths the cats had made through the thickets of weeds, like maggots in cheese.

'Good riddance to these old places,' Frank said. 'Let them smash the lot!'

'They'll do you out of a roof.'

'More power to them! I need to get off my arse soon, anyway.'

He nodded towards the fireplace. 'What do you reckon on the timepiece?'

A square-cased clock stood among the clutter above the fire. Ralph stepped over and lifted it down. The casing and glazed front were coated with years of dust. He turned it around and opened the little door at the back. The mechanism had been silenced with a roll of something which he found to be an old kid glove. He fumbled in the dark interior for the pendulum.

'This is the old man's room,' Frank said, 'but he won't mind.'

'You know what he wants to sell?'

'Thing is, we're thinking more of a clearance than punting the odd item. It'll be quicker and cleaner that way.' He jerked his thumb towards the outside. 'Or else those buggers will take it anyway.'

'Who's we?' Ralph asked.

Frank pushed out his barrel chest. 'The Fishburns and I.'

He laughed, taking pleasure in the phrase. Ralph looked towards the narrow fireplace. He saw the end of a candle rooted in its own grease and the dark corner of a picture frame half hidden by a pile of old books. A black thread of wire led to a bracket tamped into the wall.

'Can I see the picture?' he asked.

Frank followed his eyes, then turned away. 'You can look to your heart's content. Those downstairs will have forgotten our existence.'

The wire was caught about its screw so that he had to lift the frame to unpick it. The picture seemed to be glazed in dust and he cleared the face gently with his fingertips. An engraving on foxed yellow paper pictured a square-rigged ship passing a island crowned by trees and bushes. A small house stood at one end close to a wooden landing which extended into the water. A pair of what might have been dogs or pigs stood on the flat space in front of the house. The ship was sailing away from the island, its high stern just clearing the last of it. It looked out of scale or as if it were seen from a greater height than the rest of the view. The sea was calm except for little wrinkles of waves. There was a fainter coastline above the ship's mast. Apart from the ship and the dogs or pigs, there were no signs of life.

He brushed off more of the dust. There was a line of italic script under the block of the picture. *Merchantman off Capt. Wilson's Island. From a watercolour by C. Standfield. W. D. Rooke pinct.*

122

'Found something there?'

'Just an old print. Must be of Wilson's Island.' He put it back on its hanger and turned around.

'I've been there and it's not worth seeing,' Frank said.

Ralph rubbed at his hands to get rid of the dirt. 'You took a boat over?'

'I walked.'

'You can walk on water?'

'The currents have changed and you can make your way there at low tide now.'

'Was it worth the walk?'

'I got my shoes soaked through and the only thing I found was a turd in a kettle.'

'What?'

He nodded, pleased with the memory. 'I took a stroll around the place. There was nothing left to see except this big enamel kettle left under a bush. When I looked inside someone had done the job there.'

Sixteen

'I'd like to sleep now,' Joyce said.

Cliff sat in the chair, staring down at his pale, plump legs. He didn't move.

'What was the reasoning behind this place?' she asked. 'There's not much to recommend it as far as I can see.'

'One of the men at work told me about it.'

'Oh yes? I'm sure those two women in the lounge bar were prostitutes,' she said.

'They were just waiting for someone.'

She smiled at him from the yellow satin pillow. She'd combed out her hair and tied it back. It looked tight and shiny against her skull. 'You've only to look at the way they dressed,' she said. 'No woman would dress like that unless there was a reason behind it.'

She reached to turn the lamp out at her side of the bed. He was left sitting in his own circle of light.

'Have you any experience of prostitutes?' she asked.

'What kind of question is that?'

'It seems a fair question to me.'

'Then the answer's no,' he said.

She was turned away from him now. He listened to her shallow breathing in the darkened part of the room. Music came from the rooms downstairs: 'Come Fly with Me'. He could just make out the words. The afternoon's drinking had left him with a teasing headache and a feeling of heat on the surface of his skin. He looked at the rise of her hip and shoulder under the covers. He thought of her skin as having a slight down to it, almost a nap.

'Are you sitting there all night?' she asked with a sigh.

'You think I'm foolish,' he said.

She didn't answer. 'Could you turn off your light?' she asked.

He stretched out his arm and pressed the little button. The glow from the car park still shone through the blinds. He'd asked for a room overlooking the estuary, and had thought of them watching the lights of passing freighters.

'I don't know if you're foolish,' Joyce said. 'Not yet. But being the other thing isn't a bed of roses.'

'What's the other thing?'

'Being wise: I wouldn't always choose it.'

She was perfectly still. For half a minute he couldn't hear her breathe.

'I have to choose then?' he asked.

'Now you do . . .' They listened to a woman's laughter from the front of the hotel. 'That's the one who asked you for a light,' Joyce said. 'She's met her friend, you see.'

He heard the man's deep voice and then a car door slammed. The engine sounded throaty and expensive.

'You were anxious to show off that lighter of yours,' Joyce said.

'I was being polite.'

'She gave you such a look!'

'She could see we were a honeymoon couple.'

'You were preening yourself in front of her. She gave you a look only a tart would give.'

'If you say so.'

She sighed to herself, a sound of ease. There were more voices below. 'It sounds like everyone's leaving,' she said. 'Are you coming to bed tonight?'

'I'll sit for a while longer.'

The lights from a car went through the room. He could feel the coolness of the air now. He thought it must be past midnight.

'I'll kill it if you want,' Joyce said.

He stared at the shadow of her. 'What?'

'There's still time to get it done. Then all your worries would be over.'

Water was running through a pipe somewhere. The sound set his bladder aching. 'I won't hear of that.'

'If you're sure,' she said. She turned towards him. He could not see her face, only imagine the expression she might have. 'You have to tell me you're sure.'

'I'm sure,' Cliff said. 'I'm certain.'

'There's a smell from the river: a sort of chemical smell. Is the window closed?'

'I think so. I'll check it later.'

'So what do you wish for? A son or a daughter?'

'I don't care.'

'Men always want a son.'

'Not necessarily.'

'You are foolish,' she said. 'I've decided.'

Early evening. Ralph drove back through the town. The air had a smell of vinegar and cooking fat. A horn sounded behind. He looked into the side mirror and saw a tiny clear image of Charlie Sanderson with an arm through the open window of his carnival-orange Cortina. The car's bonnet was lifted on the black motor.

Still watching, Ralph swung the stick into reverse and backed up fast, the motor whingeing. He stamped on the pedal at what he judged was a couple of feet short of the Cortina's chromework, wiped his hands on the cloth he kept handy and climbed down.

'Thought you weren't going to stop,' Charlie said.

'Sorry.'

The front of Charlie's shirt was smeared with grease. His fingers were black with it. He beckoned Ralph, then spoke in a whisper. His eyes turned big and doleful towards the propped-up bonnet. 'I'm taking my mum somewhere and I have trouble with the bastard motor!'

Ralph glanced through the wet windscreen and saw the powder-white face of an old lady. She looked away when he smiled and nodded.

'You won't get much out of her,' Charlie Sanderson said. 'She's deaf and dumb.'

'I'm sorry.'

'Why are you sorry? Why's that?' Charlie nudged him gently with his elbow. 'People don't think, do they, Ralph? They say these things without considering.'

Ralph looked at the old girl again. She was busy with something on her lap. 'So can I be of help, Charlie?'

Charlie shook his head. 'Don't bother. The AA's on its way. It wasn't for that I stopped you.' He squinted towards the lights. 'I was hoping to speak to your dad but you seem to be the one in most circulation.'

'I was always circulating, Charlie. Just not around here.'

'So, well done. How is Cliff, anyway?'

'I'm not sure about that, Charlie. That's a thing that's difficult to pronounce on.'

126

'I know what you mean,' Charlie said. 'My thoughts on it exactly.'

They stood in silence for a second, looking the same way along the road. A car blared its horn as it passed, trailing the thump of a stereo.

'The world's full of these people,' Charlie declared. 'That business the other day, for instance. I hope your dad didn't take it too much to heart.'

'What business is that, Charlie?'

Charlie took a scrap of cloth from the top of his radiator and started to clean his hands with it. He frowned as he worked it carefully into the spaces between his fingers.

'My mother's eighty-two. I was taking her to see my sister.'

'You're from a big family, Charlie?'

'Two lads and a girl. And my elder brother's dead.'

'I'm sorry.'

'There you go again . . . We were talking about Cliff, weren't we?'

'That's right.'

Charlie smiled as if they were at last on the right track. 'Something happened there that didn't need to – no necessity for it at all. Just somebody exercising his authority where it didn't extend. Do you understand me, Ralph? Do you get the drift of what I'm saying?'

'The egg business?'

'That's it!' Charlie said brightly. 'Do you think you could communicate what I said to Cliff? With my apologies?'

'I will, Charlie.'

Charlie bunched the rag and threw it down into the gutter in front of the car. 'That's it then; that's the best that can be expected. Have you met my mother before, Ralph?'

'I don't think so.'

Charlie gazed at him with wide, fading eyes. 'I don't think so too.'

He led the way round to the passenger door. The woman turned to watch them. The window was closed and he made a twirling motion with his hand. When nothing happened, he did it again. The window slid down and Charlie's mother leaned towards them so that she could be seen in the light from outside. When Ralph held out his hand to her she took the ends of his fingers gently and then released them.

'Pleased to meet you,' Ralph said.

'Profoundly deaf,' Charlie reminded. 'Has been since birth.'

Ralph nodded at Charlie's mother again, smiling. After a second she wound up the window again.

'Tell that to Cliff, anyway,' Charlie said. 'Tell him it was all near-enough bollocks.'

'I'll do that. Only there's another thing, Charlie.'

Charlie looked surprised for a second, then smiled. 'Got a query, Ralph?'

'Do you know anything about the other business? The phone calls.'

He lifted his chin. 'What type of phone calls, Ralph: threatening or obscene?'

'Just breathing, that sort of thing.'

'A breather? If I was Cliff I wouldn't worry about that type too much. Breathing is as low as you can go: a breather is next door to a dead man.' He touched Ralph's arm and pointed up the road. 'Look, here comes the bloody US Cavalry.'

The revolving lights of the breakdown truck were shining in the shimmer of lights at the junction.

'So I'll see you at the match,' Charlie said.

'The match?'

'The darts match. Don't say he hasn't told you.'

'He probably did and it slipped my mind. Is the other one your man, again?'

Charlie shook his head. 'I've no more than an interest in him. Take care then, Ralph. Tell that old man of yours not to give himself an ulcer.'

The phone went while he was lying in the bath. He decided to let it ring but a few minutes later it went again, chirruping like a child's toy. The second time he found it too irritating to ignore.

'Are you there?' Jean asked. 'Am I talking to the wall?'

'I'm here.'

He wondered if she was ringing from her flat and then wondered what time the boy went to bed. Nine? Ten? He didn't know the bedtime of his own son. He looked at his watch and it was nearly eleven.

'I thought I'd talk to you,' Jean said. 'Before something happened again like the other day.'

'You mean that little friend of yours?'

128

'That, yeah. He wouldn't even tell me what he'd done. I had to get it out of one of the other men.'

'So what's a kick up the arse between friends? Have you spoken to Cliff since?'

'I think that's our business.'

'Yeah? Seems like there's some kind of overlap.'

He heard her sigh. When she spoke again her voice sounded tighter, more controlled, as if she'd thought this part over, repeating it to herself. 'If you're planning to stay, then we need to talk, Ralph. I don't want to be waiting in here for you to make a move. I want my own input.'

'Who told you I was staying?'

'You're still here, aren't you?'

He stayed quiet, not admitting to it. He could hear Alma Drean's bold laugh from the flat downstairs. She must have guests around, family.

'Did you want to see the boy?' Jean asked.

'John?'

'You remember his name, then? Yes, that's who I'm talking about.'

'He's one person.'

'One of many?'

'One of a few.'

'It sounds anyway as if you can take it or leave it.'

'I mean that I'd like to see him.'

'Excuse me a second—'

She might have been checking that a door was closed. When she came back he could feel her settling herself, making mental preparation.

'His school's having a gala soon. A water gala.'

'What?'

'Swimming. Water sports.'

'And he's swimming?'

'He's in a race and then there's a spectacular at the end. A *son et lumière.*'

'And he's in that?'

'That's right. Are you interested?'

'I'm interested, yeah.'

'Good. So we've established that. The condition is that you don't approach us – him or me. Not at this stage. You can watch but you keep your distance.'

'Watch but don't touch, is it?'

'That's it. I want to see how you behave first.'

'I could turn up anyway.'

'You don't know when or where. You don't even know which school he goes to now. Do you, Ralph?'

'I could ask Cliff.'

She allowed herself a little laugh. 'You're sure about that?'

'What's the point of this, Jeanie?'

'*Jean,*' she corrected. 'Call me just Jean. The point is, I have my hands on the wheel. As simple as that. It's my right to decide when these things happen – as I'm his sole parent nowadays.'

'So thanks for making that clear.'

She sighed. 'It's just a fact for me, Ralph. It's everyday.'

Seventeen

'So he's robbing them blind,' Cliff said.

'He helps them out, runs errands. He keeps an eye on them.'

'Anything he gives they'll pay him back a hundred times. Was her ladyship there?'

He glanced over to the muted TV.

'At first,' Ralph said. 'Then she went to her job. She does a couple of shifts in a laundrette.'

'He's living off her then?'

'I don't think so.'

'You speak well of him. Why's that?'

'Just trying to be fair.'

Cliff laughed, waving away smoke.

'They've got a houseful of the stuff,' Ralph told him. 'We should go and see it together.'

'Go with Colin again – he's good enough. Take a little bit of cash and buy the rest with promises . . . You're sure he's the one you played?'

'I'm sure.'

'Charlie's still not pleased with him. Does he know that?'

'He didn't say.'

'Thinks he's safe there, probably. Maybe he is . . . Sounds like it's the rest of them who ought to watch themselves.'

'I saw Charlie: he was broken down.'

'When?'

'Last night.'

'What did he have to say?'

'He mentioned a match you'd fixed for me . . . And he said the egg business was taken care of.'

Cliff looked relieved for only a second. 'I thought it might be. I had a feeling it was a mistake.' He laid back his head, swinging the chair slightly. 'Anything else of interest?'

'I asked about the one on the phone. The dog.'

He stopped his swinging, his mouth half open. 'Ah. You see, you

131

had less right there, Ralph, it being more of a problem personal to me. I thought that was understood between us.'

'It was news to Charlie, anyway.'

Cliff nodded, gathering the flesh at his throat. 'I'll bet it was, Ralphie. And now it's news all over.'

Eric levered the cap off a bottle of stout. The foam ran over his fingers before he could get it in the glass. He watched himself pour, smiling at his own clumsiness.

'The air in a birthing room,' Ma said. 'You could bottle it and send it to the sick.'

He set the glass upright and handed it to her. 'Was it a particular birth you have your mind on?'

She stared at him over her fleshy drinker's nose. 'You know I mean my grandson.'

'He could have used some health himself,' Eric said. 'He was like a hairless pup, I'd say.'

Ma closed her eyes. 'He was brighter than a diamond.'

'He was born as himself, I think. The way he stared about, you could see he could take it or leave it.'

'A morning baby,' Ma pronounced. 'That's what they're like – with that freshness set in them.'

There was some drink still in the bottle and Eric stood it on the table at her elbow. 'Then that's strange because I recall him as arriving one evening.'

Ma felt weary with him and his contradictions. 'In the *morning*. We went to see her in the afternoon and it was already getting dark outside, if you remember. A nurse was walking along closing the curtains.'

'Then I must have been thinking of that,' Eric admitted. He sighed. 'A miserable long place, that was. I've always detested any place longer than a normal room.'

'You're particular in this matter of rooms,' Ma said.

Eric began to frown. 'And where was that husband of hers? I've no clear memory of him in the vicinity.'

Ma took up the schooner of stout. He watched her drink and then tease the froth from her upper lip. 'He escapes my mind, as well.'

'Outshone, no doubt.'

She stared at him. 'Are you being sarcastic now? Anyway, he had this knack of self-effacement.'

'He seems to have lost it since . . . It was such an early birth anyway and probably caught him unprepared: mathematics not being his strong point.'

She still stared but he held her look. He could hear the breathing of the cat somewhere, that dirty animal.

'You're gut-full of implications,' Ma said. 'But you'll never announce yourself, only shilly-shally.'

'There was no time for any announcements. Not with that woman at the bedside to put her seal on it.'

'All children are God's: there's no room for doubt there.'

He shook his head. 'That kind of statement only makes me laugh.'

'Alice Foster came by taxi to bless him. She laid a fingertip on both his temples.' A little moth was flying against the window. The woman in the next bed had been delivered of twins.

'It's a wonder they let her proceed with that nonsense!' Eric said. 'I could see the sister looking over but she looked away again. It made me lose all respect for them!'

'She must have seen that it was none of her business.'

'Then she ought to have thought of the lack of hygiene – that stuff in the bottle. A screw top as if it had been hair tonic, and murky with a brown sludge in the bottom.'

River of Life. She had quickly made the mark on the child's forehead. Eric saw it shine for a second and then it was gone.

'Like water and a duck's back,' he said. 'When I looked back at the bottle there was something in it: some swimming thing the size of a fly.'

'There was never a fly – it's just your fancy.'

'I could see she'd been drinking. Her good eye had that look to it.'

'You slander a good woman: she was only joyful.'

'And the boy started to cry! He must have been terrified of her leaning over him.'

Ma shook her head. 'You've things arse-about as usual: the tears were before that. As soon as she touched him, he calmed. He looked up at her as if he would have spoken her name.'

When Cliff found the place, he parked across the road and watched her moving behind the windows with their stickers and Sellotaped announcements, doing her own circuit from washer to dryer to counter and back. A path in life she'd made for herself.

133

He groped with his free hand to find a cassette, slipping them about in the glove compartment. He shoved one into the machine, listened to it for half a minute and then ejected. He found another, and kept fiddling with the balance.

Alison gave change, set up the washes, presented a guy in a suit with a numbered bag. She would have known the car but she never looked beyond the window with its notices. As if she'd lost the habit or didn't care. He wondered, Does she have music in there? It seemed important to know, though he would never set foot. Her doing her work with just the scrape and swish of the machines made his blood run cold.

At a quarter to four, or near enough, the other assistant came – a tall black woman with shining golden nets over her hair in a style he'd never seen before. She spent about ten minutes in chat and apology and then bought a couple of coffees from the machine so that it had turned four when Alison was able to take off her grey overall and step out.

She zipped up her suede jacket, not for warmth but to keep the world out. She wore jeans and low shoes and she looked tough in that outfit. He turned down the tape and watched as she stepped off towards home or wherever, walking with her head down and that end-of-shift slump to her shoulders.

He waited until she was out of sight behind parked cars and then turned on the engine. Another car was parked tight behind him now so that he had to make two stabs at leaving the kerb. He caught sight of her again not far from the bus stops. A youngster asked her for money; she shook her head and passed on.

No love left in her heart, you see.

He overtook her near the lights as she waited to cross the road. He watched the way she put her foot out as if testing the water. His belly gave a twinge and a lurch but he did the trick of slowing his breath for a few seconds and it was OK.

She stepped out. A bus was going the other way and he lost her then, couldn't find her in the mirror. He wound down the window and risked a backward glance but she was gone from her spot and invisible on the parade where the drinkers sat on benches near the raised flowerbeds. A disappearing trick she'd done on him. His belly clenched again, did its party trick of turning on itself, attacking its own tissues. He was too used to it to be worried. He squeezed the leather thonging around the wheel, twisted it in his grip. He kept his eyes on the vehicle in front and felt the sweat break out.

Eighteen

Ralph found a child's pink sock on the last flight on his way downstairs and climbed back up to the middle landing. He could see Alma Drean and one of her grown-up daughters through the glass panel of her door. They must have seen him too because they stopped their conversation and waited. He pushed the sock quickly through the letterbox and turned away.

Cliff was leaning against the bonnet of the estate talking to Sammy Curl. He nodded at Ralph over the other man's shoulder and pushed himself away from the car so that Sammy had to step back quickly and almost lost his balance. He straddled the kerb, his crippled leg pushing out stiffly, staring at Cliff and then at Ralph, his mouth open.

'Evening, Sammy,' Ralph said.

Sammy swallowed and nodded. His face was as pale as the front of his shirt.

'What did you say to him?' Ralph asked in the car.

'Did I have to be saying something?'

'From the look on his face you were.'

'I told him to mind what he said.'

'So what was that?'

'Oh, various things. He's as many stories as a dog has fleas.'

'He's just a poor bastard,' Ralph said.

Cliff started the car. 'I've told you once: no one's just anything.'

A feller on the Fender, strumming his stuff through the old favourites with the box of tricks behind set to tango or cha-cha or waltz time. Spade-shaped hands and fingers ending in pads like a wall-climbing lizard. A hollow face with the skin drawn tight so that his eyes were narrow and strained. He struck mirror-trained poses with a look of having lately outgrown his strength though he was well into his thirties. He smiled towards a woman of his, say wife, who sat on the near end of a bench, looking towards him with her hands in her lap. For a few bars he directed the song to her and she moved her shoulders in her dusty velvet jacket, her face tilting into the light. She didn't smile but a look went between them that made Cliff envious, turned him wistful as if it had pressed the wrong button. He shivered. Goose over his grave.

Charlie Sanderson had been at his ear a lot after it had turned eight and the place had shifted from after-work to the dressiness of Friday night. Charlie had come over all concerned, leaning over his table with his hands planted, putting a soft mouth to his ear like a true confidant. For a second Cliff felt like a fish drowning. For relief, more or less, he took a look at Charlie's dartsman – twenty-five or so and drinking with friends in the corner. He had a fat and sloppy look of mother-love and hot dinners, wearing shiny tracksuit bottoms and a red short-sleeved shirt with a fancy silver toggle at the throat.

Charlie clapped his shoulder and went off, picking his way between the tables because the place was filling up now – pinching an arm, trailing his fingers across the nape of a neck. It made your flesh crawl to watch. Cliff diverted his eyes towards Ralph, who sat with his back to him at the bar, visible and then not as the crowd shifted. He pressed his inch of cigar into the tin ashtray and went over, pushing himself into the space beside his son's elbow.

Ralph turned in a slow way, implying that he might have chosen not to. There was a glass of clear liquid by his elbow.

'What's that stuff?' Cliff asked.

'Water.'

'So people are drinking water,' Cliff said. 'You're quiet so far. Do you feel up to it tonight?'

'Does it matter?'

'Depends on who you're speaking to. I have to say that the other lad's the favourite so far.'

'Charlie's boy.'

'Not his boy exactly. Sometimes he likes to keep a certain distance.'

'Like hell he does.'

'You're not helping, Ralph. These funny moods you get don't assist things.'

'I'd like to know more about Charlie.'

Drinking water. He took a sip, a swallow. He had a disdainful way with his throat, the rise and fall of his adam's apple.

'What's to know?' Cliff asked. He pointed over his shoulder. 'Look at him – round and about like a blue-arsed fly!'

Ralph watched through the mirror. Charlie had stopped to take out that long diary of his, mouthing to himself as he worked with the little pencil. A tray of sandwiches and cocktail sausages was circulating and he helped himself to a couple of portions, holding them between finger and thumb.

'It's time he bought himself a new jacket,' Ralph said.

'That's Charlie; he'll wear that one till it's a rag.'

'All the money he's supposed to have.'

'You shouldn't believe what people tell you.'

'He's got a lot on this match?' Ralph asked.

'He might have, I don't know. I suspect he's just being bookie tonight.'

'He's putting himself about.'

Cliff laughed. 'The poor sod doesn't know another way.'

Charlie went up to the act, the guitar hero. After an exchange of words and gestures to the dead rhythms from the box, he peeled out a tenner and stuffed it into the pint mug on the edge of the stage for donations. The thin feller signalled to his girl, did a last run down the fretboard and then pulled the jack on his instrument and lifted it from his shoulders.

'What about you?' Ralph asked. 'How much have you on this?'

'Enough to make it worthwhile but not more than I can afford to lose.'

'I see.'

'I need to bear that in mind,' Cliff said. 'As no more than a possibility.'

His son nodded as if he were satisfied with that. Cliff was in a mood for him to go on for once, show the kind of curiosity that might be construed as giving half a shit, but instead he settled himself and stared towards the optics, turning things over maybe but keeping his own tight counsel.

He lets me down, Cliff thought. When I need him to come forward, to comment, then he lets his silence speak.

Ralph gripped the dart with a look of tender disgust, like a father holding the penis of his infant son over a gutter, the little finger raised like a whisky drunk's. He threw. The next. The next. They were clapping, cheering, jeering, the bar in agitation with chairs scuffing back and glasses spilling, a little dog like a permed rat scampering between the tables. He acknowledged nothing, only retrieved his three darts and swiftly detached the flights before returning them to their pouch. He looked towards his father at his table, gave him a look with nothing to respond to and then stepped down.

The other player's manager was a thin-faced, balding type, looking like the elder brother of someone richer and fatter. Charlie was talking into his ear, rubbing a fold of cloth in his sleeve between finger and thumb. Ralph passed them by and Charlie broke off to give him the thumbs-up sign.

He lounged in the car seat, his legs stretched and his head back with a shaver's rash across the throat.

'This is yours,' Cliff said.

He looked surprised at the amount but not enough to stay his hand. Getting used to it now, Cliff thought. Scenting the possibilities.

'There's money in the game, you see, Ralph. A lot more than there used to be. It's one of those things that are getting bigger instead of smaller.'

'That's interesting.'

'I'm glad you're interested,' Cliff said.

He turned on the engine. He was slow-wheeling out of the car park when he noticed the other dartsman coming up on the passenger side. He stopped with a little squeak of the brakes and leaned over his son's lap to wind down the window.

'Something the matter?' he asked.

The player gave a pouch-cheeked grin and pushed through his open hand. For a second Ralph stared at it as if it were a dead fish he'd been presented with. The second he waited made Cliff feel squeamish but then Ralph caught hold. Red-shirt pumped his hand half a dozen times, angling down his cheery-beery face. The toggle on his collar swung loose and rapped against the lowered glass.

'You had it too easy,' Cliff said, out on the road. 'You should have to struggle more – it's character-building.'

'No thanks.'

'What I mean is, people like to see more of a match.'

He shook his head. 'They like to see somebody hammered.'

'Fair enough. We could go for a meal; Indian, Greek, say. Just to celebrate.'

'I'd like to sleep.'

Cliff drove to the flats. Alma Drean's lights were on. He could see the big paper globe she used as a shade.

Ralph already had his hand on the door.

'You have your mother's face,' Cliff said.

He let his lids droop, as though he'd been forestalled. 'That's only natural.'

'Is it? Seems like a bloody miracle to me,' Cliff said. He stayed silent for a while. Ralph was staring at him, not hostile or impatient, just waiting. 'I see her sometimes, you know. Not seeing exactly . . . Not as cut and dried as that.'

'I don't want to go on with this conversation.'

Cliff nodded. 'That's your right. That's your prerogative.'

There was music from Alma's flat, which had the windows open – sweet, settling strings.

'Say when I'm rinsing a cup and all of a sudden she's there. Rinsing the same cup, if you follow,' Cliff said.

'I don't.'

'That's OK. It's difficult. That kind of thing's not for everyone.'

'I'm tired,' Ralph repeated.

'I'm that myself. And a bit pissed. I'll be rinsing a cup, say. And I want to continue to do that but I have to stop in the nature of things. So when I turn the tap it's over again. Back to square one—'

'I'd get some sleep, Cliff.'

Something was attacking Cliff's smile at the edges, making his lips twitch. 'And you, son.'

He reached past and pushed open the hefty door.

Charlie Sanderson drove into the yard the next afternoon, passing through the gate on a sharp note of his horn and nosing into the space beside the caravan. Ralph was helping Colin to unload the van and he noticed cinder-white fumes blowing from the back end of the Cortina and drifts of the same from under the bonnet. Charlie eased himself out as the engine clattered into silence.

Colin was on the other end of a chest of drawers. He looked up, then poked his head into cover again, backing himself up the ramp. The chest was blocking the doorway now but Cliff pushed by, squeezing his shoulder as he went, striding into the yard with one finger hooked into a mug of coffee.

'Do yourself a favour, Charlie – buy a new car!'

Laughing, shaking his head, Charlie lifted the bonnet and propped it up. He waved his hand to clear away the fumes. 'Truth is, it'd break my heart to part with the thing, Cliff.'

'Break your heart to part with the cash,' Cliff said.

He drained his coffee and threw the dregs on the gravel. Charlie winked at Ralph. 'Your old man's got a wicked lip.'

'I know it.'

Charlie and his father stood looking down at the cooling engine for a minute. Then Cliff called, 'Colin?'

There was no answer.

'Where is that boy?' Cliff asked. He dragged a hand across his mouth.

'He's inside,' Ralph said.

Cliff smiled. 'Then would you please go and get him?'

He found Colin sitting in a plastic-covered wing chair, staring towards the hall's side wall with a mild look on his face.

'Did you hear that, Colin?'

Colin looked as if he were deaf at that moment.

'Cliff wants you.'

Colin sighed down his nose and straightened himself from the chair. One broken-soled shoe slapped as he went outside. Ralph followed.

'Seen anything as piss-poor as this lately?' Cliff asked.

Colin shrugged but wouldn't step closer than a yard away.

'The boy knows a quality machine,' Charlie said, passing it off. He reached to lay a hand on Colin's arm but Colin turned away.

'Something the matter?' Charlie asked.

'It's just his way, Charlie,' Cliff said. 'He doesn't make friends easily.'

Charlie made a popping noise with the corner of his mouth and then gripped Cliff's arm just above the elbow. 'Let's have a talk together.'

'A talk's always a good thing,' Cliff said.

He started to sing something under his breath and led the way into the office. Ralph waited a couple of minutes, standing by the car. The fumes had disappeared but there was still a smell of burning. Then he went inside and sat on a couch in the second row of suites from where he had a view through the open door of the office. Charlie was sitting in the other chair with his back to him and, from Cliff's nods and the odd head-shake, seemed to be

140

doing most of the talking. There was a bottle on the desk between them, and little glasses. After a minute Cliff came to the door and closed it.

Ralph went back outside. Colin was sitting in the back of the van with his legs dangling.

'They're setting the world to rights in there,' Ralph said.

Colin shook his head.

'So what have you got against Charlie?'

'Nothing.'

'With a face like that, it can't be nothing.'

Colin said something Ralph didn't catch.

'What?'

'He's a murderer,' Colin said.

Ralph stared. Colin was looking at his hands in his lap. 'Now that's interesting. D'you know that for a fact?'

Colin shook his head. 'Only I know the type.'

The two men must have been cabined together for an hour. When they came out, both looked flushed and Charlie was smoking one of his father's panatellas. He gazed vaguely about the yard and then pointed to Ralph sitting in the broken armchair under the awning.

'This one is starting to scare me.'

'Been scaring me for a long while,' Cliff said.

Charlie rolled the cigar between his finger and thumb. 'He'll find a golden road before him. He just has to listen a bit to his old man.'

Cliff said nothing. Colin was busy in the corner, his head in the cabinet of a washer-dryer. Charlie hitched up his trousers and went towards his car. The engine would be cold by now. He knocked back the prop and pressed the bonnet down, leaning his weight on it until the catch engaged.

'Leave it here,' Cliff told him. 'I'll get Colin to take a look.'

Charlie shook his head. 'He just has to touch it and my life's not worth ninepence.'

He laughed and pulled open the car door. He had to sit down first and then draw his legs inside. Cliff leaned his elbow on the open window and they talked for a while with their faces close together as if they couldn't bear the thought of parting. Just as Ralph was starting to wonder how long this was going on, Charlie switched on the engine. With a last wave he swung across the gravel and passed through the gates.

Ralph stared at his father.

'You needn't look at me,' Cliff said. The broken veins stood out on his cheeks. 'I just have one thing to take care of.'

He walked over to where Colin was working and slammed his fist down on the top of the cabinet. The noise must have reverberated for half a minute. As it was already dying away Colin stood up slowly, wiping his hands on the tops of his leggings.

Cliff pointed, though they were separated by just a yard. 'Any time you want us to part company, then just say the word.'

Colin's face was dead white except for a smear of grease. Cliff turned away and went back towards the office. When Ralph looked towards Colin again, he saw he was shaking.

'Why don't you just go home, Colin?'

'If I did that I wouldn't come back.'

He spat into the dust of the yard, a disgusted gob of something he'd been keeping to himself. Ralph went into the shop and through to the office. His father was sitting behind his desk with the chair turned so that he could watch the TV. He'd cleared away the glasses and what was left of the bottle but a sweet smell still hung in the air.

'Why did you say that to him?' Ralph asked.

Cliff wouldn't move his eyes from what was on the screen – the flush of the drink or something else on his gills. 'He was disrespectful.'

'To you?'

'Doesn't matter about me. To Charlie, I mean.'

'He's got a right not to like the man.'

This time his father glanced at him, looked him up and down in a quick judgement. 'Think so? Well, that's just where you're wrong. Colin needs to know where his interests lie. Behaviour like that is a luxury he can't afford.'

Ralph watched him watching a snooker game. His eyes flickered when the balls collided. 'What about me? What if I don't like the sick old bastard?'

Cliff turned in the chair, then laid his fists on the desk either side of him as if it were a vehicle he was steering. His face had changed like that time when cement passes from fluid to solid.

'So what's the future hold for you, Ralph?' he asked in a quiet voice.

'Is that a serious question?'

Cliff gave a slack-mouthed smile and spread out one hand,

showing the open palm. 'That wife and kid of yours, for example. What about them?'

'Ex-wife,' Ralph said.

'If you like. But no such thing as an ex-kid.'

'Maybe not.'

'So is it the old girl you're relying on?'

'That isn't worth answering.'

His father blew out his cheeks. 'You must know that you won't have long to wait: you must be able to work out that one.'

'What are you talking about?'

'A windfall would be poison to someone like you, Ralphie. You haven't got the character, you see. A person like you can only drown in money.' He stood up, involving himself in some awkwardness between the desk and the swivel chair. He freed his hips and nodded towards the doorway of the office. 'What do you see out there, Ralph?'

'You know what's out there.'

His father sighed. 'You won't play any game but yours, will you?'

'A few fridges then. Kitchen appliances. Bits of furniture.'

'That's right. Only you're not using your imagination.' He blew a breath down his nose, almost a laugh. 'You could call this place a way forward.'

'Only your way, Cliff.'

'And after me?'

'After?'

'It's simple: I mean behind me there's you.'

Their faces were inches apart now and Ralph could smell the sweetness of the gin. Maybe his own breath was something worse.

'I've made some arrangements,' Cliff said. 'To that end. For instance, I don't want any rubbish walking in here and saying that half of it is theirs – or three-quarters, or all of it.'

'So it's as bad as that?'

His father lowered his head so that he could see the way his hair was arranged across his pale scalp. 'Let's say it was as bad. It's more in hand now – I'm taking steps. When the day comes I want this place to be as clean as a whistle.'

'What day?' Ralph nearly shouted.

Cliff didn't answer but looked down the length of the showroom. The tube he'd never fixed was still trying to kick itself into light, setting up a flicker at that end. Then he started to murmur to himself below his breath.

Ralph stared at him. 'You all right, Cliff? You OK?'

He looked up laughing. The alcohol shine was still on his face but his eyes were clear, sharp as glass suddenly. 'You'll have to help me on this one, Ralph.'

'But how can I do that?'

He was still smiling, pursing his lips. 'You just have to be your own sweet self.'

Nineteen

Ralph nursed a mineral water and kept looking towards the door. Whenever someone came in from the street he looked towards the door with its frosted panel. He couldn't stop himself even though he was expecting no one.

The barman said 'Same again?' and he said no and left. It was getting dark with a fine rain drawing a shine from the pavements – the fag end of the rush, two lanes of traffic heading for the junction but not much in the other direction. When he reached the road barriers he stopped for a second and rested the underside of his wrist on the beaded metal. The cold of it started to draw out the heat he felt. Under floodlights in the centre island there was an excavation with a crane working.

He crossed by an underpass and climbed the ramp to the entrance of the sports centre. A man and a woman were talking inside a booth with Perspex security screens. The man was in uniform and had his cap before him on the counter. He picked it up and put it on peak first, smoothing back his thin hair. The woman was eating a sandwich. She put it down as Ralph approached and turned towards him, smiling. He thought for a second that it was Alison but then saw that it was nothing like her.

He bought a ticket and went through the turnstile. Following the sign for the cafeteria, he went up a couple of flights of stairs towards the shouts of kids in the big space above the pool. The counter was still open and he bought a roll and a coffee. He took it to the rail and looked out over the water divided into lanes by ropes and coloured floats. There was a balcony or viewing area opposite with banks of orange plastic seats, a spread of what looked like parents mostly on the top ranks and then a crowd of kids below who were pressing themselves against the glass and painted metal of the barriers.

Nothing seemed to be happening around the pool except a short man in a suit talking to a teenage boy in a costume and a swimming cap. An announcement was made which set up several echoes.

A bored-looking lifeguard sat in his chair on the high platform, padded headphones clamped to his ears.

After a minute a tone sounded and more kids began to file out from below, from an entrance he couldn't see, stepping into sight at the end of the pool where the lanes were marked out with numbers. He stared at them, leaning over. Older than John? Younger. It was difficult to tell with their skinny, smooth bodies and the tight caps most of them wore. He thought his son wasn't among them anyway. He sipped at the coffee, resting his arm along the rail. He glanced opposite, at the parents and the kids in their grey sweaters and dark blazers.

This time he saw Jean sitting high up near the exit sign, looking down at a programme held between her knees. He wondered if she had noticed him first and decided yes. She didn't look up from the programme.

When the race began, the kids in the gallery started to cheer and yell. The noise was amplified under the angled panels of the ceiling. Ralph went to the counter again for a squash to kill the taste of the coffee. The place was already closing but the assistant poured him the drink anyway and he took it to one of the tables. He knew the race was over because the yelling reached a peak and changed suddenly into whistles and jeers. The winners were announced over the fractured public address system. He checked his watch and then changed tables, choosing one from which he would have a better view of the start of the race. The assistant was lowering the metal shutters in front of the counter. A new set of swimmers filed in – girls this time, as thin as boys in simple black or grey costumes, the caps making their faces small and tight.

He watched that race and the start of the next, going to the rail again and looking over. Boys of about ten or eleven were swimming backstroke, kicking the water up high. The schoolkids opposite were pressing against the rails and screaming. He looked towards the place where Jean had been sitting but she was gone. The race was over suddenly with three of the boys reaching the end of the pool at almost the same time. They waited in the calming water as the stragglers came up. The announcements were made and the boys began to climb out and remove their caps and goggles. He couldn't see his son but his eyes were watering because of the fumes from the chlorinated water and there was a rainbow band around everything.

When he looked around again, a uniformed security guard was

standing near the swing door, another man than the one who had been eating in the booth – an older man with a florid, friendly face.

'We're closing off this section now, sir. If you like, you could watch from the other side.'

On the way out he saw that his plastic beaker was lying on its side on the table. The orange juice had spilled and was dripping through the perforations in the plastic top to the floor. He righted it as he went past.

'Don't worry about that now, sir.'

The guard held the door open for him and then locked it behind him with a key from his bunch. He followed him down the stairs, tapped his shoulder and pointed. 'Down there and then across and up a flight.' He stared closely into Ralph's face. 'Are you sure you're all right?'

Ralph stepped away from him, feeling as if he had slept and woken too abruptly. His eyes were still prickling from the fumes.

The guard caught him up. 'I'll show you. We'll start locking doors soon, and I don't want you getting lost.' He laughed. 'There was a boy had to stay the night in here once. The telephones were all locked up and he didn't have the nerve to set off the alarms.'

He hummed to himself as he went along, the soles of his shoes squeaking energetically against the rubber tiles.

'You've got kiddies yourself here, sir?'

'My little boy, yeah.'

'My daughter's girl goes to that school. How old is he?'

'He's eight. Nine.'

'Nine, is it?' He laughed.

They came to another landing. There was the entrance to washrooms with the door propped back by a chair. Light and a woman's high voice were spilling out. The guard winked at him. 'That's Ina. She's as musical as they come.' He pointed his thumb upwards. 'Another flight and then you'll see the doors.'

'Thanks.'

'Nine, you said?'

'Eight or nine.'

He nodded. 'It's easy to lose track.'

The lights above the water had been dimmed and the balcony was nearly in darkness. Ralph went down a flight of broad steps between the rows of seats. The kids were silent, standing in intent groups against the glass barriers. When he reached the rail he saw that an odd light was coming from below the water, from coloured panels set in the pool's tiled walls and bottom. Music sounded from speakers suspended from the tubular framework of the roof – classical stuff, gloomy and stirring. He looked above him to where the adults sat but he could see only clusters of shadows. There was a pain in his sinuses now and at the back of his head.

He found a gap between two groups of kids and leaned against the rail. The pool was still empty but the music began to change, becoming louder and shifting from one speaker to the next. Then it stopped, leaving only a hiss from the speakers.

He watched the kids file out – maybe a dozen this time – boys and girls in costumes of their own choosing rather than the regulation dark. A couple of them stayed at the head of the pool but the rest arranged themselves around its sides, so that there were three or four to each, spaced around the perimeter. The invisible adults began to clap. The kids made a few whistles but the sound was more respectful this time, expectant.

He laid his chin on his arm and watched. The music began again with a jolt and the kids dived at the first note, slipping into the water so smoothly that he thought they must have practised for weeks. But even so the surface rocked for a minute, sending out coloured sparks before it settled again and he could see below it the boys and girls gliding silently towards the pool's centre, not moving a muscle. Small bubbles were leaking in trails from their mouths. Their arms were stretched before them with one hand resting over the other, legs straight with the toes pointed. He couldn't see their faces, only the polished backs of their heads, but he thought their eyes would be closed tight against the chlorine.

Ralph sat for a while in the van. Alma Drean's flat looked to be in darkness. A very young couple were sitting on the low wall in front of the courtyard holding hands and talking. He turned on the ignition again. The engine was still warm and started at once, rumbling and shuddering below him, shaking the chassis. The vibration only subsided when he let out the clutch.

He drove past the Lamb. The tables in the little yard were crowded and he saw Sammy Curl punting stiff-legged between them, his arms full of empty glasses. He glanced up at the van and then turned abruptly away, as if the sight of it offended him. There had been an accident on the main road and a section of it was blocked off, an ambulance and a squad car in attendance. A

148

policeman in a luminous orange jacket waved Ralph on. A white Volvo estate was stalled at an angle by the kerb.

When he checked his watch it was almost eleven. He had the feeling that he had lost a couple of hours but when he thought back he found he could account for every minute. He drove by the exhaust centre with its shuttered front and then left the main road. The sky had a red tinge and he could see the outline of the port buildings above the roofs of the terraces. He turned at the boarded-up cinema and something silvery – a fox or a big cat – ran low across the road in front of him. It disappeared below the front but he did not feel an impact.

The Eagles was closing, a dark group making their goodbyes outside. One of the pub's guard dogs was trotting between them. There was the light of a fire on the waste ground to Ralph's left, the smoke leaning back in the breeze and sparks ascending.

He parked and walked down the hill, towards the fire's glow. The yellow cabins of the demolition men reflected the lively light. He could hear the crack of burning timbers and the air was sweetened and woody. The blaze was set in the newly cleared space opposite the surviving terrace. He saw the commotion in the flame as someone flung on an end of timber.

Rose was sitting on her front step, talking to a couple of friends. They turned towards him as he came close. She smiled at him and lifted a spliff in her twisted hand.

'No thanks.'

'Are you looking for Alison again?' she asked.

'I was passing this way. I thought I'd see how you were.'

She smiled, not believing him. 'You look like a man with his mind on a woman – you have that shifty look about you.'

One of her friends laughed and reached to take the spliff from her. 'Is she about?' Ralph asked.

'She's asleep,' Rose said. 'She's had a busy day. So have I. Frank's in there somewhere if you'd like to see him. On the other hand, you're welcome to sit with us.'

He looked back towards the fire, seeing people in its light. The camper van was still parked against the kerb, its tyres removed and the hubs propped on precarious stacks of bricks. Someone was strumming a guitar, stopping to tune a string.

'What's this – community singing?'

She was still staring up at him. 'You're all on edge tonight.'

'Am I?'

'I'd say so, but I won't try to read your mind.'

'Thanks. I'll look up old Frank, I suppose.'

'Then be quiet when you pass our door,' she warned. 'Lizzie's finally asleep.'

'I will.'

He stepped past her. Her wheelchair was folded and leaning in the entry. The front door stood open and he went inside. The house seemed to be in darkness and his shadow flared for a second as someone threw more timber on the fire. The window was open on the turn of the stairs and he stopped to look out over the dead space at the back of the house with its isolated lights. There was a faint noise and when he turned someone was standing on the landing above him.

'Frank?'

Frank flicked one of the brass switches. The lamp over his head seemed to fill quite slowly with light. He wore his limp suit and the unravelling woollen cap Ralph had seen him in after the darts match. When Ralph reached the landing, Frank held up his finger and pointed upstairs.

'Did you come to see her?'

'Not just her.'

He grinned, stretching his mouth. For a second his face looked broader than it was long. 'I'll wake her if you say so.'

'No, don't bother.'

He let his smile snap back. 'You can make do with me, then.'

His room was longer than Alison's and faced the front of the house. He beckoned Ralph in fussily, making a show of opening the door wide. There was a fire of splinters and ends of wood.

'You're sitting in the dark?'

He waved his hand. 'I had the start of a headache. It's gone now.'

He pointed towards a low armchair and eased himself on to the mattress, leaning back against the wall and stretching out his legs. He yawned, letting his mouth gape as if he were too weary to close it. Then he dabbed at his pockets and produced a packet of cigarettes with the wrapper still intact.

'Still don't smoke, Ralph?'

'I haven't changed my habits, no.'

Frank took out a shiny lighter with a stone set in its side. He flicked out a flame and regarded it for a second before he put it to the cigarette.

'Nice lighter,' Ralph said.

'It is, yes.' He closed the flame and dropped it back into his pocket.

'Has she any kids?' Ralph asked. 'Alison.'

He sat up. 'That's a funny thing to be curious about.'

'It came into my head to ask.'

Frank stared at him, then nodded slowly.

'So where are they?'

'Every question, there's another one behind. I'm not the encyclopedia.' He lifted his hand, fending. 'Oh, we haven't discussed them. I saw her belly one day and she has the marks.' He laughed. 'It's these little things that give the game away.'

'Little things, yeah.'

'And where there's a mother there's a father,' Frank said. 'Except that sometimes there isn't. Your own pop, for instance. Being on first-name terms with him. Some people would say you were being too familiar.' He laughed at himself, stretching in the seat again, pressing one ruined shoe against the other. 'He's a saint, your old man. You realise that, don't you?'

'Someone else told me that.'

'It's common knowledge, you see. I was brought up a Catholic so I know all the signs. What about your mother?'

'What's your question?'

'Alison said your grandmother brought you up.'

'What else did she tell you?'

'It was a struggle getting that out of her. I'd say it was a strong woman to bring up two sets of kids. Is the lady still with us?'

'She is, yes.'

Frank nodded, turning that over. The light from the fire occupied his face.

'And your own father?' Ralph asked.

Frank took the lighter from his pocket again and looked at its shining side with the stone. 'Oh, my dad was a statue. An old statue of someone dead with pigeon shit on the shoulders. You'd pass him by without a glance and a good thing if you did—'

'He's still alive?'

He stayed still for a second, bending over the lighter. 'No, I'd say that he wasn't . . .' He looked up, smiling. The lopsided look of his face was exaggerated by the light from the fire. 'I know that because I killed him myself.'

151

Ralph laughed. He felt drunk suddenly, delighted.

'It was a ridiculous thing,' Frank said. 'We were together one day and I killed him.' He closed his eyes for a second. 'Did I say that?'

'That's what I heard.'

Frank sighed as if he were caught in a difficulty, as if his tongue had tripped him. 'I'll stand by it then, yes.' He smiled at Ralph. 'You're looking at me as if you want me to say it again.'

'That's all right.'

'Thank Christ for that.'

'So how did you do it?'

'Maybe the question of how and when is between me and the person concerned.'

'But was there violence in it, for instance?'

Frank laughed and clapped a hand against his thigh. 'You persist, don't you? Well, there'd need to be a degree of it somewhere along the line. Don't you think?' He put his head to one side, listening for something. 'But if I'd really done this thing, then maybe I wouldn't like to talk about it.'

'You'd need to tell at least one other person. That's human nature.'

'You're being too clever now. I might be one of these types who'd go to their grave with it.' He looked up, troubled by the thought. 'Not that I'd be ashamed of it, though. I'd do the same again this minute. If I'd two fathers, then I'd do for both of them.'

'Then that's fair enough.'

Frank nodded, easier with himself now, his face full of comfort. 'And what use are they, after all? We're pushing the bastards aside as soon as we're born, so why not speed things up a bit? Where's the harm in that, I ask you?'

'None that I can see,' Ralph said.

Frank smiled at him, pleased, then lifted his finger. The slam of the front door seemed to travel up through the house. 'That'll be Rose and the queer feller.'

'Is he her boyfriend?'

Frank bounced his thumb against his breastbone. 'I'm her boyfriend. Same as with the other bitch.'

'You've a harem here, then?'

'I have. And I hope to add to it.'

Twenty

The Drean family was taking the sun. The sisters lay on either side of a red plaid rug, a radio between them with the spike of the aerial drawing sounds from the skies. The younger sister had her baby sleeping on a lemon shawl by her hip. A toddler was playing in the unruly grass with a plastic digger as big as itself. The rabbit was quiet in its hutch, its white side tufting through the open mesh of the wire. Alma had set up her lounger a few yards away from the girls and their music, near the back fence where ragwort fought the clematis. She lay on her side in a grey knitted dress and baggy black tights with pale holes at the toes, frowning at a paperback through big-lensed sunglasses. A glass jug stood at her elbow. Sliced lemons in sun-struck liquid. She turned to favour her other elbow and looked up. Or maybe she'd been aware of Ralph standing there but hadn't cared to acknowledge him. She sent him a smile before he stepped back from the window.

He left his flat a few minutes later and saw her climbing towards him, carrying in her hand a wedge of something he took at first for the book she'd been reading. When she was a step below she held it out to him. It was a brown envelope, bursting with its contents.

'Those photos I promised you.' She'd slipped her sunglasses up on her hair. Her eyes were heavy from the sun.

'Thanks.'

The package was held together by about half a dozen rubber bands and he saw that it was not one envelope but several, one inside the other. The paper was soft and torn along its creases.

'My mother gave me these,' Alma said.

'Your mother?'

'Alice Foster.'

He leaned back to look at her.

'You'll never see a resemblance,' Alma said. 'I take too much after my father. I was glad to escape from it. Her looks were always too forceful.'

'They were that.'

He started to unpick the bands. The rubber was perished and slack. Alma laid her hand on his wrist. Her fingers were chilly and he wondered if she was at that second nervous. 'Hang on to them for a while. I can see you're on your way out.'

'I could stay.'

She shook her head. 'Take them with you. Keep which ones you want and throw the rest away.'

'I won't do that.'

She shrugged. 'The girls aren't interested in that stuff. I tell them about it and they laugh – you can imagine.'

'What stuff?'

'Whatever it was she saw.'

'The man, you mean?'

'If it was anyone at all.'

He shook his head. 'I wasn't there to witness it.'

'Nobody was. Or it was just the two of them. And if she saw him he must have seen her. Across the water . . . The war was just over and there were men all over whose minds had been affected.'

'And you think it was one of those? That he was a madman?'

'I suppose there's a few reasons why a man might be naked,' she said.

'More than one, at least.'

He smiled at her but she seemed impatient. She nodded at the bundle of photographs. 'Those are yours now. I'm not sure that I'm doing you a favour.'

He leaned over the head of the stairs and watched her go. The lenses of her sunglasses shone back at him. He noticed that her feet were bare.

'She was back here nearly every day. Her and the boy.'

'Nothing wrong there,' Eric said. 'It's only natural that a girl should visit her mother.'

Ma nodded, her hands teasing the ruff of the cat. However she pulled, the beast would only purr. 'Not when you could see she didn't want to leave. They were hardly wed, remember. Or only a six-month.'

Eric laughed. 'The bed still warm, or should have been . . . Then it was habit with her, say. You can't change your life overnight.'

She looked at him wearily. 'Is that your opinion on it?'

'Or marriage didn't suit her; I'm only suggesting there.'

'It didn't suit me but I persevered.'

'She hadn't your application then.'

Ma felt the seeds of tears behind her eyes and had to blink. She felt a fool for doing so.

'She wouldn't explain herself,' Eric said. 'And with her being married, you couldn't enquire too much.'

'You were a fly on the wall, anyway.'

He laughed, a little noise that came out hollow. 'I sometimes think a fly would be promotion.'

'She'd talk for a while,' Ma said. 'Then she'd take the child up for a feed. When I'd look, both of them would be asleep.'

Eric looked at her gently, with sympathy. 'And it never set you thinking? Your powers must have failed you there.'

Ma shook her head. The movement was too much for the cat and it jumped from her lap. 'We've had all this before, haven't we?'

Eric looked hurt. 'I was only asking, wanting to get things straight for my own satisfaction.'

'If you need me to repeat myself,' Ma said, sighing. 'It doesn't work with what you love: you look at them and you have no penetration. You only see yourself coming back.'

He scoffed. 'A lot of use that is then! And what about your other half?'

'You know her name,' Ma said.

He shifted in his seat and took the round tobacco tin from the back pocket of his overalls. As he tugged at the lid, he glanced up at the draped portrait, her one-eyed stare through the polished glass. 'I could have said Lady Muck but I bit my tongue. Didn't she see what was coming?'

'If she did, she didn't say,' Ma murmured.

'A good friend to you then!'

Ma pulled herself more upright. A book slipped from her lap. 'There was more on her mind than my affairs. More than that silly girl's doings . . .'

She'd fall asleep with the child and Ma would cover her with the quilt, wrap a corner around her so that her legs would not be cold. She could sleep with her face towards the ceiling, her lids so clear that you could see the colour her eyes made below.

'Mrs Foster and I'd be playing gin rummy downstairs. She was a fair player but a terrible cheat. I'd feel the warmth of her fingers when I picked up my cards again. "Your turn, Marion." Mine, is it? The one girl she had, like me.'

'Then it would be him on the phone,' Eric said. 'I'd answer from the shop and pass the line upstairs.'

'"*Is she there? Should I come . . .?*" She's sleeping, I'd say. They both are. No, just a little catnap. I'll wake her with some tea, presently.'

'And he'd make his own dinner? Standing in the kitchen after a day's work!'

Ma shook her head. 'It'd be the tearooms for him. He had the stomach anyway that prefers that type of food.'

'To think of him sitting there with the bachelors,' Eric said, 'then going back to a cold flat.'

She smiled. 'He'd always make his way here to collect her.'

'Collect is the word. He'd park outside and wait, as if he were the taxi driver.'

Ma agreed. 'There was always something of that about him.'

Twenty-One

A dark-blue council minibus was parked outside the Fishburns', the exhaust leaking thin blue fumes. Half a minute went by and then the old man stepped from the house in his chalk-striped suit. He stood blinking on the top step. A couple of the demolition crew watched, lounging at the stump of a wall opposite. One of them was reading a paper and looked up only every so often, more interested in the sport.

The door of the minibus opened and a woman in a dark two-piece climbed down. Opening the side door, she smiled up at old man Fishburn as if she were worried that he might change his mind. Mr Fishburn began to turn with his stick, shuffling his feet into position. Ralph looked towards Alison's house and saw the face of the little girl in the window. Walter was joining his father now, separating himself from the shadows in the doorway and looking saucer-eyed about him. Old man Fishburn held out his hand, scarcely glancing at his son. Walter took it like an infant, looking distrustfully at the woman and the waiting van.

The Eagles was a dark hall with a horseshoe-shaped bar at one end. The barman read his paper and ignored the TV. Racing from somewhere, the horses galloping along the straight.

A darts game was going on in the corner of the hall and that was where Ralph found Frank – sitting by himself at one of the copper-topped tables and watching the play. He had a glass before him, already two-thirds empty, grey froth trailing from the edge where he'd sipped.

Ralph pointed to it. 'Want another?'

He stared as if the question was more complicated than it might appear. Then he gave a careful nod. 'I've a thirst on me today.'

Ralph went to the bar. The red-headed barman poured the drinks and avoided Ralph's eyes when he thanked him.

'You're still on the water?' Frank asked, teasingly.

'Still . . . I see the Fishburns are moving.'

Frank nodded. 'They've given me a set of keys so it'll be business as usual. And I've worked out with the opposition that they'll stay their hand.'

'For how long?'

'Well, if we want to clear the place I'd say it's tonight or the first thing in the morning. They mean to flatten it after that.'

'And your house?'

He looked amused that he should have been asked. 'We'll just have to make our own arrangements, won't we?'

'What about Rose and the kid?'

He pulled a face as if that didn't concern him. 'A woman usually has friends she can go to.' He smiled and nodded towards the board. 'We'll need to have that match soon. These no-hopers are an insult to the game.'

The man chalking the score must have heard because he glanced over at them. Frank smiled and nodded, easy in himself.

'Not now, though.' He leaned forward in a confiding way. 'I hear there's an opportunity for you there.'

'What opportunity?'

'I've heard that Charlie Sanderson is interested in taking you over.'

'Then you know more than me,' Ralph said. 'I didn't think you and Charlie were still in touch.'

'Only through third parties.'

'And why should he want that?'

'Rumour is that he's bought into your dad's business. A sleeping partner as they say.'

Ralph could feel a little tic at the corner of his mouth. 'No. Cliff's always a one-man band.'

'Has been. Charlie paid off some debts for him.'

'To call that bollocks would be an understatement,' Ralph said.

'Then you've eased my mind on that matter. I'm still having my own difficulty with Charlie, you see. He won't seem to respect my need for independence.'

'I think he's got problems with that.'

Frank nodded. 'I'm trying to work through it with him slowly. At the end I might need to pay some kind of forfeit. Though what I have left I don't know—'

'A forfeit?'

'For being a bad lad. Some scrap of myself I'll need to hand over.' He drained his glass and then picked up the fresh drink. 'Cheers.'

They sat in silence for a while, watching the darts. The game ended and Frank brought his hands together in a dull clap. Ralph glanced over to the bar and saw the barman staring at them with a look of loathing which he didn't bother to hide.

'He has me down as a troublemaker,' Frank whispered. 'Watch you're not tarred with the same brush.'

Ralph stared at his grinning face. It had a gloss on it now, trapped heat forcing out little beads of sweat. 'The other day you said you killed your father. Does that still stand?'

He gave a yap of laughter. 'Why, that's old history now!'

'You mean you're going back on it?'

Frank shook his head. 'No, it's not a thing you should deny.'

'So why did you do it?'

'Why?' He made a humming sound between his lips. 'Do you need a reason for these things? I suppose you could say it was a personal thing between us. Sometimes you get stuck with people and they require a little shove.'

'And how did you apply it? This shove?'

Frank looked uncomfortable for a second, as if he considered the conversation had become too intimate. He adjusted himself in the chair, scuffing it across the thin rug. 'It was a thing invented on the spur of the moment.'

'Would you recommend it, though? Would you recommend it to other people?'

He gave a little bashful smile. 'I'm not sure that I want the responsibility of putting it forward. Let's say, I don't think it's the solution to everyone's problems.'

'But it worked for you?'

'For me, yes.'

'And your mother? Where was she?'

He put his finger to his lips. 'I wouldn't talk of my mother in that context . . .' He smiled over the table. 'What about your own?'

'Mine?'

'That's right. Your own, I said.'

'I don't have one memory of her.'

Frank reached to slap him on the arm. 'Then I'd say your coast is clear.'

They went on to a close smoky place and Ralph sat at the bar

159

drinking Coke and lemon. Frank was with a crowd around the pool table, not playing but laughing and joking. He was sarcastically drunk.

When the game ended, he came back over. He stood swaying on his feet, delighted with himself. 'This place is as poxy as the last. We've still time to move on—'

'I'll stick with this, I think.'

He stood so that he could look over Ralph's shoulder at the photographs spread out on the bar. 'Why the picture gallery?' He reached over and took up one of the small photographs. 'Who's the old girl, for instance?'

Ralph didn't answer but tugged it out of his fingers.

'No need to break my bloody wrist!'

They stared at one another but then Frank shrugged and smiled. There was another spell of shouting and laughter from the people around the table and he went back and looked over that way, his face turning hopeful.

'I have a pain,' Ma said.

'The same one or different?'

'*Here*.' She laid her hand on her chest. 'In the same place exactly.'

'Then see a doctor.'

'Whatever's happening there doesn't need their assistance.'

Eric got up from his chair, sighing, exasperated. 'I'll bring you two tablets.'

'If you like.'

'They're not for me to like.'

In the bathroom he broke them in half between thumb and finger and watched them fizzing in the tumbler. When the liquid was clear he carried it carefully upstairs.

'Those machines have been squawking like hens,' Ma complained as he stepped through the door.

'Then someone's been lucky. If it upsets you, then you ought not to listen.'

'And why should it upset me? Every pound they win, they put back two.'

'Oh? Is that the proportion of it?'

She let her eyelids droop. 'You know how those things are worked as well as I do.'

Eric laid his hand on the back of her chair. She looked at him

160

askance until he'd removed it, then took the glass from him and drank. She handed it back to him still half-full.

'You ought to drain it, Marion.'

She shook her head. 'This stuff does no bloody good anyway.'

He stood over her, carrying a mouse in his pocket which he'd found on the stairs. The bastard cat brought them in. 'I'll wait here until you do,' he said quietly.

'You'll be there until doomsday, then.'

He sighed and left the glass within reach on the side table. He felt the mouse give a twitch, it was not quite dead. The movement jogged his memory.

'He'd come after his dinner?' he asked.

She looked at him so blankly that it set him worrying.

'Cliff, I mean.'

Ma stared and swallowed. The stuff she'd taken was tart in her throat. 'He'd take care of his own needs, I suppose – change and wash himself, feed his face.'

'And she was never at home for him?'

'The place he called home wasn't that, you see. Only a mockery.'

'The lad was doing his best,' Eric put in. 'Your life's never your own in furnished rooms.'

'Mrs Dorling's. Two rooms off the first landing.'

He nodded. 'The fixtures and fittings are the landlord's and so are you. That's the psychology of it: your arse is on their seats and the rest of you follows.'

'The Mrs was only by way of courtesy anyway. By reason of her station.'

'Mrs Dorling was no one's darling,' Eric said. 'She went about with no heels to her shoes and a face like she thought something had gone off. And all the time it was her that had. She'll be dead now: gone to her reward.' He laughed.

'Don't speak of it so lightly. It was something like dysentery and her insides turned to water and ran straight through her.'

'And out through the holes in her stockings.'

'You were out at work,' Ma said. 'I might have needed your help but I never saw you from one day to the next.'

'A morning here, an afternoon there. Odd-jobbing. I had that moped, if you remember. Eighty miles to the gallon, it was cheaper than walking. I'd park it at the kerb twenty yards down the road while I made sure that the coast was clear.'

161

'What do you mean?'

'The Foster woman I'm referring to.'

'Woman, was she?'

'I could see her from across the road: sitting like an ugly idol at the window. It was summer and warm. The casements would be open and sometimes I could hear her voice.'

'She liked to sit where there was light,' Ma said. 'She'd read to me in a way that gave things a new slant. My eyes were always opened. When I looked at the same page myself it'd be dead to me – just words on paper.'

'In that case I'd take a stroll. If it was fine I'd go between the houses and beside the pub that was there.'

'Bloody fellers spitting and cursing,' Ma said. 'Playing dominoes and darts.'

'You know I was never one for that nonsense.'

'No, you were too careful with your money.'

'So is there a fault in that?'

There was a yard at the back with a bench and a couple of rabbits in hutches, Eric remembered. A bit of an aviary in the summer with canaries and white doves. He'd take the path across the meadow. There were market gardens before he got to the foreshore.

'All sorts used to go on in that place. Even in the daylight you didn't know where to look,' Ma said.

Seven in the evening or just turned, the sun going down behind the houses. People walking dogs and youngsters with their bikes. That whirr and rattle the chains make in an open space. The sky had been the grey colour of glass. An old thin feller in a feathered hat sang something, standing where the lumpy grass ended and conducting himself with his arms.

Eric put a knuckle to his forehead. 'Now, what tune was it?'

'"Jesus' Love",' Ma said.

He smiled and reached his hand to her. 'Then you were there?'

'You've mentioned it more than once.'

He nodded, still pleased with her. His fingertips touched her wrist. 'Now, the funny thing was that he had only one lung. His voice wasn't loud but carried more than you'd think. When you walked along the shore you could hear him for a mile or more.'

A thin voice that came back off the water. Eric carried his motorcycle helmet with the gauntlets curled inside for safety.

'He knew how to project himself,' Ma said. 'But we are straying from the subject.'

'Then I beg your pardon. I saw Cliff pushing the pram along the gravel path above the foreshore. I didn't know him at first because his face had changed. I only recognised the baby carriage.'

'A Silver Cross they still had to pay for. It was beautiful, though.'

'The Rolls-Royce of prams,' Eric echoed. 'With that black lacquer finish you don't see now. I went up to say hello and he couldn't bring himself to speak. I could see him making the effort but it always caught in his throat.'

'He couldn't manage a word?'

Eric shook his head. 'We just stared at one another. Soldiers in misfortune.'

'You bloody fellers with your pity,' Ma said.

'Something that he'd swallowed. A lump of it.'

She nodded to confirm it. 'Choking on himself because she'd left him.'

Twenty-Two

At about ten thirty, a quarter to, Cliff saw Janet Drean or the younger one – hard to tell in the piss-green light – come up the stairs in slip-soled shoes with the kid in the crook of her arm wrapped to the nose in lemon woollens. Boy was it, girl? Youngster, anyway. She froze that second before she knew him and gripped the kid so tight she squeezed out a cattish, quavery cry.

'Janet,' he said. He perched like a gremlin on the steps above, his arse asleep from the glazed concrete.

She laughed with her mouth open, dangling her keys, only a safe step from the door. Music was seeping through the panel. '*Linda*, actually.'

'Sorry, Linda.'

She laughed again. 'I thought you were that boy of yours!'

'Thanks for the compliment.'

She angled the kid on to her hip and slid the key into the lock. The woollen snood thing slipped from the baby's face and it fixed him with its china-blue stare.

'Seen him tonight?' Cliff asked.

She shook her head. 'Mam says she never knows when he's here.'

'He's not sociable, is he?'

'No, not like you, Cliff.'

When she opened the door, the noise whooshed out: hi-fi, backchat between lounge and kitchen, the other girl and then the mother in fine form with that singing voice she had. An Italian in a former existence.

'A gathering of the clan, Linda?'

She smiled and passed the baby to someone, the kid chortling. A second after she'd followed inside, Alma pushed her head around the door. Her hair was pinned up, shiny and damp after some sort of treatment. She gave him a look of stage surprise.

'I'm waiting for that son of mine,' he said.

'You could sit there all night for that one.'

164

He shook his head. 'Not true: he's teetotal and regular in his habits.'

'Then I hope he knows what he's missing.'

Cliff laughed, his hands clasped between his knees. 'You cheer me up, Alma! I don't know why.' He squinted at her glossy pile of hair. 'Been improving on nature?'

'I just whisk this stuff through the grey bits. Like weeding a garden. Hint of a tint.'

'Very nice.'

'And you'll give yourself piles like that. Why don't you come and join the fun?'

'I'll give him just a while more, and then I'll go.'

'You want to suffer for love, then.'

'Do I?'

She nodded, standing half on the landing now, a long brown robe with a look of Lady Macbeth. 'Don't be a mug for your own kid, Cliff. You'll find it doesn't repay you.'

'Words from the heart there, Alma.'

'Good advice that you'll ignore, I know.' She glanced into her flat, towards the squalling of the baby.

Well after twelve he heard the crash and rebound of the doors downstairs. He leaned his head against the iron uprights and caught sight of his son's flat hand springing and unspringing as he levered himself up the first flight. He took a quick drag on his smoke, waiting. Ralph pivoted tightly on the landing and took him in without a pause. He climbed the steps in twos and was already passing.

'Cliff,' he said.

Cliff looked down at himself. 'That's right.'

'Coming up?'

Cliff trailed after him up the last flight and stood a yard apart while he did the business with the Yale. Ralph went inside, snapping on the lights. The blinds were still at half mast from the night previous or the one before that. The place didn't look lived-in, or not by a person anyway. Spermy smells of damp hovered and on the floor by the chair was half a cup of coffee with a solid raft of scum.

Cliff couldn't help telling him. 'Remember you're looking after this place.'

Ralph nodded. 'Be better than he's used to lately.'

165

'What kind of remark is that?'

He didn't answer and when his father sat down he stayed standing.

'Been visiting?' Cliff asked.

'What?' He looked lost for a second, wall-eyed blankness on his face.

'Are you going deaf, Ralphie? I asked if you'd been visiting.'

He shook his head. 'Been doing a bit of work. Clearing a few bits.' Like a dreamer he fished a bent filtertip from his jacket pocket.

'Taken up smoking again?' Cliff asked.

He looked down at the evidence. 'Suppose so . . .'

'Have one of these instead.'

He held out the flat tin of panatellas. Ralph hesitated for a second and then took one, levering it out of the row. Then the plastic wrapping defeated him.

Cliff shook his head. 'Sometimes I can't believe you, Ralph. I see it but I can't believe it.' He took the cigar from him as from a child, found the little red strip and unpeeled it. 'Here.'

He lit it for him. Ralph drew on it and coughed.

'Take a seat,' Cliff said. 'It's a waste of energy standing when you can sit.'

Ralph looked about as if the place were new to him. He took the couch with its dented hide upholstery. Cliff could recall buying it at the market, lugging it with Colin up the stairs.

'I take it you saw Alison,' he said.

'No.'

'But the boyfriend was there?'

'I saw him, yeah. We put some furniture in the back of the van.'

'That's good, Ralph. That's handy. So what do you think of him?'

'Not much.'

Cliff blinked his eyes. 'It comes with practice, Ralph. Seeing through the shite. No skill's more valuable in the business world.'

'I dare say.'

'The trouble is that Alison takes it all in – not out of stupidity but as a policy. She isn't businesslike, you see. She's got an open heart and that's the worst kind.' He took out his stuffed wallet and unclipped it, fingering through money, receipts, scribbled

166

addresses, little reminders of this and that until he found the card. 'But I think you can help with that, Ralph. I think you can do me and her both a favour—'

'What's that?' Ralph asked.

'Just take it!' Cliff found himself shouting. Ralph read the card and turned it over. It had a nasty little map on the back.

'Only an hour away,' Cliff told him. 'Even in that heap you drive.'

'What if it is?'

'She phoned me yesterday. In reply. She was talking about getting a taxi but I took the liberty of mentioning your name. It's a funny thing, but me and Alison only have to talk together and we start to fight. I wish the opposite was true but we're like cats in a bag at the moment.'

'What's the opposite?'

'That's what I'm trying to bring about. We need to spend some time together when the pressure's off. When she's away from a certain party.'

'And you want me to cabbie for you?'

Cliff laughed, making little of it. 'You have some influence with her. Friendship might be a better word.'

'Pimping would be another,' Ralph said.

Cliff brought his hands together. 'I'll let that pass, Ralph; I'll let that go. Let's just say I'm hurt by your choice of terminology.'

They sat quiet for a while. The TV was still on downstairs, Yank voices booming. Then Cliff tried again. It was a couple of hours since he'd swallowed a pill but the sweat was starting again on the back of his neck.

'Ralph, I don't like to talk in terms of favours.'

He glanced up with this wise look he'd dredged from somewhere, canniness about the eyes. 'Don't then.'

'But you force me to. There's such a thing as bad faith.'

'Not in my dictionary.'

'So what did you have when you came here, Ralph? And what was it you were getting away from?'

'That's my business.'

'I asked you no questions, don't forget that – but you force my hand now. And I know one thing already.'

'What's that?'

'This is the last place you'd choose if you'd a choice at all.'

Twenty-Three

'Money isn't the same now,' Eric said.

'Why, what do you mean?'

He showed Ma his thumb, which was black from counting. 'I mean that the ink comes off on your hands like dirt.'

'The better it sticks, the better you'll like it.'

He shook his head. 'Not true – not true at all!'

'Did you take it to the bank?' she asked.

'Except for a float for the morning. I'll put it in its place later—'

'Only you needn't disturb me.'

'So you'd have me down on my hands and knees?' he asked.

She laughed, leaning on her elbow in the bed. When the sun came through the windows, he could make out the face of what she had been, like reading the time through the scratched glass of a watch. There was a smell of linctus in the room and an open brown bottle of it stood on the table by the bed.

'I'll massage your back later,' he suggested.

She shook her head. 'You won't start that nonsense! After keeping me up half the night with your scratching and hammering.'

'I was never hammering.'

'When will you finish up there? Doomsday?'

He grinned at her and pushed his white-stubbled chin at Alice Foster's portrait. 'She'd know all about that.'

'You lower everything to your own conception,' Ma said.

He still smiled. 'She'd have needed a telescope, you know.'

'What tripe are you talking now?'

'That feller on the island. To see him properly – to see him in the condition she claimed.'

'It was a vision she had. The air cleared before her and condensed like a lens.'

Eric snorted. 'To magnify his piddle? That was the only way she could have seen it.'

'You're dull like a feller with only one joke,' Ma said. 'A penis on God is not the same as a penis on a man.'

He made a noise between his lips. She stared at him, then turned away, sorrowful. She thought for a second that she might shed tears.

'Maybe she dreamed it,' Eric said to placate her. 'That and a vision are much the same.'

'The picnics then? Did I dream them? Did I dream that the spirit moved among us?'

'No, I can vouch for those: every year on the dot of it.'

She started to laugh, a phlegmy sound captive in her chest. 'Then it's everything else that doesn't ring true.'

A couple of the fitters were working on a car on the ramp at the rear of the building. Ralph thought at first that another woman was sitting at the desk behind the partition but when she lifted her head he saw that it was Jean with something about her expression that had prevented him from recognising her. The red-faced man he'd spoken to on his last visit was standing near to her, peeling an orange over a waste bin. He looked up.

'I thought you might have been clever enough not to come back!'

'He's a bigger threat to himself than to anyone else,' Jean said. 'If you could just spare me for a few minutes, George.'

'A few minutes, George,' Ralph said. 'You can't object to that.'

George frowned down at his orange. 'If it comes to sarcasm, I could destroy you with a word.'

Jean opened a little cupboard beside her desk, and took out a black leather bag and tucked it under her arm. She wore a green full skirt with a sleeveless blouse of the same colour. The material had a watery shimmer to it.

The fitters stared at them as they went through the door. Jean's heels squeaked on the greasy concrete.

'What was that stuff about being a threat to myself?' Ralph asked.

'Oh, I just said that to set his mind at rest.'

'I see. So where's your other friend today?'

'Who's that?'

'The short-arse, I meant: the one who's handy with his feet.'

She stopped on the pavement and turned round to face him. 'He's attending his mother's funeral, Ralph.'

169

'Is that the truth?'

'I wouldn't joke about it, would I?'

'How old was she?'

'In her eighties somewhere. They're a close family.'

They walked towards the van which he'd left on a yellow line. She nodded towards it. 'Cliff said you live in that thing really.'

'Did he?' He liked the feeling of walking with her again but thought he wouldn't get used to it. 'So you and him keep in touch?'

'Of course we do.' She nodded at the van. 'What's that stuff you've got in the back?'

'Furniture.'

'I can see that. You're involved in the business then?'

'Now and again. Sometimes I leave it for a few days. I don't care to be close, myself.'

She nodded. 'I could have killed you, you know: I would have had no compunction.'

He laughed in a light way but felt it cut his throat a little, like something with not enough sugar. 'When could you have killed me?'

'Any time in these last few years. Up to the other night, say.'

'So what made you change your mind?'

'Because I saw you as pathetic. I'd never seen you as that before. Not in that light, you see.'

'You're the one who called me. You arranged it.'

'That's right. I did that as a favour to Cliff mostly. I was helping him, not you, straightening out his life for him. He's in a mess, I think, and I wanted this one part to give him satisfaction.'

'Which part?'

She hesitated, not wanting to couple the two things, as though words might carry a contagion. 'You and John.'

'You were brave then.'

'Brave, yeah.'

'So when I left, Cliff stepped in?'

She looked across the road and gave someone a quick wave. Ralph kept his eyes on her face. 'Cliff was delicate about it. Gentle,' she said.

'Tactful, you mean?'

'Gentle will do. He found me a job. And when that finished he put in a word over this one.'

'Why should he do that?'

'Because that's his style. You know, I was certain you'd turn up stinking the other night.'

'Why's that?'

'Because it would have been the worst thing. Then, when I saw you, I had to laugh.' She stared up at him as if trying to memorise his face. 'Have you seen that film? Where the guy comes back from the wars?'

'I don't like films, they're not like life.'

He looked across the road and saw the fitter who had kicked him staring at them from the other side, holding a white paper bag against the front of his red overalls. Jean smiled and waved, then took Ralph's arm, as if to turn him away. The fitter was still staring.

'I was lying to you about the funeral,' she said. 'I feel as if whatever I say to you doesn't matter any more.'

She laughed to herself and her face looked beautiful for a second. She tugged at his arm and then let it go, turning around to face him.

'You didn't know him, did you?'

'The runt over there?'

'No. *John*.'

He shook his head. 'He wasn't in the pool.'

'He had a cold, that's why. But I mean later, when you came upstairs. You didn't know him and he didn't know you.'

'He was there?'

She nodded. 'You were standing right next to him.'

Ralph laughed. He watched the little mechanic crossing the road towards them.

'You'll laugh till you cry,' Jean said. She peered at a little watch on the underside of her wrist. 'Well, I think our time is up.'

Twenty-Four

The comb-and-paper band again – the woman in her raincoat leading with her tambourine, the thickset man behind with the baton. The kids piped their tune in almost a monotone, the tissue flapping in their faces. 'Isle of Capri', was it? You could tell only from the buzzing rhythm. They were walking away from him, passing diagonally across the cleared spaces as if they were following a buried road.

A fire of rubbish was burning not far from the Portakabins, its greasy smoke lolling over the ground. The Fishburns' door had been torn from its hinges and left lying across the front steps. Dust was lifting through the broken sashes of the windows.

The wind was in the other direction but Ralph could still taste the smoke. There was no answer when he knocked at the door of Alison's house, and so he climbed back into the cab and closed the window against the stink of the fire. The weight of the photographs was against his chest and he drew them from his inside pocket. The envelope was split along one long edge. He slipped off the rubber bands.

The photos were small and square, curling in on themselves. Their glossy emulsion had a crackle to it, a net of fine lines. He slid the first from the hollow of the pack. A black dog stood against a background of grey over grey and a man's glossy shoes were just visible at the top of the picture, sliced from their ankles by the white border but sharply in focus, brass eyelets shining. The hound was softer, though, closer to. A tongue of mist lolled from its jaws. He peered without recognising it, then slid it to the back of the pile.

Ma and Alice Foster sat heavy-legged on a spread cloth, a bowl of fruit before them, then little plates of sandwich crusts, the tartan column of a thermos. The women's loose summer dresses were decorated with bold designs of flowers. Ma's arm was around the shoulders of her friend and she aimed her smile at the lens while Mrs Foster looked one-eyed away from it. Her blind eye was as grey as cement and she was saying something sideways on, turning

172

words into the ear of Ma. The shadow of the picture-taker had invaded her lap.

A shrieking like teeth being drawn came from the Fishburns'. Ralph looked up in time to see a toilet pan teetering on the sill of one of the upstairs windows. He watched while it toppled and dropped. It hit the top of the low front wall and shattered.

He turned back to the photograph, holding it against his knee. The hump of the island was midstream, threatened by a shoulder from the left. The elbow was bent, holding something in its crook. A child's sandal pushed into frame. The one thing sharp was the silvered buckle of the sandal.

He started the engine and turned slowly in the road. A digger was at work at the back of the house, rooting up the garden and leaving a wake of torn soil. He drew away. A few cars were parked outside the Eagles. The Dobermann stood guard upon the roof, front legs braced against the parapet. The red-haired barman was at the front, throwing a bucket of suds towards the road.

Alison loaded clothes into one of the dryers. She did not see Ralph at first or pretended not to. She pushed change, three different coins, into the slot and then turned around and looked at him briefly before carrying the basket she'd emptied to the other side of the room. She slopped it into a stack of others.

'I wasn't expecting you,' she said.

'Who then?'

'I thought he'd send Colin.'

He shrugged and sat on one of the row of chairs. 'He thinks I owe him this. I'll sit here and wait, shall I?'

She nodded. 'The other woman will be late today. She has to take her little girl to the clinic.'

'OK.'

He went over to the machine and tried for a coffee. It swallowed twenty pence and spouted grey water.

'I'll make you one,' Alison said.

She leaned over the counter and jammed a lead into the back of a kettle. The lights dimmed for a second. He watched while she found a couple of mugs and spooned in coffee from a catering-size tin.

'I suppose he thinks you might get lost.'

'That starts to feel the better option.'

He looked around the place. There was a stain on the ceiling in one corner where water must have dripped from the floor above.

'Do you like working here?'

'Tell me why I should.'

She poured milk from a carton and handed him his coffee. She stood in front of him holding her mug against the belly of her blue overalls.

'You don't look well. Haven't you been sleeping?' she asked.

'I sleep when I want to.'

She nodded. 'Are you going to help me fold a few sheets?'

'All right.'

'Wash your hands first.'

There was a covered yard at the back with a door to a toilet and washroom. Supplies for the machines were stacked on metal racks. He could see misty blue sky and the floating shapes of clouds through the corrugated plastic of the roof. He rinsed his hands and dried them with a paper towel.

'I thought you weren't coming back,' Alison said.

'It's nice out there. Restful.'

She started to laugh.

'What's the matter?'

'Nothing. You just made me laugh.'

He held one end of the sheet while she gave him instructions from the other. He went the wrong way a couple of times but then got the knack of it.

'How long is it since you did this?' she asked.

'A while.'

He put the sheets into a pile for her. They were warm and pleasant-smelling from the washing powder. 'The boys are in the Fishburns' house,' he said.

'First thing this morning. Frank said you got out what you wanted.'

'That's right.'

'He'll miss that place – it was an income for him.'

'Does he know about this little trip you're making?'

'You mean did I tell him?' She seemed irritated now, walking from one side of the room to the other, checking the progress of the machines, tidying. 'I can't abide a liar,' she said. 'When it gets beyond a certain point.'

'We all need our little lies,' Ralph said.

She shook her head. 'He does it out of contempt for people.'

'Blarney, you could call it.'

'You could. Except that he isn't Irish.'

174

He stared at her.

'Not an iota. Can't you hear the way his voice floats about?'

'I'd noticed, yeah. I thought he'd been around himself.'

'He's just lousy at it, can't keep it up. What else did he tell you?'

'Bits and pieces.'

'He reckoned he had you eating out of his hand.'

'Did he say that?'

She made a shape with her mouth. 'I've got some washes to finish . . .'

The other woman came at about four fifteen. She chatted to Alison as she changed into her overall and put a sort of golden net over her hair to keep it in place. At some point she worked out that Ralph wasn't a customer and gave him a look.

'Don't mind him,' Alison said. 'He'll be leaving with me.'

The woman continued to stare at him. Alison passed her a bunch of keys, reached behind the counter and pulled out a holdall. One of the handles was frayed so that the string loop was showing.

'That all your luggage?' Ralph asked.

'That's the stuff.'

'Do you want to change? I could run you home first.'

'He thinks I should make more of an effort,' Alison said to her friend.

The woman smiled but said nothing. Alison took off her grey overall and pulled on a suede windcheater which was stained and too large for her. A man's jacket. She unzipped one side of the holdall and stuffed her work clothes inside.

'I don't want to lose this because the boss would make me pay for it. Wouldn't he, Chloë?'

'That's right,' Chloë said. She waved to them as they were going through the glass door. 'Enjoy yourselves.'

He kept looking at her as they were stuck in the traffic queues, glancing at the side of her face.

'Stop staring for a second,' she said. 'Stop looking at me.'

'I was wondering how old you are.'

'How old do you think?'

'I'd say thirty-four or five.'

She nodded. 'Then that's how old I am.'

'You ought to marry Cliff. You won't get a better offer now.'

She looked away from him. She had kicked off her shoes to give

175

her feet some ease. 'You're a charmer,' she said. 'I didn't think there was much of him in you but I was wrong.'

'Much of Cliff in me?'

'Much of your father.'

'Then you're another one who doesn't like him.'

'Am I? Who was the first?'

'Do you know about the phone calls? Some guy rings up and breathes at him.'

She nodded. 'I listened in once. While Cliff was out of the office. I had an idea it might have been a woman.'

'Why a woman especially?'

'Just a feeling I had: I thought it was more of a woman's silence.'

They passed through the heavy traffic near the docks – cars heading for the terminals and foreign lorries with shuddering loads under canvas. They went past the high walls of the docks with their topping of razor wire, the river visible at the gates. She put her hand on his arm and then took it off, as if she'd wanted to ask a question but thought better of it. He wished he had cleared the mess of newpaper and chocolate wrappers from underfoot.

'What sort of place is it?' Alison asked.

'Hasn't he told you?'

She took the card from the dash and bent over it. 'It says "parties catered for". Do you think we make up a party?'

'I think it's just you and him.'

They had turned a little away from the river and there was derelict land on the side of the road. He could see the towers of cranes across the empty lots.

'You're a couple of fools,' she said.

'Do you think so?'

She nodded. 'One of you will cut the other's throat.'

'You're psychic then?'

'I've been listening to the way you talk.'

The estuary was in sight now, a dazzle above it as if the air were confused. The brightness made him blink. 'I owe him a few things first.'

'You'll always owe him,' Alison said.

He shook his head. 'There must be an end to it: there's no justice otherwise.'

'That's a funny word to use.'

'It just came to mind.'

'So what happens when your debts are clear?'

'I have a choice then: he couldn't object to anything.'

'You hate him, then?'

He was uncomfortable with that. 'Not exactly hate.'

'There's another word for it?'

'There should be. Hate doesn't do the job.'

All evidence of the town had vanished except for the road, which seemed to continue beyond its function. A slush of water shone in the waterlogged fields. There was a tight cluster of cooling towers inland – fat brick spindles with a scurf of smoke.

'You can let me out here,' Alison said.

'What?'

'I said, let me out.'

They were passing the long fence of a warehouse. The buildings behind were painted a light grey. Cables wound on huge wooden armatures were stacked in rows and lamps on silver posts shone brightly even in the sunshine. Alison tried to open her door but he reached across her and pulled it closed.

'You'll take the skin off your arse like that!'

She pushed at his arm for a second, then let herself fall back. She looked at the low buildings going by, then big advertising boards on hoardings – so much per foot, per year, rent-free periods.

'Are we nearly there?'

'We're close.'

They could see the river again and a distant line of lead-white where the land stopped and they were looking out to sea. The engine lurched and the noise of the exhaust went up a notch so that it would have been difficult for them to speak. The tarmac was new and felt spongy under the tyres. The road acquired a long kerb and the verges with a few young trees, temporary-looking because the land was too open and bright for them. The smoke of the cooling towers was still visible like a long trail of cloud. They passed a metal sign with swan-necked lamps above it: HOTEL 500 YDS >>.

177

Twenty-Five

Eric followed as she went up in the creaking stair lift, keeping always a step below – a page in the wake of a queen.

'You spoke to him,' he said.

'Is it a crime to speak?'

Ma's legs hung in wrinkled flesh-coloured stockings over the seat. She'd have tugged down her dress but she was past caring.

'You had a bloody nerve to be so interfering,' Eric said.

'Where my flesh and blood were concerned?'

'His blood as well, wouldn't you say?'

He stood below as she turned in the tight space of the half-landing. The chair almost stopped, then extricated itself and continued up the other flight.

'He had a look like death,' Eric added. 'I asked him if something was wrong but he couldn't bring himself to answer.'

'A sign that you should mind your business, probably.'

'Did that woman advise you?'

She sent him a severe look while ascending slowly to the whine of the motor. 'What woman? Who?'

'The one you adore,' Eric said, with a little simper.

'You'll overstep yourself one day,' Ma warned. 'You shouldn't presume too much on the years we have in common.'

'You came between the child and him.'

She shook her head. 'I came between nothing, only offered my help. I had the capacity, so why not?'

'And what did he say?'

'He considered, then told me he would be grateful.'

The lift had reached the landing now and Eric helped her down, taking her weight on his arm for a second. He had the chance to speak close to her ear. 'He told me that the boy was changed against him.'

She found her feet and wrenched herself away from him. 'Why, how was that when he was always welcome?'

'Oh, there's nothing worse than being made welcome: that tea-and-biscuits style of it.'

'What else was I to do? Turn my back on the child?'

'I didn't say that.'

'You thought my time would be better spent on you.'

He shook his head. 'You're turning spiteful now, Marion—'

'Am I? It makes my flesh crawl the way you think you're indispensable.'

He stepped towards her, puffing out his thin chest. 'So dispense with me!'

She wanted to reply but could not say the words. Her balance was uncertain and she gripped the banister rail.

'*Marion?*' He saw a quiver cross her face, as if he were seeing it through water. 'Marion? Aren't you well?'

Cliff stood in the mostly empty car park. There was a children's area beyond with the top of a slide seen above slanted red railings, then a couple of three-storey blocks with claddings of bleached stone and shallow first-floor balconies of fancy ironwork. A striped canopy led from the glass entry of the nearest building into the open space before the parking slots. The breeze was billowing one side of it. Every so often there was a snap as the fabric adjusted. Cliff's dark suit looked new or at least seldom worn, more sober than his usual cut. Alison was slipping her shoes back on, keeping her head down while Ralph parked the van. He jumped out and went around to open the passenger door but Cliff was there first.

'Thank you,' Alison said quietly as she climbed down.

Cliff took her arm but let go of it the second her feet were on the ground. Ralph found himself grinning, leering like a fool at them.

'If either of you is peckish, then I'll order a meal,' Cliff said. 'Or we could forget about food and have a couple of drinks.' He smiled from one to the other. Someone out of sight was trying to start a car, turning over the engine, waiting, turning it over. 'Well, plenty of time to make up your minds . . .'

He had his hand on Alison's arm again, not gripping it but restraining her by a touch. He began to guide her towards the striped canopy, as if he thought once under its cover the way would be eased and she would follow him willingly. Ralph was hanging back. His father sent him a troubled look and then leaned closer to Alison, whispering something as a gust got under the canvas.

She stopped, resisting him. 'I'll have to talk to you, Cliff.'

'That's why we're here, isn't it?'

179

She shook her head. 'Talk now, I mean.'

Cliff took hold of her shoulders. She loosened her grip on the scruffy tartan bag and it tumbled close to her feet. Ralph took a step towards them; she glanced at him and put her hand to her mouth. It looked for a second as if she meant to bite it.

'Not even on the same floor,' Cliff was saying earnestly. 'As far as they're concerned, we're two separate people.'

Ralph scooped up the holdall and held it out to her. She stared at it but didn't take it.

'She needn't stay,' Cliff said, looking his way. 'If that's what she wants she could go straight back with you now.'

Alison took the bag and tucked it under her arm. 'All right.'

'Sorry?' Cliff asked.

'I'll stay. To talk with you.'

They were under the canopy now. A red runner ran between brass kerbs to the doors of thick tinted glass. One door was hinged back into darkness set with tiny bright lights. Cliff bent to her again and she seemed for a second to lean against him.

'You're not joining us, Ralph?' Cliff asked.

'I'll take the air first.'

He watched them from a dozen feet away. The menu was on display at the entrance, set on a stand in an inclined frame of lacquered brass. *Table d'hôte.* Alison stopped to stare at it, as if she found it curious or sinister. Cliff was smiling now. Cat with the cream. He slipped his arm around Alison's shoulders and shepherded her inside.

Shepherd not the word.

Twenty-Six

A black-hulled freighter beat towards the port, moving so slowly that it seemed to be at a standstill until you took your eyes from it and looked again. The bell of the lightship was cutting about on the breeze, sending its fragile chimes. Something made Ma sneeze.

'Bless me,' she said, laughing.

Alice Foster pulled a face as she fixed her teeth into a sandwich. Mrs Cromer leaned to pour ruby wine but she put her hand over the glass.

'No more.'

'Very wise,' Ma said. 'Though I need fortification against this air.'

She watched as her glass was filled to an inch of its top. She was happy suddenly so that words failed her. The sunshine pierced her like a ray. Eric was standing before them, feet spread in the chalky loam with the Kodak tight against his belly. He squinted one-eyed into the viewfinder.

'Look at him with his box of tricks,' Ma said. 'Did you ever see such a man for fussing?'

'If I didn't fuss you, who would?' Eric asked, his thumb against the lever. He stared down at their stamp-sized group. He saw Cliff on the edge of frame in his striped suit. He was peeling the boy an orange.

'So smile, then!'

He leaned forward. The sun was behind his shoulder and he saw with pleasure that the Foster woman was touched by his shadow. The boy moved just as the shutter made its dry clack.

'*Snap!*' he called in triumph.

They stayed still for a second, Ma's free arm over her friend's shoulders. Mrs Foster had turned her blind eye to annul the power of the camera. She knew how the emulsion would fail at that point, would not register an image. She watched with her sighted half as Eric wound on the film, then clipped the camera into its polished leather case. She turned away and looked instead at her daughter walking Mrs Cromer's Colin towards them, her plump hands gripping the infant's wrists as she walked bent behind him. Alma caught her look and smiled back. She called to them over the toddler's rattling laughter.

'I could eat him! I could eat every little limb of him!'

'You'll do no such thing,' Mrs Cromer said. She noticed that his little knees were muddied. A glass toppled beside her, spilling ruby. She tugged away the hem of her dress with a cry of annoyance.

'These lads are perpetual motion!' Ma said, laughing. She grasped the hand of Ralph who knelt thunderstruck on the fringe of the cloth, then winked towards his father. 'Take him away for God's sake! Tire him out somewhere!'

Ralph started to sob, dismayed by the spreading stain.

'You know I'm only a famous old woman,' Ma said, relenting. She wasn't sure what she meant. 'Look!' She palmed a fat plum and revealed it in her hand an inch from the boy's nose. 'Take that with you and forget that I spoke.'

Cliff stood over them. He had a hulking look although he was small. He saw that the Foster woman watched him carefully, glancing at his hand as it rested for a second on his son's head. Her dead eye had a shine to it like fly wings. It moved like a fly, never settling.

She spoke to him, for the first time that day. 'Everything's behind you now, Cliff. Except you and the boy. And that's a tie that never can be broken.'

He frowned at 'never can'. What did she mean by talking arse-about like that? He could not be bothered to fathom it. Instead he took the boy towards the water. Ralph was still snotty and smeared about the eyes, dragging his feet in their Sunday sandals across the mud and pale ribbings of rock. Cliff held his squirming hand and saw Eric heading their way, Ma's bollicky boy. The sound of the lightship's bell was being carried towards them.

'Hear that?' Cliff asked.

Ralph stared up at him.

'You must hear the bell!' Cliff said. 'To warn sailors that a shoal is there. You know what a shoal is, don't you?'

The boy shook his head.

'Where there's something below the water – a rock or a sandbank. Could even be the wreck of a ship.'

Ralph turned towards the sound but the lightship was a

mile upstream and hidden by the wooded hump of the island. He shuffled on his feet, kicking against a little knob of flint which proved solid. He sniffled again. Eric stepped up to them, unsnapping the camera.

'I know you can smile,' he said, beaming. 'I've seen that at least.'

Ralph uncurled his hand from around the plum and looked down at it. It was split at the side and the soft flesh was oozing. Eric eyed the women a hundred yards away, then sidled crabwise closer, diffident but then coming to it, talking side-mouthed towards Cliff's ear. 'You should get the lad away from them, you know. Soon as you can.'

Cliff stared back at him. He mightn't have heard.

The sun came out of a dragging roll of clouds and turned the water into fishscales which then stopped their jostling and went still. Eric struggled with himself, scuffing his feet. 'The shite those two are spinning, what chance does he have? If it was just a question of religion there wouldn't be so much harm in it.'

Cliff looked at his son, who was holding the shed carapace of a crab to the light, squinting through it like a lens.

'It's not so much Ma as the other one,' Eric went on, 'who's got her under the thumb. If I didn't know better I'd say it was unnatural.'

'How's that?'

Eric squirmed a shoulder. 'The way they behave sometimes like a pair of lezzies. Holding hands and that business—'

'She gives him a home,' Cliff said, impatient with him. 'Neither of us could do that.'

Eric slipped a hand on his arm, just the thumb and forefinger. 'Find yourself some woman, Cliff. Take him away with the pair of you.'

'I couldn't.'

'Couldn't you?' Eric sighed and stayed the swing of the camera. There was laughter from the picnicking women. 'Ma's talking about selling her stock, you know. She wants to try new lines.'

'Oh aye? There's always some scheme of hers.'

'This time she's talking about giftware. *Giftware,* I ask you!'

'There's nothing wrong with giftware,' Cliff said.

Eric sucked at his lip. 'Not in itself but what sort of world will the boy think he's growing up in?' He smiled at Ralph, who was staring at them from one to the other. 'What have you got there, Ralphie?'

The boy held it up towards them, his answer caught in a stutter.

'A crab house but the crab has gone!' Eric said gently. He laughed, his eyes shining, and lifted the camera. 'Stand near your father now and I'll take a snap.'

Ralph stood uneasily before his father's legs, then felt himself lifted into the air. He was held, his feet dangling. One sandal was loose and might fall. He tightened his grip on the brittle shell and caused it to shatter. His distress came as a hiccup.

'There's the spirit!' Eric said. He stared down at the little image. 'If you can't say "cheese", say "gorgonzola".'

Twenty-Seven

Hungry, gagging on its own juices, the cat pushed against Eric's leg and he pushed it away. He listened for the bell from upstairs, but heard only the fridge chugging, a tick of rain on the window and the little singing of the pilot light.

'Marion?' he called from the hall. 'Marion?'

He went to the foot of the stairs and listened, his hand on the turned ball on top of the newel post.

'Marion, your tea's ready!'

He listened again. A car or a van passed in the street, its draught sucking at the front door. He withdrew slowly into the kitchen, one foot after the other, his intent face still turned to the stairwell. The cat came to him again and he pushed it away with his foot.

The hotel grounds formed a bowl in which cold breezes circulated. A small alpine garden set with picnic tables occupied the shaded side of the building. Scraps of blown paper were caught in the shrubs and little conifers. From where he sat, Ralph could see an older structure of dark brick, joined to the rest of the hotel by a glazed walkway. A woman in a dark-green uniform was guiding an empty trolley along it. He watched as she turned around so that she could push backwards between sprung double doors. She looked at him once before she disappeared. The doors flapped shut after her and in the same second a yellow lamp came on above him.

He looked up and saw a row of them shining along the perimeter fence. The car park, which was almost empty now, extended from the rear of the building towards a pair of boxlike garages. Behind them the tarmac ended at brownish land with dark water in its creases. The doors of the garages were hinged up and out and their insides were lit sharply. A man stood at the open front of the middle garage, looking out with his hands in his pockets. After a while he turned on his heels and stepped back inside – a heavily-built man with a rolling walk. The wind altered its tack and carried a tremble of music.

Ralph went over. His arse was numb from the edge of the bench. Two of them were staring at a section of gearbox under an angled lamp. The radio was playing and the thickset man was explaining something to a youngster, talking into his ear. Their backs were to Ralph as he stood in the doorway. He looked into the other half of the garage and saw a worn-out dartboard. A handful of darts spiked their shadows. A car was high on a jack with a couple of lamps clipped to the back of a chair set underneath in the trough.

The music stopped for a traffic report. The youngster turned and saw Ralph. 'If you want to try that,' the older man said, 'I'd say you were brave or stupid.' He laughed.

Ralph stepped past the end of a workbench and up to the board. He tugged out the darts and compared them. He picked out three and laid the others on the top of a filing cabinet. A line of yellow paint was half hidden by grease on the cement floor. He stood up to it and started to throw, aiming loose towards the top of the board, retrieving the darts and then starting again to more purpose. He settled himself and narrowed his aim to the little oblongs of the trebles.

The young man was standing behind him as he turned back from the board, smiling as though he'd witnessed some act of foolishness. His face was dead white with deep pocks of acne across the cheeks. Ralph gave him a nod and then threw again, grouping the darts close so that he could wrap his hand around them and tug them out as a single stem.

The youngster was standing in the same spot, holding a heavy screwdriver by the blade. 'We're closed now. As it happens.'

Ralph looked behind him. It was getting dark outside. He decided he'd throw for real. Rattle off a game. The other man stepped through, carrying a pair of mugs. He was dark-faced, with the beginnings of a beard. He handed one mug to the youth and then stood to watch.

'Exhaust, is it?' he asked.

'That's right,' Ralph said. 'Blown a little hole behind the silencer.'

The man took a sip and nodded. 'We heard the racket when you drove it in.' He glanced at Ralph's scuffed jacket, the slacks with their map of grime. 'Staying here, are you?'

'I was delivering someone.'

'That's right,' he said, as if he'd thought as much. 'It's nothing but a bloody knocking shop in there.'

The youth sniggered over his tea.

'We'll take a look if you like,' the older man said. 'It's too late to get a part so it'd have to be another patch.'

Ralph laughed, lining up a shot. 'Patch'll do fine.' His wrist was loosened now and the points went in hard, burying themselves up to the cheap alloy bodies.

'It's a miracle you're getting those things to go straight,' the older man said.

'A knack I've got.'

He threw again. Two trebles and a seventeen. The kid stared as if it were algebra but the other knew he was on a finish by the swoop down from the top of the board.

'Treble eight, treble nine, double nine, is it?'

'That's it.'

'Don't you believe in missing, pal?'

'Sod that for a religion.'

He laughed, watched. Ralph threw, one shot chasing the other. He picked off the first trebles, then steadied himself for the final dart. The bed of the nines looked as spacious as a swimming pool but then the wire on the outside edge caught the light and he went instead for that, shot for the shine of it. He heard the twang of the metal and saw the bright pock the point left as the dart rebounded towards the floor. It flicked backwards and then skittered over the concrete.

The older man bent grunting to pick it up. He went to the board for the rest. He looked sorrowful as he came back.

'So we'll take a look at that van . . .'

Ralph missed the wild knocks and splurgings of the exhaust. When he stopped at the first set of traffic lights the engine sounded the quiet ghost of itself. He had just left the dual carriageway when he spotted Rose waiting in her chair on the edge of the pavement. She was bending over something in her lap, studying it although it was fully dark. A book? A map? He thought of stopping to see if she needed help but a few yards further he saw Colin and the little girl. Colin was standing tall and protective beside her, holding her hand. He gave the van a glance but didn't seem to recognise it, or he was indifferent now. The little girl's arm in the sleeve of her navy duffle-coat lifted straight over her head, her hand lost in Colin's fist.

He reached the flats and then drove past. Alma Drean's flat was in darkness. A tall copper was talking into his radio at the end of the street. He glanced up as Ralph waited at the junction.

The Lamb was brightly lit with fuzzy rectangles of light falling into the narrow courtyard at the front. A woman in a white blouse and slacks sat on the low front wall drinking from a bottle.

He found a spot a few yards up the road and walked back. A match was going on in the bar – a local league fixture. Quartered sandwiches and cocktail sausages spiked with toothpicks were circulating on trays with paper doilies. He took one of the sausages and swallowed it almost whole.

He was drinking before he knew it. He had one at the bar and then another. A pint of the sweetish fizzy lager and then a different beer which had more of a taste. He beckoned the barman and ordered a whisky to go with the second drink. He watched the game until the players broke for the interval. When he turned away he caught the eye of Murdo, who was sitting by himself at a corner table. Murdo picked up his drink and came over. He looked darker and slighter without his apron, hollow-chested as if he were bending over nothing.

'I didn't see your dad today,' he said.

'You wouldn't – a couple of days' break for him,' Ralph said.

'A rest will do him well,' Murdo said. 'Will you be opening the shop yourself?'

'I think Colin will be taking care of that.'

'A nice lad but no head for figures,' Murdo said. There was a smell of bacon fat about him as if his pores were saturated with it. It was the same smell his café had in the early morning. He watched Ralph's throat twitching as he swallowed. 'Cliff told me you were teetotal but I knew he was joking.'

'But it's no affair of yours,' Ralph said. He reached out to a passing tray and took a sandwich between finger and thumb. 'Is it?'

'No,' Murdo said. 'If you put it like that, then it isn't.'

He stayed standing at the bar but looking the other way for a couple of minutes, until there was only a slop of drink left in the bottom of his glass. Then he took it back to his table.

The phone stopped ringing as Ralph let himself into the flat. He stood with his hand over it for a second but didn't pick it up. The room was as he'd left it, the blinds open. The darkness outside looked glossy and fat, pressing against the glass. A ripe smell in the air made him think of cat food. Couldn't be. He went into the bedroom and took off one shoe but didn't get as far as the other.

He dreamed about the old guy with the supermarket trolley. When he woke up he had no memory of it, only a recollection he couldn't place of the reek as the black bags had burned, melted into stinking vapour under the attack of the fire.

The phone had started to ring again. It was getting light but the darkness hadn't given up, just pulled itself tighter. His head and jaw ached as if his teeth had been loosened. He got up from the bed and walked lopsided to the window. The brightest thing outside was the fat white flank of the rabbit pressed against the mesh of its cage.

The phone was still chirruping, settling in for a long campaign. He went into the lounge. A man was asleep in the armchair, his head fallen to one side and his hands clasped in his lap. A string of drool was making its way from the corner of his mouth. A grey suitcase, strapped to a wheeled trolley, stood canted on the rug beside him. Ralph stepped past it and picked up the phone. 'Hello?'

'I was trying to reach you all last night.'

'I'm here now.'

Eric left a silence. 'It's your grandmother,' he volunteered.

'What?'

'Something's wrong with her.'

'What's wrong? Eric?'

'I don't think I should have to explain myself,' Eric said.

'What are you talking about?'

'I've been dealing with this on my own while you and Cliff chose to make yourselves scarce.'

'Dealing with what, Eric?' Ralph looked down at the head of the man sleeping in the chair. His hair was dark and thinning, the scalp showing through. 'You're telling me she's been taken ill?'

Eric laughed his breathless little chuckle. 'Oh, I'd say she's ill all right.'

'Eric, if she's been taken—'

Eric put down the phone. Ralph saw that the visitor had woken and was looking at him over the back of the chair.

'You know who I am?' the stranger asked.

'I know. But I can't recall the name.'

The man laughed. 'That's ripe, isn't it?'

His beard was growing in pinpoints of stubble. He was fully

189

dressed except for his shoes, which lay where he'd kicked them, the laces still tied. He wore grey socks, holed at the toes. His greasy waterproof jacket was zipped to the collar, a seam split at one shoulder.

He looked about the room. 'A pig's arse you've made of this place!'

'I'm not much of a homemaker.'

He nodded, the curl on his lip getting deeper. 'I used to dream about this flat. Having it to myself. Taking care of it. Does that seem funny to you?'

'Not exactly funny.'

'I expected Cliff to be here. We've got a few things to talk over, you know, and I was hoping he'd be around.'

'Cliff's had a lot on his mind lately,' Ralph said.

The stranger thought this over. Then he smiled, as though a happy thought had occurred to him. 'Ever heard of a vacuum cleaner?'

Ralph went into the bedroom to find his other shoe. His head swam as he bent down to tie the laces. He went back into the lounge and looked for his keys on the floor near the couch. The man watched him as he picked them up. Ralph remembered his name now.

'So how's the old king-turd nowadays?' Terry Wordsworth asked.

'Cliff?'

He rolled his eyes. 'Cliff, yeah.'

'He's OK.'

'He's OK? Is that all you can say on the subject?'

'Sorry, Terry, but I've no time to chat.'

Terry Wordsworth stared at him, then smiled as if he thought that was reasonable. He called out when Ralph was almost at the door. 'Hey!'

Ralph turned.

'When you see Cliff, tell him he should have got a woman in this place.'

Twenty-Eight

Cliff's nose started to bleed. He felt the warm gush of it in the dark, and a taste of salt and metal at the back of his throat.

He stood in the tiny bathroom and tried to stem the flow with a strip torn from the toilet roll. The blood turned the tissue into red mush. When it seemed to be stopping, he made a little wad and stuffed it into his right nostril. He smiled at his ridiculous face in the mirror above the basin and then went back into his room and stared at the big drops of blood on the pillow. He was impressed by their startling redness. When he kinked the blinds he could see that it was light outside.

He picked up the phone. 'Room twenty-one, please.'

He waited. A woman. 'Which room is calling, sir?'

He couldn't remember. He squinted at the tab of the key in the door. 'Room twelve.'

'Just a moment, sir.' She left him for a good minute. He could feel the pressure of banked blood behind the plug in his nose. 'The guest left early this morning, sir.'

'It's early now.'

She gave a laugh. 'Then I mean late last night, sir.'

Too early for the morning rush. Slanting rain was falling, although the roads were not yet damp. The engine turned quietly and without fuss as Ralph crossed the town. Gulls were shrieking and cawing, fighting over a damp bundle in the road. He parked outside the florist's shop.

The rain was little needles on his face. The arcade's painted metal shutters were closed and padlocked. Upstairs the blinds had been pushed back and there seemed to be a light in every room. He pushed the button of the bell. The chimes sounded in a different part of the house.

He pushed it again, standing out of the rain. He stepped back and looked at the brightness upstairs, then hammered on the panel with the side of his fist. A flake of paint was dislodged

191

and fluttered down. He heard the bolts being withdrawn, top and bottom.

Eric said nothing, just stood against the wall, averting his eyes with a sulky look. He wore his old red dressing gown over striped pyjamas buttoned to the throat, his bare feet pushed into heavy brogues so that his ankles looked ridiculously thin.

'Ma's in her room?' Ralph asked.

He let his eyelids droop. 'Where else would she be?'

They went upstairs, the old man following at first, then edging past, making a noise of impatience in his throat. He waited on the landing, under the yellow light. He was panting with the effort of the climb.

The draught excluder brushed against the rug as Ralph pushed back the bedroom door. The bed had been moved away from the wall and now seemed to take up most of the room so that he had to squeeze between it and the edge of the door. The overhead light shone behind its fringed parchment shade. Ma's face was so pale that he did not see it at first against the white pillow.

'You see the condition of her,' Eric said with satisfaction.

A vein was working at Ma's temple, like a little blue signal switching on and off. She lay with her eyes closed and the covers drawn almost to her chin, head a little to one side. Her body seemed hardly to disturb the bedding, as if she'd lost two-thirds of her weight.

'Have you called the doctor?'

Eric sniffed, as if he thought Ralph had misunderstood the situation. 'You can see that she's sleeping.'

'It's not sleep.'

Eric shook his head. 'You know her thoughts on doctors. You know she hasn't a kind word to say . . .' He reached out. It seemed to Ralph that he stroked Ma's hair against its growth.

'What happened to her?'

Eric twisted his neck against the buttoned collar of his pyjamas. 'I had her tea but I couldn't wake her. I left it there but when I came back she hadn't touched it. Stone-cold and I had to pour it down the sink.'

'She might have had a stroke, Eric.'

'I know. D'you think I'm ignorant?'

'Was it you that moved her bed?'

Eric smiled and carefully closed the door. Ralph saw that the cat was curled asleep on the quilt close to Ma's hand. Every few seconds her middle finger would lift and tremble.

'I'm going to call an ambulance.'

'Be that on your own head,' Eric said.

'What do you mean?'

Eric looked smug, as if he'd cleverly gained an advantage. 'Only that it was your idea, not mine.'

Ralph used the phone in the living room. When he'd finished he felt the cat winding itself about his ankles. It followed him downstairs and into the kitchen. There was an open tin of meat in the fridge and he scraped some into a bowl with one of the knives and watched it gorge itself. Then he peered through the little curtained window into the garden. He was surprised to see Eric standing on the square of lawn. He opened the back door and went outside. It was still raining and Eric's thin hair was shiny with wet. Ralph watched as he made a putt from about four feet. It missed the hole by a couple of inches and overshot.

'The ambulance'll be here soon, Eric.'

He grinned painfully and struck the ball again. This time it swung around the hole and spun out into the grass. He stared at it and began to massage his wrist. 'I suppose you think she has no rights in the matter now,' he said.

'I don't want to argue about that.'

'This place is all yours if she goes – but you'll know that, won't you?'

'I didn't.'

Eric smiled and positioned himself again. 'Fuck-all is my portion but then I'm not in the family. She always made a point of telling me.' He looked up suddenly, smiling on one side of his face only, the lines gathered around a shining sarcastic eye. 'I was her sex slave for twenty years, you know.'

'Her what?'

'Her slave in that particular. Until she lost all interest.'

He carefully made the stroke, watching the ball as it trickled away. Ralph caught at his arm and forced it down. For a second it looked as if he might resist but then he let the putter slip and dropped to the turf on his knees, his legs folding suddenly.

Ralph stood over him. The old man was watching him carefully. The looping siren of the ambulance sounded as it entered the top of the street. They both listened.

'If you're going to do something, you'd better do it now,' Eric said.

He waited. Ralph saw the dimpled ball nested in the hole close to his shoe. He bent down and picked it out. He balanced it on his palm for a second then closed his hand and flung it, high over the wall at the back of the garden. He saw the speck of it against the sky before it dropped.

'You wouldn't give me even that satisfaction,' Eric said.

He stood up painfully, pressing himself upright in stages. There were grass stains on the hip of his dressing gown. He looked down at himself, grinning.

'Your mother was the same but it was looks with her: a look would kill you.'

The siren had stopped its racket. Ralph listened for the doorbell. He noticed Mrs Foster sitting neatly on the kitchen step, cleaning its muzzle with a paw.

A man of about his father's age and a younger woman took a rolled stretcher upstairs and then carried Ma awkwardly down towards the open door. 'This is against her wishes,' Eric said as they passed by.

'We've given her an injection,' the man said, ignoring him. 'That'll make her heart beat stronger.'

Ma was secured to the stretcher by two broad webbing bands. The man was at the head end, directing the woman as she stepped backwards.

'Where are you taking her?' Ralph asked.

'St Hugh's. It isn't the nearest but the facilities for stroke are better there.' He spoke to the woman. 'Now mind the step this time.'

'Right you are,' the woman said.

Ralph followed them out. The ambulance was parked at an angle to the pavement, its rear doors already open. When Ma was laid safely on one of the bunks, the woman stepped down again. She had removed her cap and was holding it against her chest. It had left a ridge in her fair, wavy hair. The man was still inside the cabin, sitting at the foot of the other bunk, leaning towards them.

'So which is the relative?' the woman asked, looking at them both.

Ralph gave Eric a little push in the small of his back.

'It can be both of you or none,' the woman said. 'You can only decide that for yourselves.'

194

'Then it's me,' Eric said.

She glanced at Ralph as if she needed his confirmation. He stared past her to the open doors where the ambulance man was waiting. She sighed and replaced her cap, then climbed into the cab.

'Go on, then,' Ralph said.

Eric stepped forward. The lights of the ambulance dimmed for a second as the driver started the engine. Its blue lamp began to turn in silence. A van had stopped outside the newsagent's and was unloading papers.

'I'll need the keys,' Ralph said.

Eric stopped with his foot on the step.

'If you go with Ma, I'll need the keys.'

Eric began to drag them from his pocket – a chain of Yale and mortice keys and the small silver keys of the games machines.

Ralph took them, surprised by their weight – a plumb line with a settling swing. He gathered them with his other hand. 'Thanks.'

'Don't thank me,' Eric said.

The ambulance man came forward to offer his hand but Eric shrugged it away and climbed aboard with a look of purpose. His brown shoes slopped loosely at his bare heels. The ambulance man smiled at his rejected hand, then at Ralph. He leaned out to pull the doors closed.

Twenty-Nine

The phone rang. Ralph thought it would stop in a second but it went on with a clamour that put his back up. He searched the kitchen cupboards until he found the bottle he knew would be there: Martell four-star. Medicinal. He poured a good measure into a mug and added a splash of water from the tap. The telephone stopped but it was a few seconds before he registered the fact. The cat came in through the open door to the garden and rubbed against him. He pushed it away. The drink tasted strong and cleansing.

The doorbell sounded as he was on his way upstairs – a short chime at first, then a longer tone, the thumb left on the button. He considered for a second and then went back down. Whoever it was had left the door and was rattling the front shutters. He squinted into the fish-eye but could see only a circle of dullness with rain falling through curved paths. The shutters shivered into silence. Then someone called mournfully for Eric.

He opened the door to a thickset man in full evening dress, a trimmed goatee almost like a line drawn around his mouth. There was a small round scar below one of his eyes as if someone had dug there with a potato peeler. Ralph recognised the man who had stood in the booth.

'Eric in?' He had a fresh scent of aftershave.

'He's out.'

He stretched himself to look over Ralph's shoulder, not disguising it. 'Mrs Orr then?'

'She's been taken ill.'

He stepped closer, almost into the doorway, staring with his dark-lashed eyes. 'What do you mean? When you say ill, what do you mean?'

'She might have had a stroke,' Ralph said. 'Eric's gone with her to the hospital.'

The other man's eyes seemed too mobile and clever for his broad face. He glanced away and then back, leaning with his

196

bulky shoulder forward. 'You mind me asking who you are yourself?'

'But you've seen me before,' Ralph said.

'I might have but my memory isn't much. Tell me again and I'll go.'

'I'm Ralph, her grandson.'

'Grandson?'

'That's right.'

The man slipped a hand into his inside pocket. The lining of his jacket caught the light. He took out a notebook and a slim silver pen. He clicked the pen and wrote on a leaf of the diary, then tore it carefully from top to bottom.

'I'm sorry about Mrs Orr. That's my number if you need it.'

He stepped back from the house again and stared at the upstairs windows, as if there might be something contrary there. Then he turned and walked back to his car.

The phone rang again as Ralph was unlocking the door of the office. He waited for the tremble of his nerves to die down and then stepped inside. The second he flicked on the light, the phone stopped.

The office was a small room which had been his own. Because of the ground plan of the house it had an unusual shape. The back wall with its single window diverged from the side to form a sharp angle at the outside corner. A cheap oak-veneered desk was set diagonally across this, leaving a triangle of space behind. An office chair upholstered in black plastic stood before it, swung around so that it faced him. A gash across its seat had been repaired with black insulating tape which was peeling away now to show the foam stuffing. A four-drawer filing cabinet stood in the opposite corner.

The thin curtains were closed on the window. He tugged them a little apart. Eric's putter was still lying across the lawn. He closed them again carefully then pulled out each drawer of the desk in turn and tipped the contents on the desktop. He found rubber bands and paperclips, a dry ink pad, a child's wooden ruler and a man's single black shoe, specked with white paint.

He turned his attention to the cabinet. It was locked. He searched along the key chain and separated one of the smaller keys. When it did not fit, he tried a couple of others. The barrel turned with a dry rasp of brass. He began at the bottom, pulling out each drawer.

The first two held a mess of papers and files, which he pulled out in handfuls and flung to the floor. In the third drawer he found a mask of black leather and a rusty engineer's hammer. He held the mask against his face and peered through the eyeholes. The leather was dry and stiff, impregnated with a vague scent. He threw it down. It was so desiccated and light that a draught made it scutter crablike across the boards.

He went upstairs, carrying the hammer. The cat was under his feet for a second, almost tripping him. He looked over the banisters and saw it gliding down the last flight. There was a ripe, fruity smell in his grandmother's room. He turned back the covers on the bed and laid his hand palm down in the hollow she'd left. He tried to decide if there was still a warmth.

The smell troubled him. He crouched down to peer below the bed and saw round pellets of cat shite. The fan heater was still blowing warm air. He switched it off. A dog-eared corner of the rug extended just below the line of the bed. He tugged at it and a section came loose with a suck of underlay. The turds rolled towards the skirting.

The square door of the safe was flush with the floorboards. The metal had a bluish matt finish which made him think of ice. The keyhole was outlined in brass. A recess at one end served as a handle.

He tugged at the bed. It swivelled easily on its casters which must have been oiled. He turned it until it was almost blocking the door and then squatted before the safe. Dust caught in his throat and he swallowed but wanted instead to spit.

He laid the key chain on top of the curl of the rug. Extended, it was about the length of his arm. A short key of machined black metal was fitted on a ring at its end, like a plumb weight for the rest. He teased at its link and removed it altogether. It fitted the lock so nicely he felt a slight suction. He slipped his fingers into the sunken handle and tugged. There wasn't a trace of movement and he turned the key again. The door opened, up and back. It was an inch thick but surprisingly light, backed with some rough layered material like wafers of honeycombed metal. The compartment was shallow, about a foot square, offset from the door so that he had to reach under the surround.

He brought out one book and then another, leaning down with his cheek to the boards. They were narrow and deep, their covers a mottled blue with a dull crackle to it. When he opened the first he saw columns of figures in both pen and fading pencil, crossings-out, amendments, sections cancelled altogether with cross-hatching. He threw them out of the way, against the wall. He was panting with exertion. Nerves, was it? He could smell the cat shite strongly.

He found the metal cash box and lifted it out. It was unlocked. The interior shone with little metallic flakes. He drew out a roll of notes – fives, tens. Some of the dust was adhering to it and when he brushed it off, the tips of his fingers began to shine. There was also a little bottle with a metal cap, which might have held medicine. He shook it. The clear liquid inside filled with a cloud of pale grey. He held it to the light for a second, then dropped it back into the safe. He pushed the money into his shirt pocket without bothering to count it.

At the bottom of the box he found a wad of greetings cards – Christmas, New Year – not many, half a dozen, say. Some were in their torn envelopes, others free. A dust of glitter fell as he examined them.

Dear Mam Dearest With Love XXX My Darling Mam XX
My love and best wishes

The glitter stuck to the sweat on his palm. The hinge split as he opened one. Its edges were dark with handling, the ribbons gone stiff. The writing had big open loops he didn't recognise.

Best Wishes with love XXX
XXX. Your Joyce
XX

He stared at the date on an envelope – *12/58*. The stamp had the young Queen. He squinted at the roundel. The ink was faded into the paper. *Kilmarnock*. He took out the card and blew away the sparkle. Christmas robins. He read the message *XXX* and then pushed it into the pocket of his shirt along with the money. He needed to bend it so that it would fit. His hearing must have been very sharp because he heard the slap of the cat flap in the kitchen door downstairs.

Ralph stood on the stairs and waited. The cat halted on the step below him and began to cry, a little sound out of scale with its thick body. Hungry again. When he didn't respond, it tried to pass below him into Ma's room.

He swatted at it with the hammer and it lay down at once soundlessly on its side. Its snout was blunt and closed. X. Then the ends of its limbs started to twitch. He threw the hammer down the stairwell and it rattled against the banisters.

Thirty

The motor stopped and Cliff tried the key a couple of times with no result, other than the starter going into spasm. He cruised along with the tape deck turning until he reached to switch that off and could hear the air against the car's body, the tight little whistles it was making.

He started to drift to the side of the road, making use of the slope of the camber. An overtaking lorry sounded its horn. The car's body leaned in the space of dead air the lorry left. He tried the ignition again and didn't touch the brakes until he was on the hard shoulder. He cancelled the indicators and sat in silence, hands in his lap. He could smell unburnt petrol. Another lorry went by with its dragging wind. Cliff thought, if today doesn't kill me, nothing will.

He tried the ignition again and kept at it until the battery started to flatten. His jacket lay across the passenger seat and he reached inside for his tin of cigars, then recalled smoking the last. The ashtray was stuffed with cigar butts and he thought about lighting one up but decided against. A pain had started in his gut and he stuffed his fist into it, bending over.

The door was stiff and he had to push at it with his shoulder. He breathed in the fine rain, then planted his hands on his knees and stayed like that for a while because of the battle going on in his belly and bladder. In that position he thought about Alison and pictured her body with those lines a kid had left, her hair he had taken in his mouth. Every time something passed he leaned in the wind of it. He wiped the rain from his lashes. The pain in his gut overwhelmed him.

One foot forward and then the other. The stiff grass of the verge caught at his ankles. He stepped over a bird reduced to a mat of feathers. Behind a thin hedge, run through with wire, the sloping field was ploughed into black ridges with an oily shine to them. Empty yellow sacks were strewn over it, with rainwater in their folds.

The sacks made him smile. The ugliness of the way they were spread as far as he could see. The soil had the treacherous look of rich cake, a shallow slope running up to a dark clump of trees with white sky showing between their trunks. Their shape reminded him of something he couldn't place.

He took a glance both ways at the empty road and then unzipped himself. For a second nothing came but then it started, spattering into the hedge, which was hung with little glassy berries. He didn't like the colour of it, its cloudiness and slowness of fall. He thought he'd take a pill anyway, have to. A car was slowing, coming to a stop. He glanced over his shoulder. They turned on the siren for a second – a single whoop, just a signal of their intent.

He didn't bother to look. Best not to. No stopping now, anyway, as if he'd completed some circuit and the flow had no end. He stared towards the dark trees, holding himself in a cloud of his own steam.

He held the kid on the beach, leaning against the breakwater, feet planted in the mud and broken chalk. Feeling the lad's warm head against his cheek.

'See the island?'

'Those trees?' That singsong to his voice, rising to nothing. Air across an edge.

'One with the trees, yeah,' Cliff said. 'That's Wilson's Island.'

'Does anyone live there?'

'Not now. They might have done once.'

'There's a house.'

'It's not a house, only an old shed. If you look you can see daylight through the roof.'

He squirmed, peering. 'Can we go there?'

'We'd need a boat.'

'Can we get a boat?'

'We can't today.'

'Can we get a boat tomorrow?'

'I don't think so.'

The boy twisted to look at him, squinting against the light and wind, another question in his throat. You could hear the trapped wingbeat of its stutter. Cliff lowered him to the ground, keeping a grip because of the slipperiness of the mud. He looked back at the others. Eric was arranging them for another photograph.

202

The Foster girl was still fussing the toddler but the women were gathered around her mother.

Cliff crouched down, holding his son's shoulders. 'A woman saw someone there once. A sort of man.'

'Who?'

'I don't know. Just a man, and and that's why I'm telling you. Other people might say different.'

'Who might say?'

He laughed, uneasy with himself, glancing over to the women in their flowery dresses. 'Other people might tell you all sorts,' he said.

Watching the child watching the island, he squatted behind him, feeling the sharp bones of his shoulders under the cloth of his navy coat. He might lose him the second he let go but he unlocked his fingers anyway.

The boy stepped away, smiling, picking his way in his new sandals. He turned, raising his arm to make an arc. 'What was the man called?'

'He didn't say – he was only there for a second.'

He looked impatient. 'The other man. The man with the boat.'

'*Ah*. Wilson.'

Ralph frowned. Cliff heard Eric's raised voice and the laughter of the women – the old fraud keeping them amused. The child was teasing something with his toe, a shell or something. 'He doesn't live there now?'

'No, son. He doesn't.'

Thirty-One

Charlie Sanderson sat in the Lamb making notes in his pocket diary, jotting down figures, adding and subtracting. He leaned over the page, breathing down his nose with the effort of it. Then he closed the book and laid his fist gently on it like a paperweight, sitting back and smiling, satisfied.

'I need to take care of these things right away or my memory starts playing tricks, Ralph. I look the next day and sometimes I can't credit my own figures . . .' He looked about, cold-eyed, taking in the new arrivals. 'And the mother is chesty. It's an awful thing to listen to. It was touch and go if I'd be here tonight.'

'We've illness in the family as well,' Ralph said.

'Oh? Nothing too serious, I hope?'

'It's being taken care of.'

Charlie nodded and gazed around again. He took in Ralph's half-empty glass but said nothing. Information he might act on later. Then he frowned, as if something was amiss. 'So where's your father so far? Or is he the poorly one?'

'*Cliff,*' Ralph said. 'You'll find his name is Cliff.'

Charlie smiled with just the sides of his mouth. 'Whatever name you like.'

'He'll be here. You know he cuts things fine.'

'That doesn't always give the best results.'

'At least I'm here, Charlie.'

Charlie laughed, still staring across the room. 'But in a few minutes I shouldn't be seen with you.'

Ralph looked over his shoulder – a row of backs at the bar, nothing more. Sammy Curl was acting as potboy and sent him a nod and a wink. He nodded back. The big screen in the corner of the bar had been turned on but showed nothing but flecks of light.

'Because we're on opposite sides of the fence,' Charlie said. 'At least that's the popular view.'

'What's yours, Charlie?'

'Mine?' he asked, as if that could be of no interest, his pale toper's eyes still roaming. 'Mine is that your prospects might improve beyond that.'

Ralph finished his drink, then went over to the bar and found a space between the elbows. It was nearly nine, he guessed without looking at the clock above the optics. He ordered and then turned back to see the edge of a smile from the man beside him. Youngster in a blue shirt with already a drinker's slack belly.

'Nice to share a joke,' Ralph told him. 'Let the air to it.'

'If you say so,' the youth said.

He turned back to his friends. There was a boil on his barbered nape like an inflamed nipple. Ralph had an impulse to reach out and recall him to the conversation, but just then Sammy Curl got between them and started to stack glasses carefully along the front of the bar. When he'd done that he dried his hands on the cloth he used to wipe the tables.

'Those characters aren't worth the breath,' he said.

'No?'

He shook his head. 'Not a bit of it. I tell you that because of the good times I spent with your father. Years ago when he used to look up to me and thought the sun shone out of my arsehole.' He made a thin smile to himself and wiped his fingers on the cloth. He turned slowly, his leg dragging. 'Talking of which, I don't see him yet.'

'He'll be here any minute.'

Sammy squinted towards the back of the bar, swaying on his feet very slightly, as if he had to make that movement to keep his balance. The barman came in from the other room and started to carry glasses four-in-hand towards the sink.

'He could have bought and sold us any time,' Sammy said.

'That's the family business.'

Sammy half closed his eyes, picturing it. 'That's right. A funny sort of occupation.'

Ralph watched him move stiffly away, then turned back to the bar. There was a pool of spillage where he might have leaned his elbow. He glanced at the mirror and spotted Charlie coming towards him with a fat-faced man in a pink sleeveless shirt.

'No sign of him?' Charlie asked.

'Not this minute.'

'Pity.' He extended his hand towards the sleeveless character. 'I'd like you to meet my boy Vince. Vince, this is Ralph, who I think you've seen in action.'

They shook hands. The other man was the shorter by a couple of inches. He sent a single look up into Ralph's face.

'May the best of you win,' Charlie said. 'Though I can't say it matters much which.'

He laughed, enjoying himself. The other player looked uncomfortable, fidgeting on his feet. Over his shoulder Ralph saw Frank and another man walk through from the front bar.

'Seen a ghost?' Charlie asked.

'Nearly.'

He turned to look and smiled to himself. 'That trash shouldn't trouble you, Ralphie.'

The dartsman sniggered but Charlie gave him a sharp look and he sucked in his lips. Ralph watched Frank making his way through the crowd towards the back of the bar. The friend was queuing for drinks – a man with pale hair whom he didn't recognise.

'Well, something seems to be happening,' Charlie said.

He nodded at the screen. The electronic snow was gathering into a picture. Ralph saw the back bar and the raised walkway with the board at its end. A couple of casuals were already busking – some minor match to gather the crowd. People were moving, drinks in hand, towards the double doors and he spotted Frank talking to a dark-haired woman in a white fluffy top. One of his hands was bandaged. It was his left hand and the dressing passed diagonally across the palm and between the thumb and forefinger.

Clapping and a few jeers. Ralph ducked his head to it. The doors to the other rooms were hooked back and people were still moving through. A bar had been set up in one corner, dispensing spirits and bottled beers. Charlie was talking to a group in the centre of the floor now, holding forth. His hand darted out to touch a sleeve or a belly. The overhead lights started to dim and one of the bar staff blanked the screens of the machines along one wall. The level of noise dropped as the MC came forward.

The first game was easy. Ralph's hand was heavy at first with the drink he'd had but then gained lightness. The MC called the scores into his microphone and some citizen in a starched shirt and dicky made the amendments with a squeaky chalk. Ralph took the winning double with the other player marooned in the two-hundreds. He smiled at him as he drew out the darts, rubbing it in.

He won the second game but dropped the third when Charlie's player had a run to leave a finish on the nine. When he took his eyes from the board, he saw Charlie and his father alone at the same table, heads together. Charlie leaned back and sipped at his brandy and Babycham. His father continued to talk, spinning something out with a glaze on his face under the reddish lights. He seemed to be staring at a point on Charlie's throat.

Ralph picked up his darts and crossed with the other player. Charlie's man nodded at the pair below them.

'Thick as thieves, those two.'

'Thieves is right,' Ralph said.

He took his position and threw again. The treble. He brought up the next dart.

Cliff wore the same formal suit but without a tie. He looked out of place, as if he'd stepped from somewhere darker and colder. He made his way over to the stage, turning looks aside with his lowered head, then mounted the steps almost at a run. His shoes and the hems of his trousers were covered with dried mud. He still hadn't smiled.

He caught hold of a fold of Ralph's shirt. Ralph looked down and saw that the front was dusted with little sparkles of glitter.

'So where is she?' Cliff asked thickly.

He was in doubt for a second, not sure. 'Who?'

'Don't fuck me about,' Cliff said. 'I called at the house on the way back and no one answered the door.'

'I've got the keys if you want—'

Cliff stared at him. 'Why should you have the keys?'

'Eric gave me them. Because Ma's been taken into hospital.'

Cliff touched himself in the middle of the chest as though he had a pain there. 'When?'

'Early this morning – I called an ambulance.'

'And Eric went with her?'

'That's right.' He watched the other player taking up position in front of the board.

'Where did they go?'

'St Somewhere.'

'They're all St Somewhere.'

'St Hugh's.'

'And how is she now?'

'I don't know.'

Cliff stared at him as if something was happening to his face. Another ear, for instance, pushing from below the skin. 'Wait here.'

He went towards the phones in the other bar, shoving people aside with the flat of his hand. Sammy Curl watched him as he left the room, holding a stack of glasses against his chest.

The other player had thrown. Ralph went to the mark without bothering to check the score. He hit a pair of close trebles, the second dart whistling against the flight of the lead. Then a slacker twenty, fallen away but still in the tail of the bed. A hundred and forty. There was slow clapping because they hadn't liked the way he'd kept them waiting.

He was sitting in his seat when his father returned. Cliff didn't climb the stage but stepped close behind so that he could talk into his ear.

'Eric's still there.'

'Did you talk to him?'

'I spoke to them about him: they were calling him Mr Orr.'

'Orr?'

'Her husband, you understand – he's been giving out he's her husband.'

'So how is she?'

'You know the shite they give you,' Cliff said. 'Stable for the time being, they'd only tell me that.'

A woman in the body of the room laughed. Charlie's man had fixed two darts into the twenty and was aiming the third. He dropped his arm for a second.

'So how was the weekend?' Ralph asked.

Cliff shook his head. 'Don't ask me that now.'

'Where's Alison tonight?'

Cliff didn't answer but stared at the glass in Ralph's hand. 'You're drinking that stuff again?'

'We could leave this place and find out about Ma,' Ralph said.

He watched his father struggling with himself. Pathetic, the way it showed on his face. 'We can't afford that.'

'Afford?'

The lounge was closed now and the long room was packed. The barman and a couple of extras were busy behind the makeshift bar. The crowd was buzzing again, impatient with the delay. Ralph stayed in his seat.

'We can't afford to walk out of the match,' Cliff said.

'You mean you can't.'

'It comes to the same thing. Charlie gets the cream whatever way we play it. Whatever we win, he wins more.'

'And if we lose?'

He lowered his head and looked up again. 'We don't – we don't lose. There isn't room for that.' He took a quick glance at the rest of the hall over his shoulder. There were whistles now, shouts and laughter. The sweat was squeezing from his pores. 'You'd better go up there.'

Ralph nodded, holding the darts loosely. 'One more thing, though . . . Have you ever been to Kilmarnock?'

He watched his father's blank moon face. 'Not to my knowledge,' Cliff said. 'Should I have?'

He went up to the mark and threw quickly, one dart after the other, into the margins of the board beyond the wires. He waited for the next, until the room was quiet, only someone oblivious ordering loudly at the bar.

Lager. Lager top. Guinness. Gin and Italian.

He threw for the wire between the five and the twenty. He heard the loud little thrum of the tensed metal as the dart rebounded. It skittered nearly to his feet.

'*Nil,*' the scorer announced after a pause. 'Nothing scored!'

There was silence for a couple of seconds then someone stood up quickly so that a glass rolled and broke. Ralph picked up the fallen dart to jeers and whistles. He looked towards the back of the room and saw the thin guitarist and his blonde girl sitting on one of the benches. He sat down facing the board so that he did not have to look at anything else. There was still a buzz to the place and he felt someone tug at his sleeve. He looked down, expecting his father, and saw the sweating face of Sammy Curl. The potboy grinned with his lips stretched thin.

'You're a piece of shite!' he said.

Ralph turned in his chair to face him. 'What?'

He worked his mouth, relishing something. 'You're a piece of shite like your old man.'

Thirty-Two

Ralph felt drunk but a second later he felt sober.

The dogs on the roof of the Eagles started their racket as he walked from the van. A moon was showing and fragments of broken glass shone on the surface of the road. The Fishburns' house had already been reduced to its ground floor with the stumps of walls standing ragged. A high-sided skip was parked by the kerb, filled with bricks and sooty timbers.

A cat fled so quickly he might have imagined it. The butchered camper van was still parked at the kerb, its bodywork coated with builder's dust. He thought there wasn't a light anywhere in the house. He peered through the side of the bay window until he saw the leaning comma of a flame on the other side of the glass.

Alison came to the door with the candle in a little china saucer. The flame turned the body of the saucer into a luminous disc. She made him wipe his feet on the mat.

'What's happened to the lights?' Ralph asked.

'They found our supply next door and cut the cable. All we've got left now is the gas and a box of candles.' She looked at him crooked over the flame.

'Aren't you nervous?' He nearly said 'afraid'.

'It's Frank they're really after.'

'I saw him tonight but we didn't speak.'

She nodded. 'Then you're fortunate . . .' She stood back to let him in. 'So why are you here, Ralph? Anything in particular?'

'To say hello. Isn't that enough?''

She didn't answer. He watched while she took care over the bolts.

'When did you get back?'

'Earlier,' she said.

'When?'

'Earlier today.'

'Cliff arrived just a couple of hours ago.'

'We travelled independently.'

She led him into Rose's room. A square table and a couple of chairs stood under the window. An armchair was pulled close to the fire and a few ends of wood were burning in the grate, he thought more for the light than for the heat.

'I saw Rose and the little girl,' he said. 'With Colin.'

She put down the candle. 'You're everywhere, aren't you, Ralph?'

The air had a warmed, smoky smell. His eyes started to prickle. He laid a hand on her waist and she stepped away.

'Sorry – I've enough to do with that other no-hoper.'

'No-hoper? Is that what I am?'

'I think of you and Frank together – you occupy the same mental space.'

He grinned and took the cans from his pockets. He stood them along the edge of the table.

'I thought you didn't drink,' Alison said.

'You can help me out with them.'

She took the other chair. Burning wood snapped in the hearth.

'Nothing like a wood fire,' he said.

'Give me a blow heater any day . . . Where did you see Frank?' she asked.

'At a game I was playing. He must have left before the end.'

She nodded. 'Did you win?'

'No.'

'Pity. I got the idea Cliff was relying on that.'

He opened the cans and passed one to her after the foam had subsided.

'Your health then,' she said.

'Likewise.'

He drank and wiped the froth from his lip. He found it easier to talk at her now that something had happened between them. 'You shouldn't be here on your own.'

'Shouldn't I? My choices are limited then.'

'Not necessarily.'

She smiled as if he'd said something absurd. They listened to a car coming up the road. Slices of light fanned across the ceiling. The dogs of the Eagles started to yap.

'Tourists,' Alison said.

212

'A courting couple.'

The noise of the engine stopped a few yards down the road. The lights died.

'See?' he said.

'Very good. So how was Cliff?'

'Are you interested?'

'You think I've no right to be?'

'What did you do to him?'

She shook her head. 'No. The other way. The doing was all in my direction: he had these plans for us.'

'You must have known he would.'

'Do you know why he chose that place?' she asked.

'Because he liked the service?'

'He said he went there with your mother.'

The dogs were quieting themselves with croons and growls, sharp little yaps, passing through all their possibilities of sound before they could be silent.

'Did he say anything about her? Anything of interest?'

'He said she's always there for him. Whenever he rinses a cup, he said.'

'A cup?'

'She's rinsing the same cup.'

'Ah.' He tipped back the can and finished it. Alison was still sipping hers. He wished he'd brought more. He was drunk and then he wasn't.

'These threesomes never work, I told him. Someone always ends out on their ear.'

'Yeah. And this time it's him.'

'He'll survive: I have that feeling about him.'

'You might be wrong there.'

She nodded, allowing that. 'Anyway, I'm sure *she* will.'

He was nervous of her suddenly and glanced out of the window. There was a gleam on the roof of the camper van, stray light gathered from he didn't know where.

'So what are your plans, Ralph?' she asked.

'For the future?'

'My interest doesn't run so far. I meant more for tonight.'

'I've a stranger in my flat,' he told her.

'The tenant?'

'That's him.'

'Then we've both lost a roof.' She lifted her beer and put it

213

down. 'You can finish that yourself – I'm off to bed. If you build up the fire, be careful.'

She took up the candle and cupped her hand around it. Her face was in shadow but her fingers shone.

Cliff was drinking whisky and chasers. Why not? Glasses were stacked in rows on the top of the bar and the barman was taking them in turn, pushing them on to a device like a rubber porcupine, then rinsing and polishing, holding each to the bar light to check for smears. It was well after time, the rest of the room dark except for the colours of the machines which chased their own tails. Why not?

The phone. The barman picked it up left-handed, a pair of glasses between the fingers of the right. 'Hello?' His face not changing against the light from the optics. 'Hello? Hello?' He put down the glasses impatiently, clacking their sides, then killed the connection with his free hand.

'No one there. What d'you think about that?'

Cliff caught sight of himself in the mirror and looked away. Avoid self-regard – a sip of this, a mouthful of that to keep you ticking. A few people were still sitting at tables, settled in for the night now or until sleep should intervene, when they'd settle their heads on their arms. He turned on his stool, and caught sight of gimpy Sammy pushing an upright Hoover between the tables and the legs of the chairs. He watched him for a while – the painstaking way he guided the machine into dead ends and corners. Impressive, really. Lesson there. He looked past to the empty back bar and saw the lamp still shining above the stage but skewed now so that its light missed the board, falling below and to the side. He stared at that for a time, the bare patch of wall it lit. He sensed the eyes of the potboy on him.

Never forgiven me. I forget what for but he doesn't and that's enough. Can't be his leg because I know who gave him that and why.

Cliff slid down from his stool – knees holding up well, not hundred-per but OK – and found a course between the tables, past the mutterers and the midnight cribbage players, the jukebox left on low. Jim Reeves, was that?

'You know something that I don't, Sammy? You know what makes the world go round?'

214

Sammy looked at him levelly with his hands folded on top of the leather grip of the Hoover. 'I don't know what you mean, Cliff. The drink is talking, if you ask me.'

Cliff was still gripping the whisky he thought he'd left at the bar because he had no stomach for it. The potboy stared with no expression but a spark of blood-red came up from whatever store of it he kept behind his eyes.

Cliff stepped back. He dropped the glass without feeling his fingers let go and it spilled without sound on the acrylic rug. '"Night, Sammy.'

He heard the Hoover start as he walked away.

The extractor fan clattered as Cliff pissed against crazed porcelain. *Adamant Niagara* in pale-blue letters under the glaze. Moths were frittering the wired lamp. He rinsed his hands and dried them under the blower. There was a pain in his chest now, nothing to speak of but catching up on him.

Like a bastard train.

He pushed at the bar of the fire door and stepped out into the yard. Drizzle showed as floating drops in the yellow light. He felt better for a second, breathing the stuff in. Then he started to shudder.

He put his hand again on his chest. The yard was stacked with zinc barrels and empty plastic crates. There was a shine of standing water in its blocked runnel and he could smell the fermenting slops.

Started panicking a little, which you weren't supposed . . .

He was fucky-fingered from the stopped blood but he managed to fish the silver box from his inside pocket and hold it awkwardly between his first two fingers until the polished sides played a trick. It fell on the concrete paving, flicking open.

Uh.

He looked at it, stupid for a second. A gravelly sound behind him as a cistern flushed. He bent, then painfully knelt when that movement made him giddy. The oval box was open like a mussel shell. He could see from the angle of the two halves that the little hinge was broken.

The grey pills were spilt, darkening as they soaked up the wet. Chalk mainly, which goes to show. The drizzle was falling on his bare head and the nape of his neck. His knees were trembling. He reached down between them and tried to pick one up between finger and thumb. His hands as big as hams.

'—.'

He looked up then and saw her in front of him, squatting down so she could peer into his face. Her legs were smooth and bare and her face was gentle as it had sometimes been but crooked, shifted slightly to one side as if this was the price of her returning to him.

She held the pill between them, turning it to show him how it was changing to mush between her fingers. She smiled, making light of it. Her fingertips were bloody but he did not know this until she brought them to his lips.

Their metallic taste stayed with him. Joyce smiled from her fractured face, then stroked his cheek, drew down her cold fingers to soothe it.

He had not known that it still smarted.

'Thanks,' he told her. Did he speak?

Thanks, he said.

Thirty-Three

Ralph listened to Alison's feet over his head, crossing the floor and back again. The fire was at the stage where it gave out a little heat but no light. He wasn't sure how long he had been asleep. He tried to settle himself again and then sat upright. The pacing upstairs stopped, as if she were listening for something.

He went upstairs, one flight and then another. There was a masked shine from the skylight. Her door was an inch open on the final landing. He knocked and then again.

'Hello?'

'I can hear you but I can't see you,' Ralph said.

'Good.'

'Why is it good?'

'You can come in first,' Alison said.

The first thing he saw was the glow from the window in the mirror over the mantelpiece. A dark hole near the bottom corner spread doglegged cracks.

'What happened there?'

'Frank. He happened to it.'

'Was he drunk?'

'Cold sober. Will you take a look out the window?'

He could make out the shape of her now, sitting on the edge of her low bed and leaning to one side. The room had a smell of the extinguished candle.

'Is that who you think is there?' he asked.

She shook her head. 'That character isn't on my mind at the moment.'

He had to step over a corner of the bed to get at the window. He saw the paleness of her bare foot pushing from the blanket. He lifted a corner of the curtain and studied the darkness below.

'No one,' he said.

'Look again.'

A pinpoint of red showed in the garden as somebody drew on a cigarette. After a while Ralph could make out the other man's pallid nakedness. He stepped back.

'See him now?' Alison asked.

'Large as life.'

She stared up at him. He couldn't read the expression on her face.

'You said yourself he was harmless.'

'I think you were right about that. What you said about dogs that never bite.'

'Has he bitten you?'

'I went to put something in the bins. When I looked up he was watching me.'

'He's allowed that, isn't he?'

'Except he had an erection.'

'I don't think he's got one now,' Ralph said.

'Are you laughing at me?'

'I'm sorry. Didn't they move him with his father?'

'He turned up a couple of days afterwards. He must have made his own way from wherever they took him.'

'In that condition?'

'I suppose he had clothes to begin with.'

'So where does he sleep? In the shrubbery?'

'The guys on the site leave their caravan open for him. Give him food and fags, cups of tea.'

'That's nice.'

'He sweeps up, does a bit of lifting. They tell him their kind of jokes. Do you know the kind I mean? He gives me looks like they do now.'

'And Frank isn't here much?'

'He comes and goes.'

'And now he's gone?'

She turned away, propping her head against the fat cushion she used as a pillow. He stared out of the corner of the window, watching the brightening and waning of the cigarette.

'You're making me nervous yourself now,' Alison said.

'Sorry.'

'What did you come here for? Just a fuck?'

'Not just that.'

'What if I was to say that I'm not in the market now? That fucks aren't in my repertoire?'

218

'Is that to do with Cliff?'

She made some noise of annoyance. 'Ralph, could you do me a favour?'

'What's that?'

'When you talk about Cliff, could you call him Father?'

He shook his head, useless signal in the dark. 'I can't. I can't even force myself.'

'It was she who left him. Do you know that?'

'Is that what he told you?'

'Him? No. It's what I've learned from other people.'

'Who?'

'Murdo, say. Or the old guy with the lame leg. People like to talk about your mother.'

'Do they? Not to me.'

'Not to you . . . And what about your own wife? Jean, is it?'

'You know her too?'

'Only by sight. And the little boy I've seen.'

'Ex-wife, ex-kid,' he said.

'Simple as that?'

He didn't reply. He let his legs fold. There was a cushion near the window with a rough embroidered surface. He touched little beads among the stitches. After a minute he thought she was asleep. He could have slept himself. The light from the window was held by the broken mirror.

'Touch my face,' she said.

'What?'

'Touch my face.'

He kicked something with his foot, cup or something. Cold liquid spread under his stockinged foot. She guided his hand. Her skin was just warmer than his fingertips. He felt her temple, the rise of the cheekbone.

'Can you feel it?'

There was a line under her hair like the edge of broken crockery.

'Who did that?'

'It doesn't matter who. I didn't look the same afterwards. Not exactly. I tried to but I couldn't. That's the worst – being turned into someone else without your permission.'

He nodded. It felt a liberty, touching the crusted tissue.

'Not saying anything?' she asked.

'No.'

'Lost for words, are you?'

He turned away, impatient with her. She must have sensed it because he felt her hand on his arm.

'How old is your boy now?'

'Eight. Nine. I've lost track, to tell the truth.'

There was a slight staleness to the sheets. He laid his head against them. She twisted herself in the bed.

'Which hand did you use?'

'What?'

'Which hand did you hit him with?'

He wouldn't answer.

'Which?'

'The right one – I was right-handed then.'

'Then touch me with that.'

He touched her face and then her shoulder. He felt her stillness in the bed.

'I don't like to be afraid,' she said. 'You reach a point and there's no more mileage in it.'

She still wore her sweater. He put his hand below it on her side. He could feel the slip of her ribs below the skin. She took hold of his wrist, holding it between her fingers and thumb, pushing down his arm, adjusting herself against him.

'Do you think I'm a hag?'

'No.'

There was the slight suck of her flesh, the quietest sound possible. 'Yes, you do.'

'No.'

She guided his hand between her legs and held it by the pressure of her thighs. He shook his head, touching the dry mouse fur of her sex.

'That's the part that was hurt the most,' she said.

'Yeah?'

She laughed with her face turned against him. 'Is that all you can say? Is that your contribution?'

He kissed her cheek, then found her mouth. Her lips were soft and sad.

'Don't kiss me yet. Not tonight.'

'OK.'

'I think I can sleep now. Will you be comfortable like this?'

He thought about the quiet burning of Walter Fishburn's ciga-cigarette in the dark. The little crackle it would make in a silence.

'I think so.'

*   *   *

A nurse came. Eric was frightened of them, always had been. Their manner made his blood run cold.

'Mr Orr?'

He didn't recognise himself for a second. 'That's right,' he said with caution.

She bent towards him, smiling, her feet neatly placed together and her hands clasped in front of her lap. He leaned back in the stacking chair.

'I think you should go home for a few hours' rest, Mr Orr. If you leave your number with the desk, we'll call you if there's a change in your wife's condition.'

'Thank you,' he said. He hadn't meant to say that, didn't want to seem to agree with anything she'd been saying. He looked away from her, past the screen and along the ward with its dimmed lights. There was a lamp at a desk flanked by two tall vases of mixed blooms. The strong light gave the flowers a waxy glow. 'We've never been separated,' he explained.

When he looked back she was still smiling at him. Reddish hair was escaping from below her linen cap. A lot of them were reddish.

'I can rest here,' he told her. 'This is all the rest I'll need.'

A lot were reddish and the rest were black.

She made a little sigh and stepped back from him. She stood with one foot forward in its flat shoe, an expression on her face as if he were a child.

'There's no point in making yourself poorly, Mr Orr. Even the staff fall ill because of the draughts along this ward.'

The pair of slapping double doors opened at the far end and a man in a white coat stepped towards them in squealing patent shoes. As he came closer, he seemed to grow progressively younger, passing them as not much more than a schoolboy wearing heavy rectangular spectacles and a row of coloured pens along his top pocket.

He flapped his hand. 'Good evening, nurse.'

'Good evening, Dr Sellers.'

Eric rubbed his eyes. The doctor passed through the doors at the far end. A pulse of cold air brought clatter and commotion.

'Saturday night,' the nurse said with a sigh. 'We're always busy on Saturdays.'

He nodded. 'Closing time. They'll be murdering each other out there.'

'Dr Sellers is one of our best doctors,' the nurse said. 'In a few months he'll be going to work in Africa.'

Eric didn't answer but looked at the side of Ma's face. He could only see it dark against the darkness. A mask of clear plastic was held to her mouth with strips of adhesive tape. A white scrap of something inside was animated by her breath and fluttered like a small moth.

'And an African doctor will be coming here,' the nurse added. She hugged the cardigan around her as another draught blew around them.

'Then fair exchange is no robbery.'

There was a machine beside the bed like a black suitcase on a trolley. Every few seconds it gave a little squeak just within hearing, as if something was turning which needed oiling. He had worked out that this had something to do with Ma's heartbeat, although he could see no tubes or cables passing from her to it. He was mystified by this.

'Will she die?' he asked.

A nurse or matron in a darker uniform had appeared and taken her seat at the desk. Her bonnet was more elaborate. She moved one of the vases aside so that she had more room for her elbows. She looked along the ward towards them and then looked away.

'We can't really expect a recovery,' his nurse said. 'Not at her stage of life. She may not even regain consciousness, and if she does wake the chances are she will be very confused.'

'Well, I'm confused,' Eric said. 'And she was the one to set me straight.'

Thirty-Four

Ralph woke to a small explosion. He could make nothing of the sound and turned over on his side, snuggling his face into the cushion's nap. He waited until it came again and it was sharper this time, not fogged by sleep.

Frank was facing him on a collapsing wicker chair. He was cracking walnuts between the jaws of a wrench and his stockinged feet were surrounded by the broken shells. He grinned as Ralph struggled up in the bed. There were pieces of masticated nut in the spaces between his teeth.

'Morning, lover!'

Ralph stared at him, then lay back. He listened to the noise of working machinery from behind the house. Shouts and laughter.

'The boys are looking forward to a little party,' Frank told him. 'You see, once this place is flattened, they're due for a bonus.'

'That a fact?'

'The lippy bastard with the beard told me. When he made me an offer to get the Fishburns out.'

'Did you take it?'

He exploded another walnut. 'It was going begging and I reckon I did them a favour anyway.' He picked among the fragments in his palm. 'Care for a nut, Ralph?'

'Too early for me,' Ralph said.

He shrugged and tossed the kernel into his own mouth. He fitted another between the jaws of the wrench. The bandage was still around his palm, loose and dirtied now, its folds held together by a thin knot.

'What happened to your hand?' Ralph asked.

Frank stared at it as if surprised by its appearance. 'A dog, I suppose: I was bitten by a dog . . .' He smiled and nodded at the disrupted bed. 'As you can see, her ladyship had to go. No doubt she'll be back as fast as her legs will carry her.'

'Did I ask you?'

Frank showed his clogged teeth again. 'You're one of the types whose thoughts show on their foreheads. Easy as TV.'

There was more noise from the back of the house – the engine of the digger straining, cheers and laughter from the crew. Frank stood up, scuffing back the chair, brushing pieces of shell from his lap.

'You can stay and wait if you like. I'm on the move myself – before those boys bring the place down on top of us.'

'Would they do that?'

'As far as they're concerned these places are empty.'

Ralph drew his legs from the bed and cast around for his shoes. When he found them they felt loose on his feet, as if they'd been substituted by a pair half a size larger.

'Do you always sleep in your clothes?' Frank asked in a quiet manner.

'Not usually.'

'On special occasions then?' He watched while Ralph knotted his laces on the edge of the mattress. 'I'm sorry I couldn't stay to the finish last night – I'd a few things to do. Ends to tie.'

'That's OK. The other feller won.'

'That's a new departure for you – losing.'

'I found I was in a rut with the other thing.'

'That's right – it's the sort of thing you can carry to extremes.'

'So where is it you're going?' Ralph asked.

Frank put on a close look, drawing in his shoulders. 'You'll understand if a man in my position is tight-lipped about that.'

Ralph glanced at his watch, out of patience with him. The hands were stalled at a quarter to three. He could feel the roll of money against his chest. Some of the greetings cards' glitter had leaked into the bed.

'I need to make a call,' he said.

They left by the back door. The wall was broken down and its brickwork toppled into the weeds. They could see the back of the Eagles across the open ground. One of the demolition crew spotted them and nudged his workmate. Frank waved like some celebrity and strode on. The back seam of his jacket was split, showing a line of white padding. Ralph caught him up as they neared the site hut and its narrow outbuilding of a chemical toilet.

'See them there?' Frank whispered. 'They're in the mood for a party or a stoning.'

About a dozen men were laughing and talking near a bonfire of timber. Their faces were flushed under the yellow helmets. A few were smoking cigars, cocking their wrists to flick ash into the flames and streaming smoke. One of them called something out and pushed at his neighbour's shoulder. The man staggered away, laughing. The others brought out a cheer and broke their group, standing back to clear a space through which Walter Fishburn walked.

'The lad himself!' Frank called, stretching in his eagerness to witness. 'Our prodigal boy!'

Walter was dressed in an oversize orange overall, gapping in places and too tight around his shoulders and pendulous belly. His feet were pushed into a pair of dusty yellow boots, open at the tops with their tongues lolling and one lace whipping. He passed between the grinning men with a stiff, dignified stride, enormous-hipped. He ignored the grins and elbowings or else did not see them. He turned his head slowly from side to side, surveying the acres of dust. His eyes were small and stern in their deep sockets; his beard stiff with dirt and thrusting forwards from his chin.

'Alison said he's been hanging about her,' Ralph said.

Frank winked. 'That's right – like a dog around a bitch. She wanted your protection, I suppose – the manly strength you might provide.'

'She was scared. She said he'd been exposing himself.'

Frank laughed, a rush of it from his throat. 'Then I hope she was impressed.'

He led the way again, bending to his pace with his hands pushed into his pockets, scurrying almost over the humps and ridges of the ground. When a few yards separated them, he spun around and said something very rapidly that Ralph could not catch.

'What?'

His face was streaming with tears, as if something was forcing them from his eyes. 'Did you fuck her?' he repeated. 'Did you fuck my girl?'

'She isn't your girl, Frank. She's nothing like it.'

He nodded, considering that, then held out his open hand. 'Look!'

Ralph wasn't close enough to see. 'What have you got?'

He sniffed and wiped his eyes with his sleeve. 'A ring someone gave her – a ring for her tiny finger!'

225

It was in his fist now. He drew back his arm and threw, nearly overbalancing with the effort. His grunt died away. Ralph saw a glitter in the air and then nothing.

They passed the concrete pads where bungalows had stood and came to the Eagles leaning against its timber buttresses. A road of dark tarmac had been laid past the front yard with its chained benches. The air carried the smell of bitumen.

'Last time I'll set foot,' Frank said.

'Why's that?'

'Because my welcome won't extend any further.'

They went in by the side door. The room was dark after the breezy brightness outside, silent except for quiet talk from the TV on its mounting behind the long central bar. The barman was sitting with his back to them on one of the high stools. As they walked in he did not look at them but only put down his paper and raised the hatch to step through to the business side.

Frank slapped his hand on the bar. His face was still blotched where he had wiped it. 'Where's the music, Quinlan?'

The barman busied himself with the stock, stacking bottles on the lower shelves, two at a time with his big hands. 'The brewery came for it this morning, for a place across town.' He indicated a black radio-cassette player perched on the glass shelf below the optics. 'I'll put something on that if you like.'

'Not the same when you can't make your own selection.' Frank took out a black wallet worn thin and shiny and opened it to show the fresh edges of notes. 'Charlie gave me something last night to tide me over.'

'Charlie Sanderson?'

He nodded. 'There's no other as far as I'm concerned.'

'I thought you were finished together.'

'Oh, you can never be finished with Charlie – your involvement is only larger or smaller.' He showed the grubby bandage on his hand. 'If you can't pay in money you have to give blood, you see.'

Ralph stared at the dressing. Where it had loosened around the palm he could see a blue shading of the flesh.

'Blood's cheaper,' Frank said. 'You don't have to go back out and earn it.' He laughed. 'It's funny how we could have ended up working for the same firm.'

'There was every chance but no chance,' Ralph said.

Frank turned away, smiling across the bar. 'A couple of brandies for us, Quinlan. And one for yourself . . .'

Ralph shut himself inside the booth with its folding door. A couple of the panes were missing and he could still hear the TV from the bar. He went through his pockets, nervous that he'd lost the slip of paper, but then found it, folded to the size of a stamp. The pencil had smudged so that he had to hold it up to the light to make out the number. He dialled, turning his back on the bar. A woman's voice asked him to wait. He listened to her walk away – soft heels on a hard floor. After a while the pips sounded and he slipped in another coin. He looked into the bar and saw Frank talking to the barman. Then a woman with an older, deeper voice was speaking.

'Mrs Orr,' he repeated.

'Are you a relative?'

'Her grandson.'

'She's still unconscious and we're doing our best to make her comfortable. I'm afraid that at her age there's not much chance of a full recovery.'

She waited for him to say something. 'Are you still there?'

'Who's with her?' he asked.

'Beg your pardon?'

'Who's there with her?'

'Mr Orr has been here all night,' she said.

'No one else?'

She left a pause as if she thought he'd questioned her too far. 'Not as far as I know. I wasn't there the whole time.'

'OK, thanks. Thank you.'

'Sorry there's nothing more positive,' she said, laying down the phone.

Frank had the drinks set up when he came back into the room. A couple of men from the demolition crew were standing at the other end of the bar, still wearing their hard hats.

'Any luck?' Frank asked, solicitous.

'No luck at all.'

'Something the matter?'

'Nothing, no.' He leaned on his elbow and found himself looking towards the vacant board. 'Shall we have that game now?'

'I was about to suggest that myself,' Frank said.

They moved their drinks to a table in the corner. Frank signalled to Quinlan to turn on the lamp.

'We'll need something to throw,' Ralph said.

'Left yours behind?'

'They were a gift from Charlie and I gave them back.'

Frank laughed. 'Well done. You need to be careful with gifts.'

There were only the house darts in a dimpled glass. One of the demolition men marched over and tugged a leather pouch from his back pocket. 'Use these. We'll make the next game a four-hander.'

Frank took them and touched them to his forehead. The other man picked up a knuckle of chalk and stayed to score. Frank tried a few practice throws, grouping them near the bull.

'What about a tenner on it?' he asked.

Ralph took the darts from him. 'OK.'

The scorer laughed and threw his chalk into the air. 'Sure you boys can afford that?'

Frank turned to him as if ready for an argument. But he spoke softly. 'I suppose your lot will soon be finished.'

The man took his hard hat off and put it brim down on the table. The plastic band had left a white mark across his forehead. 'That depends on you and your friends, I'd say.'

'Oh, you won't find us an obstacle much longer,' Frank said.

He threw the first dart, sending it on his way as if he did not care about the outcome. It lodged close to the triple twenty. Then he seemed to turn cack-handed and sent the other two without power to the sides of the board.

The scorer chalked the result without comment.

'Some people's darts will work only for them,' Frank said, handing them over. He walked to the bar and started some backchat with the other workman, his foot up on the rail. Ralph threw and the scorer did the subtraction.

'You were a southpaw the last time we played,' Frank said when he came back to the board. 'Maybe you should have stuck to it.'

'Maybe I should.'

They struggled towards the end of the game. The scorer chalked with a look of boredom, glancing down at his watch. Frank bought a round for the four of them.

'We're playing like a pair of pigs,' he said.

Ralph picked off the final double after a string of attempts. He handed back the darts and went to the bar. Quinlan was fiddling with the TV, skipping from channel to channel. Frank took up the chalk to score. He beckoned with it between his fingers.

'We need you over here, son.'

Ralph shook his head. 'One game's enough for me now.'

The other man laughed and started to throw. Frank did the chalking with his little finger raised, forming the numbers with care. When the game was finished he came over and stripped a note from his wallet.

'Take it! It's not every day I honour a bet.'

Ralph stuffed it into his pocket. He heard a car stopping outside, its tyres crunching the new sharp gravel. Quinlan stood facing them now, his freckled fists resting on the bar. Frank finished his drink and stood the glass with a flourish.

'Another?' Ralph asked.

'No.' He smoothed his mouth with the back of his hand and leaned over and kissed Quinlan deliberately on the lips. It was an audible kiss. Quinlan rocked back an inch but didn't speak. He did not look at them as they left the bar, passing through the main doors into air that turned dull and then bright again.

The wind carried a stream of smoke overhead. The fire had been built up with dark lengths of timber. The narrow door of the chemical closet hinged back suddenly and a black-haired, stocky man stepped out, zipping up his fly. An orange Cortina was parked close to the picnic tables at the side of the pub, its windows nearly opaque with dust.

'Well, my lift's here,' Frank said.

'Charlie?'

Frank looked irritated, disappointed in him. 'I've told you that Charlie isn't a problem!' Then he grinned, his mouth twisting as if he couldn't contain the joke. 'So what are your plans, Ralph? If you'll forgive me for asking.'

'I don't know,' Ralph said.

'You must have some idea.'

He shook his head. 'I don't know absolutely.'

'But you shouldn't follow me,' Frank said in a rush. 'I think this is as far as you should go.'

The engine was running quietly, a wisp of vapour lifting from the exhaust. The driver's window was wound down a couple of inches to let the smoke of a cigarette out and Ralph could make out Charlie sitting at the wheel. Someone was in the passenger seat, leaning towards him in a frail, enquiring posture. He thought that it was Charlie's speechless mother until he made out a narrow man's face.

'The old scrotum's come for me in person this time,' Frank said softly. 'To lead me back by the hand . . .'

One of the demolition men threw something pale on the fire. It looked in the air like a child's doll. He stared in that direction, thoughtful for a second, mouthing under his breath.

'So give my love to your lady-friend.'

'She isn't that.'

'I don't care what she isn't!'

The men from the site left the pub and walked past them, jostling and joking. Still laughing, they crossed the dusty space towards the fire. Ralph watched after them until his eye was caught by an old overstuffed armchair set with its back against the sunny side wall of the site hut. Walter Fishburn lounged in its sunken seat, his legs stretched out and his head tilted back. The bright material of his overalls had a sunlit glow to it. He might have been sleeping, with his stiff tuft of beard pointed at the sky.

'Seen him?' Frank asked.

'I see him now.'

Frank nodded, pleased with something. With himself most of all. 'Well, maybe that one has the winning ticket.'

Charlie sounded his horn – a long blast followed by a short. A demand more than a reminder. Frank turned with a little shrug and stepped towards the car with a swaggering duck-arsed walk. As if nothing now could detain him.

Thirty-Five

Eric held Ma's arm. He was confused and she would set him straight. 'Rest your weight against me.'

'Am I an invalid then?'

'I'm only here to help you.'

She laughed. 'But you're the one who needs most assistance.'

They crossed the road. It had been raining and the cobbles were slippery. She wouldn't countenance one of those frame things or even a stick. An assistant was throwing a bowl of soapy water across the pavement before the fishmonger's. Fish scales glittered in the wash. The jeweller's was still boarded after a robbery.

'This country is finished now,' Ma said. 'It's fit for only thieves and chisellers.'

'We're still going strong, aren't we? That must prove something.'

'Are you sure of that?'

'Sure of what?'

'Sure that we're still going?'

Eric shrugged, pretending not to follow. The matron's bonnet was more elaborate than that of the nurse. She had moved a vase to make way for her elbow. He stepped closer to Ma as they mounted the kerb. Mr Hoseasons passed by, trailing his bow-legged black mongrel. He lifted his hat and Ma nodded, sniffing, the twitch of a smile. A white moth fluttered before her lips. There was a machine beside the bed like a black suitcase on a trolley.

'He grows like that dog,' she whispered.

Ma swallowed slowly. The movement of her throat looked painful. The sound of the machine was to do with her heartbeat.

'We'll get you to that bench,' Eric said.

They passed the Waverley with its sour smell of slops. *Happy Hour 5.30 'til 7.30.* The alley down the side had been resurfaced and the tarmac was still soft. A pool of water had collected, its surface coloured with oil.

'Did you bring the bottle?' she asked.

'You've asked me that.'

'What about the cat?'

'You and that beast! I've only just fed it.'

He held her arm, the loose nubbly material of her coat. A couple of men he didn't know were chatting in the pub's little back yard. They stopped their talk. He was proud of the stern look she gave them. The sky opened out with the light above the river. 'We might get some sun now, I'm thinking,' Eric said.

She didn't answer, couldn't care less about sun. The path was muddy, sucking at their heels. A kid passed on a bike, sounding a klaxon. The hawthorns were in coarse, spiky blossom. She stopped so that they collided.

'Are you well, Ma?'

'Don't walk so close!' she ordered. She closed her eyes.

'Must I not?'

She swallowed slowly. The movement of her throat looked painful.

'We'll get you to that bench,' he said.

She stared at him for a second and then nodded. He took her sleeve again and helped her up the slope. Her loose-sided shoes were slipping in the clay, forcing her to lean her weight against him. He could feel her distaste for her own weakness. They paused near the bench with its worn slats. He put his arm around her and felt the shuddering of her rib cage.

'Are you all right now, my love?'

She looked at him closely. 'Is there film in the camera?'

'I didn't forget.'

Eric transferred the leather holdall to his other arm and helped her to the bench. She sat heavily, depositing herself like a sack of coal in the middle of the seat, occupying it so there was barely room for him at either side.

'Well, we are here,' he said, smiling at her.

Ma squinted against the daylight. 'What? Where are we?' She looked at her hands and rubbed them one against the other. 'It's cold already.'

'The summers are no use at all now,' Eric said. He turned thoughtful. 'Do you think we'll get a card this Christmas?'

She shook her head. 'No, no more cards.'

Eric laid down the holdall and unzipped it slowly. There was a point where it would jam and he eased it carefully past. He took out the bottle with its screwtop. The rest of the bag was occupied by their wrapped sandwiches and a dumpy Thermos, his old Kodak nestled in the corner.

Crab. Potted meat. The Thermos was the type with the milk in a separate container.

'Can you see the island?' she asked, sitting among the scratchings and gougings, her big hands on her knees. *Rene sucks. Malcolm 4 Steph. Terry and Linda for years and years.* 'My eyes don't reach that far.'

'As clear as anything,' Eric lied. He perched on the far end of the bench and unwrapped the sandwiches. He unscrewed the flask and stood it carefully between his feet. There was nobody about. Who could be? 'Which do you want?' he asked. An African doctor would be coming.

'What?'

'Which kind of sandwich?'

The white specks of shore birds were chasing the little breakers, running back and forth like clockwork. She saw only the vague agitation. 'Anything that comes to hand.'

He paused in his unwrapping. 'You must have some thoughts on the subject.'

She sighed. 'The crab, if you mean to persecute me.'

Eric stripped back the tissue. 'Good: we've established that then.'

He passed her the dainty triangle of moist bread.